DARK STARS

DANIELLE ROLLINS

An Imprint of HarperCollinsPublishers

HarperTeen is an imprint of HarperCollins Publishers.

Dark Stars
Copyright © 2021 by Danielle Rollins
All rights reserved. Printed in the United States of America.
No part of this book may be used or reproduced in any manner
whatsoever without written permission except in the case of brief
quotations embodied in critical articles and reviews. For information
address HarperCollins Children's Books, a division of
HarperCollins Publishers, 195 Broadway, New York, NY 10007.
www.epicreads.com

Library of Congress Control Number: 2020951007
ISBN 978-0-06-268000-6

Typography by Jenna Stempel-Lobell
21 22 23 24 25   PC/LSCH   10 9 8 7 6 5 4 3 2 1
❖
First Edition

For Bill & Jon, because you love these books

PART ONE

"Who are you?"

"No one of consequence."

"I must know."

"Get used to disappointment."

        —William Goldman, The Princess Bride

1

DOROTHY
NOVEMBER 12, 2077

Midnight, read the note.

Water churned around Zora's Jet Ski, the black surface of it reflecting the light of the ever-shifting anil. A breeze moved over the waves, creating ripples and causing Ash's empty motorboat to rock. Seated behind Zora, Dorothy heard only the sound of creaking wood and lapping waves.

It was 12:05 now. Whatever happened here had only occurred a few short minutes ago.

Dorothy crumpled the damp paper in one hand, a muscle near the corner of her eye twitching. She felt each of those minutes as if they were hours, years. Time was such a fickle, funny thing.

She tightened her grip on Zora's waist, her breath lodged deep in her throat. It was only when she looked very closely at the water that she could see the blood. The deep red of it looked black until the anil's light caught it just so.

Dorothy could smell it, though. Even under the scent of

seawater and rot, the smell of the blood was unmistakable. She felt ill and found that she had to look away.

"Seen enough?" Zora asked. Her voice was a low rumble but, even so, the emotion laced through it startled Dorothy. She'd always known Zora to be stoic to the point of appearing to have no emotions at all. She glanced at Zora's back, frowning, wondering if the other girl was holding back tears.

And why wouldn't she cry? Ash had been her best friend, practically her brother. And now he was . . .

Dorothy swallowed, pushing the thought away. She couldn't let her mind travel to that place, not yet. Not until she had proof.

"Can you get any closer?" she asked, voice thick.

Zora hesitated. Dorothy gnawed on her lip, waiting for her to make a decision, her heart sinking a little lower with each passing second. She'd so hoped they could be on the same side, that Zora would believe her when she said that she had nothing to do with whatever had happened to Ash.

Minutes ago, Zora had shown up outside of her room at the Fairmont hotel, headquarters of the Black Cirkus. Dorothy still thought of it as her room, but she supposed it might be more accurate, now, to call it her cell. Earlier that evening Mac Murphy had taken control of the Black Cirkus and Dorothy's rule as Quinn Fox, vicious assassin and leader of New Seattle's deadliest gang, had come to an end. She'd been overthrown by her own people, held prisoner in the very hotel she had won for them.

She'd still be there now if Zora hadn't fought her way through the Cirkus Freaks standing guard and set her free.

Of course, if Dorothy had thought for a second that Zora had been there to rescue her, she'd been sorely mistaken. A moment after breaking into her room, Zora had shoved a gun in her face and produced a note that Dorothy seemed to have written herself coaxing Ash to this very spot, at midnight, so that she could . . .

Dorothy's eyes drifted back to the blood on the water. So that she could *what?* she wondered.

Stab him? Kill him?

Dorothy felt the horror of it hit her like a punch. She knew in her heart that she would never do that. Even after Mac Murphy had put a bounty on Ash's head, blaming him for Roman's death, the only thing Dorothy had cared about was finding Ash and warning him. None of this made any sense.

Was it possible for a man to survive after losing so much blood? Or was she fooling herself, thinking there was any chance that Ash could still be alive?

The Jet Ski's engine suddenly roared to life, breaking the stillness of the night. Zora brought them up to the side of Ash's boat, and Dorothy's heart lifted. Maybe they could work together after all. Maybe—

"Do I have to tell you what I'll do to you if you try to run?" Zora asked, her voice a low growl.

Dorothy's heart fell once more.

"You do not," she said, and, gathering the damp edges of her cloak in her fists, she climbed from the Jet Ski to the small, rocking boat.

She heard a *click* behind her and knew, without turning, that Zora had a gun aimed at her head. *Again.* The back of her neck prickled.

You would do the same, if you were in her position, she reminded herself. Zora had every right to be cautious. For the last year, Dorothy had been working against her and the rest of the Chronology Protection Agency, trying to steal the secrets of time travel out from under their noses. It made sense that Zora didn't trust her.

But it still hurt like hell.

Dorothy swallowed, shifting her attention back to the boat. Her throat was dry, and she could hardly hear anything over the steady beat of her heart at her temples. The boat rocked gently in the waves, and Dorothy softened her knees and leaned forward slightly, to keep from losing her balance. It was an automatic reflex, picked up after spending the last year in this watery city.

There was a spray of blood over the worn wood, a black scuff that could have come from a boot. It looked exactly as someone would expect it to look after two people had a brief confrontation and one of them had been stabbed and thrown overboard. Dorothy wasn't a detective, but even she had to admit that this was all rather damning.

She released a heavy sigh, tears clogging up her throat.

The note in her hands felt suddenly hot, like it could burn straight through her skin, and there was a part of her that wanted to throw it into the water and watch it sink, ink bleeding until it looked like nothing at all. None of this made sense. It was like a riddle without any answer, and yet Dorothy kept staring at the scene, hoping that something would jump out at her, tell her what had really happened.

She *couldn't* have done this. She was being set up, somehow, made to take the fall for someone else's crime. But who could possibly benefit from that? And why?

Her boot knocked against something hard, which skittered across the bottom of the ship. Dorothy frowned and crouched lower.

It was a gun. And not just any gun. *Ash's* gun, the navy-issued snub-nosed S & W revolver he'd brought into the future with him from his original timeline—1946. Dorothy had known him only to be without it when Roman had stolen it from him.

She picked the gun up, her throat constricting. Glancing over her shoulder, she saw that Zora was staring at it, her lips slightly parted. Emotion flashed across her face—pain, confusion, fear—gone a moment later.

"That . . . ," Zora said, in a croak of a voice, and Dorothy knew they were both thinking the same thing: Ash wouldn't have left his gun behind voluntarily.

A light appeared in the darkness, a small circle bobbing over the waves. *A headlight*, Dorothy thought, frowning. Or else a spotlight attached to a boat.

Another appeared, and then two more.

Five. A dozen.

Blast, Dorothy thought. Every nerve in her body sparked. The lights glimmered in and out of focus as they passed behind distant trees and wove around buildings. They seemed far away, but the flatness of the water caused sound to carry in strange waves. Dorothy heard voices now, laughing and talking as clearly as if they were right beside her. A series of sharp cracks broke through the night.

Gunshots. She stiffened, fear crawling up her spine.

"The Black Cirkus," she murmured, glancing at Zora. "They'll be here in minutes."

"They must've followed me," said Zora, her voice so low that Dorothy almost didn't hear her. Her dark eyes shone in the light coming off the anil.

"They're looking for Ash," Dorothy added. "Before you came for me, Mac put a bounty on his head. Every Cirkus Freak in the city will be wanting to bring him in." She didn't say *dead or alive*, but she didn't have to.

Zora lifted an eyebrow, questioning. There was more to that story, of course, but there wasn't time for Dorothy to get to it just now. What happened in the future, with Roman, was still too raw for her to think about without risking tears, and she'd be damned if she was going to cry in front of Zora.

She lowered Ash's gun so it wouldn't be perceived as a threat and forced herself to meet Zora's dark eyes.

"Take me with you, and I'll tell you everything I know," she said.

Another gunshot exploded in the night. Zora flinched. She looked at Dorothy again, and Dorothy could see the struggle playing out on her face. Zora didn't want to trust her but, just now, she didn't have much of a choice.

"Fine," Zora said, after a long moment. "We can't be found out here, anyway." She twisted the handle of her Jet Ski, and the engine growled to life. "Get on."

Dorothy tucked Ash's gun inside of her cloak and climbed onto Zora's Jet Ski, a flicker of triumph moving through her as she wrapped her hands around Zora's waist. "Do you know somewhere we can go? Where they won't look for us?"

Zora, gruff, said, "I can think of a place."

2

A building appeared in the distance, nestled between the taller skyscrapers. It looked like it was made entirely of mirrors, but thick vines crawled over the exterior, making it impossible to tell for sure. Water reflected in the outside walls, creating the illusion that the structure was moving.

Dorothy frowned as they drew closer. They were in Black Cirkus territory, only a few blocks from the hotel that served as the gang's headquarters, and yet, she'd never been here before. She'd noticed the building before, obviously. It looked almost like a giant diamond, making it hard to miss, but she'd never paid it much attention. So many of the buildings downtown were flooded to the point of being unusable.

"What is this place?" she asked as Zora pulled the Jet Ski up to the dock wrapped around the building's outer walls. The Jet Ski's headlight glimmered off the glass, the brightness making Dorothy's eyes water.

"Old library," Zora said, cutting the engine.

"*This* was a library?" The libraries in Dorothy's time had been dusty, brick structures. Nothing like this.

"Pretty, right?" Zora said, softening. "You should have seen it before the floods. It was my favorite place in the whole city."

Dorothy fisted her hands, her palms suddenly clammy. Was that kindness she'd just heard? It felt like a foolish thing to hope for, and yet she stole a glance at Zora, blood pounding in her ears. Maybe it wasn't too late.

But there was no kindness in Zora's face. Her eyes were cold and narrowed, her lips thin.

Please don't let it be too late, Dorothy thought.

They climbed off the Jet Ski and made their way inside. Mildewed books towered around the entrance, sending deeper shadows over the tile floor. There didn't appear to be any lights, or, at least, not any working lights. The dark inside was deep and perfect, but Zora was able to pick her way through the surrounding clutter easily, as though she'd done it many times before.

Dorothy followed her into a wide, open space lit with a half-dozen flickering candles. Here, she saw that they weren't alone. Chandra, a girl with dark skin, black hair, and thick glasses was playing a card game at a rickety table. Willis towered behind her, his skin and hair pale beneath black clothes. The bones in his face slanted at sharp angles, causing the skin to pull too tight over his cheeks and chin. Neither seemed to have noticed them come in.

Willis leaned over Chandra's shoulder and touched one of

her cards with the tip of his massive finger. He said, in a deep, velvety voice, "You missed the ace."

"I didn't *miss* the ace," Chandra snapped, rolling her eyes. "I was just saving it."

Willis frowned. "Saving it?"

"I like saving up a bunch of cards in a row and then, when I'm ready, I get to go *bam bam bam* and do them all at the same time." She mimed flipping a bunch of cards onto the table. "It's fun."

"I didn't realize solitaire could be quite so exciting," Willis murmured, a smile curling his lips.

Dorothy felt an ache, watching them. She'd forgotten what it was like to be around these people, how comforting it could be, almost like having a family. Once, she'd thought that Willis and Chandra could become her friends.

But that was a long time ago. She hadn't seen either of them in over a year and, since then, things had gotten . . .

Complicated.

Her smile flickered. If she'd made different choices, she might be sitting among them right now, playing cards and laughing. It was much too late for all that. The past year seemed to rise up between them, massive. She doubted either of them would consider her a friend anymore.

Still, she had to try. She took a step toward them, tentative. "Hell—"

She was interrupted by a click of metal, the feel of something small and cold pressing against the skin on her neck. She snapped her mouth shut, swallowing the rest of her greeting.

Zora was pointing that gun at her again.

Lovely.

Dorothy's mangled greeting had drawn the attention of both Chandra and Willis. They'd looked up from their card game and were staring, but Dorothy couldn't tell whether they were surprised or afraid. Perhaps a little of both.

"Try anything and I'll make that pretty face of yours a little less pretty." Zora removed the barrel of the gun from the back of Dorothy's neck, but she kept the thing trained on Dorothy's head as she moved around to her other side.

Dorothy bit back her disappointment. She was used to this feeling, after all. She couldn't think of a day in her life when some form of aching loneliness hadn't plagued her. Even when Roman had been alive, she'd been well aware that the rest of their gang had only tolerated her out of fear.

But she wouldn't have anyone pity her. She may not have a friend in this world, but she did have some pride.

"I'm not sure it's possible to make my face any *less* pretty," she murmured, a poor attempt at a joke. She motioned to the scar that cut across one of her eyes and curled into the corner of her mouth.

Chandra released a surprised laugh. Dorothy glanced at her, a flare of hope shooting through her chest, but Chandra had quickly recovered and gone back to studying the cards spread across the table before her, brow furrowed, all traces of laughter scrubbed from her face. Willis met Dorothy's eyes, but his gaze was chilly. It made Dorothy's heart hurt.

She shouldn't be so surprised by this less-than-warm

welcome, she knew. In the year since they'd last seen each other, Dorothy had fallen out of a time machine, gotten her face carved up, taken over a bloodthirsty gang, and risen to the top echelons of power in New Seattle, becoming Quinn Fox: assassin, murderer, rumored cannibal. This had all been possible because of the (quite false) stories about what a violent monster she was, but Dorothy hadn't been bothered about any of that. Power was power. She'd lived long enough without any of her own to appreciate it in whatever form she could get.

She and Roman had come up with the rumors about her viciousness to keep her safe, and they had no more truth to them than most fairy tales. But still, they'd stuck. People loved to tell horror stories.

Unfortunately, Dorothy found that they were less likely to tell the happy stories. Like how she'd tried to save the city. How she and Roman had restored electricity and brought back much-needed medical supplies, among other things. People seemed to prefer gruesome lies to the truth.

Anyway, none of that mattered anymore. Everything, all that she and Roman had built, had been taken away. In the course of just twenty-four hours, Mac Murphy had managed to steal her time machine and take control of her gang. Quinn Fox was gone, and she was only Dorothy again. Roman, her closest ally and the only person she'd actually trusted in this godforsaken city, had been shot and left for dead in the blackened ruins of the future.

And Ash . . .

Dorothy's throat closed just thinking of it. She couldn't let herself dwell on what may or may not have happened to Ash just now.

"Sit," Zora said, pointing to a stool near Chandra.

Dorothy gathered up the wet ends of her cloak and sat, chair creaking beneath her. Despite everything, she was glad to be here. Back at the Fairmont, she knew everyone wanted to kill her. Here it might just be two out of three.

"Well?" Chandra's eyes skittered toward Dorothy and away again. "What did you find?"

Willis added, "Is he really—"

Neither of them actually said the word *dead*, but Dorothy heard it ringing through the air, almost as though it were being sung on a loop.

He's not dead! she wanted to scream. *He couldn't be.*

But she didn't actually have any proof of that. She was holding tight to the fact that they hadn't found Ash's body, but that damn boat was floating in the middle of the Puget Sound. Any murderer with half a brain would've thought to drop him over the side of the boat, allowing his body to sink to the ocean floor. They *wouldn't* have found a body, no matter what had happened.

Dorothy stared down at her hands, blinking hard. She wouldn't let herself cry. Not here, not in front of these people who hated her.

"We found his boat outside the anil," Zora was saying. Her voice cracked as she added, "It was covered . . . there was blood, everywhere."

There was a beat of silence. And then—

"You actually did it," Chandra murmured. "You killed him."

Dorothy lifted her eyes and found Chandra glaring back at her, arms folded across her chest. It was like a knife twisting through her chest. She couldn't remember *ever* seeing Chandra angry before.

"I *didn't* kill him," Dorothy insisted. She looked from Chandra to Willis but found no sympathy in either of their faces. What would they do to her, if she couldn't make them believe her? Her voice began to waver. "You—you *have* to believe me . . . I was as surprised to find that empty boat as Zora was!"

Willis's eyes seemed to bore into her. "Ash used to see visions of his future," he said, very slowly. "Prememories, they're called. It's a phenomenon that can sometimes happen when you pass through an anil. The brain short-circuits, forgetting that the future hasn't happened yet. When you have a prememory, you can remember an experience from the future as easily as you might remember a real memory."

Cold dread slithered down Dorothy's spine. Her mouth felt suddenly dry.

She'd had a prememory before. When she first traveled through time with the Chronology Protection Agency, she'd had a series of short, dreamlike premonitions of her future. It had been unnerving, to say the least, when those premonitions had actually started coming true.

14

What had Ash seen? Had it been something bad about her? Had she done something terrible?

She wet her lips, her heart beating in her throat. "Are you trying to say that Ash saw his own death?"

The look in Willis's eyes suggested that she might be better off not knowing. "He did," he said, after a moment. "He had a recurring prememory, one that he saw nearly every time he entered an anil. In the prememory, he met a woman outside the anil, and she stabbed him. It was only recently that he learned that the woman from his prememory was Quinn Fox." Willis nodded. "You."

Dorothy's dread was sudden and sickening. No wonder they were all so sure of her guilt.

She touched her cloak, nerves creeping up the back of her neck as she felt the paper in her inner pocket rustle. This wasn't the first time she'd heard of someone seeing visions of their own death before it had happened. Roman had left her a note before he'd died. *I've been haunted by memories of my own death*, it read. So, it seemed, he'd been familiar with prememories, too.

She dropped her hand, refocusing her attention on Willis. "I was trapped in my room at the Fairmont until Zora showed up and took out the men guarding my door," she said very carefully. "This note that Zora found, it asked Ash to meet at midnight, but I couldn't have gotten there in time. Whatever Ash saw in his prememory, *I* couldn't have done this."

Willis studied her through slits of eyes, chewing his lip.

There was a stretch of silence, and then Zora released a low sigh.

"I did find her at the hotel," she said, resigned. "She's telling the truth about that."

"I'm telling the truth about all of it!" Dorothy insisted, though she was no longer holding on to hope that her words carried any weight here. Maybe there wasn't a chance for any of them to be close again. Well fine, she could find a way to deal with that. But she had to make them trust her on this. If not for herself, then for Ash.

She pinched her nose between two fingers, chest tightening as she thought about Ash's motorboat floating in the open sea, the waters stained red with his blood.

Her throat closed up.

"Look," she said, when she could speak again. "We all seem to be in agreement on the fact that something terrible has happened. And I'll be the first to admit that it appears that I must've . . . I don't know, come back from the future and—and attacked him, for some reason. But I'm telling you all the truth when I say that I don't know *why* I came back, or what, exactly, I did to him. I wouldn't have, I would never . . ." The words *kill him* felt stuck in her throat.

She closed her eyes, took a deep breath, and tried again. "A few hours ago, Mac put a bounty on Ash's head. Right now, every Cirkus Freak in the city will be out looking for him. Perhaps whatever happened to him has something to do with that."

"Why would Mac Murphy care about Ash?" Willis asked, frowning slightly. "He's never bothered with us before."

"That was before Ash and I broke into his brothel and shot him in the leg," Chandra said.

Dorothy blinked, taken aback. "I'm sorry . . . *you* shot Mac Murphy in the leg?"

For the first time since Dorothy arrived, Chandra looked at her with something like her old warmth. "It was awesome," she said, grinning. "Ash was all, *where do you keep your girls*, and then Mac said—"

"Off topic," Zora murmured, cutting off Chandra. Turning to Dorothy, she asked, "Is that why Mac put a bounty on Ash's head? Because of the thing at his brothel?"

"What?" Dorothy shook her head. "No, that's not it at all. Mac needed someone to take the fall for—"

Dorothy stopped talking abruptly. Roman's death felt like it had happened a lifetime ago, and yet the memory of it played in her mind like a movie waiting to be cued.

She saw Roman's chest blossoming with blood. Roman falling to the ground, his eyes going distant. And Mac's hand on the trigger. She had to close her eyes for a moment to stop tears from spilling on to her cheeks. *Oh, Roman.*

It was too much, all this pain. Just when she thought she'd gotten a handle on herself, some other memory roared up inside her mind, threatening to ruin her.

When she found her voice again, Dorothy said, as carefully as she could, "We went to the future, Mac, Roman, and

I. We'd planned to kill Mac, but Ash showed up before we could take him out. There was a fight and . . . and Mac shot Roman."

Dorothy wasn't sure what sort of reaction she'd been expecting, but it wasn't this one. Chandra released a sharp "Oh!" and threw a hand over her mouth. Zora's face fell, and something in her eyes went complicated and distant. Willis lowered his massive head to his hands.

Dorothy shifted uncomfortably in her seat, a shot of irritation moving through her. Who were these people to mourn Roman? They'd turned their backs on him, just as they were turning their backs on her now. She'd been his only real friend in the end.

More tears pooled in her eyes, but she blinked, hard, refusing to let them fall.

"I never got the feeling you all were close," she said, voice flat.

"He was one of us before everything happened," Willis reminded her, wiping a tear from his eye.

Dorothy was unmoved. "He was my friend, too. My best friend." She didn't say *my only friend*, but that's what she'd meant. Clearing her throat, she continued. "After Roman's death, Mac told the Cirkus that Ash was the one who'd killed him, and he offered a reward for anyone who brought him in. They're probably out looking for me, too. By now, they'll have seen that I'm not in my room."

"Is that why you killed Ash?" Zora asked. "To regain

favor with the Cirkus by taking out the man they think murdered their leader?"

"I *didn't* kill Ash," Dorothy insisted, but she was having a hard time mustering up the same indignation she had before. They didn't believe her. Perhaps they never would believe her. What was the use of trying to convince them?

Tired now, she added, "I'm telling you, before he showed up in the future, I hadn't even *seen* Ash, not since that night at the ball!"

There was a beat of silence, all of them staring at her. Dorothy narrowed her eyes. There was something they weren't telling her.

"You're lying," Zora said, voice flat. But, behind her, Chandra was frowning. She opened her mouth, looking like she wanted to add something, but Zora shot her a look, and she shut it again.

Dorothy kept her eyes trained on Chandra, nerves creeping up her skin. *What had she been about to say?*

"You should go," Zora said.

Dorothy could've laughed. "Go? I can't *go* anywhere. If the Cirkus finds that I've escaped, they'll *kill* me."

Zora seemed unmoved. "You can't stay here."

Dorothy scrubbed a hand over her face, standing. She tried to convince herself that none of this mattered, that she didn't need these people, that she was better off without them.

But when she met Zora's eyes, she felt a thrill of pain move through her. She couldn't lie to herself anymore.

It mattered. *They* mattered. Without them, she was lost.

"You trusted me once," Dorothy said, working hard to keep her voice steady. "You might not remember that, but I do. I wish you could trust me now."

Zora gave her a strange look. "*Trust* you? I don't even know who you are. Are you Quinn? Or are you Dorothy?"

Dorothy, quiet, realized that she didn't know the answer to that question, either.

3

Back at the Fairmont. Dorothy was careful to keep to the shadows, peering carefully around corners and walking close to the walls so that the creaking floorboards wouldn't give her up.

It was dangerous for her to be here. She couldn't think of a single Cirkus Freak who wouldn't give up her location on sight. But it looked like she was about to be on the run and, if that were the case, there were things she needed from the Fairmont. Supplies, money, food if she could scrounge up any. She would just have to be quick about it.

The hotel had the look of a place that had once been extraordinarily lovely but had long ago fallen into ruin. Ornately beautiful rugs covered the floors, but foot traffic had left them worn, the edges frayed where they met the walls. Dorothy touched one of the hotel's mahogany doors and the once glossy wood was now dull and soft beneath her fingers. The scent of rot hanging in the air like a fog. Dorothy pressed her sleeve to her nose to block the smell as she turned a corner, the hallway opening into a cavernous room.

Her heart stilled as her eyes searched the shadows for movement. There was no one. Everyone would all be out searching for Ash.

Or for me, she realized, with a rush that left her head spinning. She walked a little faster.

Columns rose from the floor, and long-decayed chandeliers hung from above, cobwebs stretched between the bulbs. Murky water filled the courtyard below. If she squinted down into it, Dorothy knew, she could see a grand staircase, an old piano, and marble countertops.

She crept up to her room using the back staircase, ears peeled for the creak of footsteps or the distant roar of laughter. Her room was on the fifth floor of the Fairmont, but it looked exactly like the one she'd been kept in when she was kidnapped the year before. Two beds, each covered in a white quilt. Wooden furniture. White curtains. Blue chair. The only item that actually belonged to her was the small silver locket hanging from her mirror. Her grandmother's locket. Her mother had given it to her on her wedding day, and it was the only object she still had from her own time period.

Dorothy slipped the locket off the wooden frame and looped it around her neck. And then she started to pack. Two pairs of extra clothes, her cloak and mask, the precious little money she had left—all of this she shoved into a duffel, which she hurriedly looped over one shoulder, eyes scanning the room for anything else she might need. Her heart gave a strange little twitch as she realized there was nothing. She'd spent a year in this hotel, and she'd been starting to think of it as a sort of home, and yet she was able to pack her entire life into a duffel bag and leave it all behind. The thought made her sadder than she cared to admit.

"Enough," she said out loud, giving her head a shake. Now wasn't the time to get sentimental. She had no way of knowing how long she had before a Cirkus Freak—or worse, Mac himself—wandered back down these halls. She had to move.

She removed the money from her duffel and quickly counted the bills. It wasn't much, she was afraid, and it wouldn't last long. There was enough to feed her for a week. Maybe. She would need to get used to skipping breakfast.

And after that? She supposed she could pick pockets, run a few short cons, lift a pocket watch or whatever other valuables people in this time still had. The thought caused a bitter smile to cross her face. She'd thought those days were behind her. Old habits certainly died hard.

She shoved the money back into her bag and slipped into the hall, easing her door shut behind her without a sound. There was still no one here, she saw, a relieved breath escaping from between her teeth. She'd been lucky, but she'd be a fool to press that luck any further. She started for the staircase . . .

And now she paused, an idea occurring to her.

Roman used to keep cash stashed away in his bedside table. *For a rainy day*, he'd always told her, ironically, with a glance at the perpetually overcast sky. In New Seattle, every day was rainy—both figuratively and literally.

Dorothy chewed her lower lip, considering. Was that money still there? she wondered. It seemed soulless to steal from the dead. But what other options did she have? Starving wouldn't be much fun.

"Blast," she muttered, and turned left instead of right, veering toward Roman's old room. He would understand, she told herself, trying to tamp down her guilt. Roman no longer needed to eat. He would think it was sentimental nonsense to let money go to waste.

Down the hall Dorothy went, and then up another staircase, to Roman's old room. Unlike Dorothy, Roman had taken the trouble to decorate. There were pictures on the walls: sketches torn from old books—Roman particularly loved Rembrandt and da Vinci—knickknacks scattered across the dressers. Pausing, Dorothy saw a photograph of Roman's little sister, Cassia, tucked into the frame of his mirror. Strange how she'd never noticed the photograph before.

She knelt in front of his bedside table and began shuffling around, pushing aside books and papers. Nothing there. *Blast.*

She tried his desk next and found more of the same: notebooks, journals, textbooks. No cash. She dug her teeth into her lower lip and was about to slam the drawer shut in frustration when her fingers brushed against something silky and thick.

A prickle of familiarity went through her. This wasn't cheap, like the other notebook paper in Roman's desk. It felt like it had been torn from a very nice journal. Heart thudding, Dorothy slid it out, her eyes quickly scanning the handwriting.

I've been over Nikola Tesla's notes half a dozen times now, and I still find that I'm too nervous to actually put his theory to the test.

Dorothy felt every muscle in her body go still. Her heart hammered steadily inside of her chest. She knew this handwriting well. She'd never met the man who Roman and Ash referred to as merely "the Professor," but she knew all about him. He'd invented time travel, and then he'd disappeared, leaving behind a journal of cryptic notes on the theory of time travel, experiments into the past and future, and a lot of questions about where he'd gone and why.

Several weeks ago (or, a year and several weeks, depending on how she calculated time) Dorothy had stumbled across his journal in some of Roman's things. She'd read the entire thing in one sitting, desperate to learn more about how and why time travel was possible. It had been like getting lost in the very best kind of novel, except that it had all been real.

Staring down at the pages she held now, she felt a prickle of excitement move through her. She'd had no idea that parts of the journal had been missing.

Somewhere in the hotel, faint as a sigh, there was a noise: a shoe scuffing against the floor, a whisper, something.

Dorothy was instantly alert. She stood, head cocked

toward the door. The sound didn't come again, but it thundered through her memory, seeming much louder than it had been in real life. Slipping the journal pages into her cloak, she inched toward the door, rolling her feet from ball to heel so as not to make any noise on the creaky floorboards. She pressed her ear to the door, holding her breath.

Nothing.

Her heartbeat began to slow, but she knew she wasn't the only one in New Seattle who knew how to move around without being heard. She lowered a hand to the doorknob, fingers curling around the cool brass.

She'd gotten to be a fair fighter over the last year. She was small and slight, but Roman had taught her how to use an opponent's weight and mass against them. And then there was the dagger hidden in her cloak—she could be deadly with that. If there was only one person waiting for her on the other side of this door, she stood a good chance of getting away. If there were two people or even three, she figured she could still fight her way through them, as long as she took them off guard.

More than that, and . . .

Well, Dorothy thought, swallowing. It wouldn't do her any good to think about that just now. She slipped one hand into her cloak pocket, fingers curling around Roman's dagger. The weight of it comforted her. It was much heavier than the signature, deadly thin daggers she usually kept hidden up her sleeves. She'd lost those when she and Roman and Mac had gone to the future, but Roman's dagger would work in a pinch. It was heavy, its blade thick. She could do some damage with it, if she needed to.

Holding her breath, she flung the door wide—

The hall was soaked in darkness. It played tricks on her. She stepped forward and, at the same time, something in the shadows twitched, sending her heart leaping into her throat. But it was just the window at the end of the hall reflecting her own movements. Nerves pricked the back of her neck.

There was no one here.

Dorothy turned in place, looking around the empty hall, the open doors and dark rooms. She tried to recall what she'd heard and found that she couldn't quite remember what it sounded like. Perhaps it hadn't been a footstep at all but merely the wind blowing against the window, or wood creaking as the old building settled and shifted on its foundation.

"Or, perhaps, I'm losing my mind," she muttered under her breath. Quickly, she hurried back into Roman's room and grabbed her duffel from the foot of his bed. She double-checked that the Professor's journal pages were safely tucked up her sleeve and stepped back into the hall—

"Did Donovan actually *say* that he saw her? Or was he only bragging, like always?"

The voice drifted up from the staircase. Dorothy recognized it immediately as Eliza, a Cirkus Freak who seemed to harbor a particular hatred for her. Dorothy held her breath, worried about making a single sound.

Somewhere deeper in the hotel, a door opened and closed, and then there was the sound of footsteps winding their way up the stairs, down the hall . . .

"He said he saw *her*," said a second voice. *Bennett*, Dorothy thought, her body going tense. "'Bout twenty minutes ago. Said she took the back entrance."

"Twenty minutes?" Eliza released a short bark of a laugh. "She'd be a fool to stay any longer than that."

Dorothy backed into Roman's room and eased the door closed. *Blast*. She closed her eyes, pushing a finger to the skin between her brows.

Think, damn it!

There was another staircase at the other end of the hall, but she couldn't risk going back down the way she'd come. If someone had seen her sneak into the hotel, then Eliza and Bennett wouldn't be the only ones looking for her. There would be others as well, probably a pair for every floor. Any route she might take back down to the docks was effectively blocked.

It would have to be the roof, then.

Silently, she crossed the room and threw Roman's window open. Eight rows of sleek glass windows separated her from the ground below. From up here, the murky brown water below seemed unbreakable, like concrete.

Dorothy swallowed and looked away. She'd been exactly here once before and, then, she'd chosen to jump in order to escape the people chasing her. This time, fortunately, she wouldn't have to attempt anything quite so dramatic.

Sliding her duffel to her back, she propped a foot on the windowsill and hoisted herself up, balancing on the edge.

Wind blew against her legs, and the world spun below her.

Deftly, she eased along the thin ledge of concrete that jutted out from below Roman's window, fingers gripping along the walls for the worn-down grooves in the rock that Roman had taught her to look for. Wind whipped her cloak against her legs, threatening to flick her off the side of the building like a child might flick a spider. Her fingers quickly cramped, and her lips quivered, but she kept going.

Past one window, and then two, until she'd reached the balcony of the room next door. She took a single moment to catch her breath, and then she began to climb up . . .

There was one floor between Roman's room and the Fairmont's roof, but Dorothy's arms still burned when she finally pulled herself up and over, legs scrambling for purchase beneath her, desperate to take some of the weight from her arms. She stayed on all fours for a moment, gasping for breath. Only when her head stopped spinning did she bother to sit up.

The whole of New Seattle spun, dizzily, below her. The corpses of long-dead trees grew up from the black waters, their white bark reflecting the light of the moon so that they seemed to glow in the darkness. From where she sat, Dorothy could make out the flat concrete saucer that was all that remained of the Space Needle, the outlines of tall buildings, and the dull black of the water that was everywhere else.

She sighed and leaned back on her elbows. In her year of living in New Seattle, Dorothy had never quite gotten used to the skyline. It looked strange and futuristic and alien, as always. The only thing that felt familiar was the moon hanging above her, close enough that she almost thought she could reach up and pluck it out of the sky.

She lifted her face, staring up at that moon. Back when she'd been new to the Black Cirkus, she often came up to the roof to think. No one else in the gang would risk climbing so high. Other than Roman, of course.

A tear touched her cheek. She brushed it away with an angry flick of her hand, but another came after it, and another. Eventually she gave up and let them come. In all her life, she'd never felt as alone as she did right now. Even during those first terrible days back in 2076, when she'd crash-landed in the wrong time, she'd still had Roman. But, now, he was gone. He was gone, and Ash was gone, and the Chronology Protection Agency wanted nothing to do with her, and her gang had betrayed her.

A lump moved up Dorothy's throat, making it hard to breathe.

She was without allies. Without hope. Without money.

For the first time in a long time, she found herself missing her mother.

"Stop it," she told herself, opening her eyes again. She pressed her palms to her cheeks, sopping up her tears. She might not have allies or friends, but it wasn't as though she didn't know what to do. She'd been hopeless before, and she'd always found a way out, hadn't she?

She just needed leverage.

There, she thought, *I might just be in luck*.

She pulled the Professor's journal pages out from beneath her cloak and began thumbing through them. The air was heavy with damp. It wasn't raining, yet, but it would be soon, and the thick pages stuck to her fingertips, the ink bleeding. She grimaced as she pulled them apart. She would need to get through them quickly or else they'd be ruined. And then they'd be no use to her at all.

Propping herself up, Dorothy began to read.

I've been over Nikola Tesla's notes half a dozen times now, and I still find that I'm too nervous to actually put his theory to the test.

Time travel without a vessel, without access to an anil, without any exotic matter.

If Nikola is correct, if these things really are possible, it means that we've only just begun to scratch the surface of this science.

But if he's *incorrect* . . .

Well. Let's just say that there are many, *many* ways this could go wrong.

For instance, if you'll recall, only two people attempted to travel through an anil without a ship before me. One was killed, instantly, and the other had his skin ripped from his body.

Neither outcome is especially appealing.

And yet . . . there's reason to believe that it *should* be possible to travel through time without a clunky machine and access to an anil. In fact, stories of time travel can be found as early as eighth century BCE.

Natasha once told me a story about a kid named Abimelech who travels sixty-six years into the future while gathering figs, all because God wanted to spare him the heartbreak of war.

And in the ancient Sanskrit epic, the *Mahabharata*, King Raivata was said to have left the earth to meet with God only to return hundreds of years later.

And the Japanese legend of Urashima Taro tells of a fisherman who goes to visit some underwater God. He experiences only a few days passing, but when he returns home it's three hundred years later.

It's occurring to me as I write this that none of these great voyagers ever returned from their journeys through time. Which is unnerving. But not as unnerving as the guy who had his skin ripped off.

I should back up a bit. Before I decide whether it makes any sense to test Nikola's theory, perhaps it's best that I lay out what it actually is.

In the 1890s and early 1900s, Nikola became obsessed with a theory that he might be able to conduct electricity long distance through the earth's surface. He took a lot of money from a lot of people, lied to everyone about what he was doing, and moved from New York to Colorado Springs to experiment with this type of research far from public scrutiny. Around this time, he's quoted as saying, "Progress in this field has given me fresh hope that I shall see the fulfillment of one of my fondest dreams; namely, the transmission of power from station to station without the employment of any connecting wires."

Spoiler alert: he did not see the fulfillment of his fondest dream. He was super wrong about everything. He spent a year at his lab in Colorado Springs, ran through all his funding, went into debt, and ruined his reputation. At one point, he seemed to think he was communicating with other planets. When we first met, he assumed I was a martian (ha!).

Now, though, while we know that it's not possible to transmit energy across vast distances using the power in the earth's surface, as Nikola posited, we do know that it's possible to transmit *mass* through *time* using an anil. Hence time travel. The research Nikola left for me seems to be a sort of mash-up of his research and mine. He argues that the earth's crust is made up of millions of tiny anils, and that it should be possible for me to harness that energy from *anywhere*—not just inside of an anil. To stabilize the energy, he recommends injecting a very small amount of exotic matter directly into my person (he's drawn a rough prototype for a tool that should help me accomplish this).

The science holds. And yet, I'm reluctant to test his theories. Nikola is well-known throughout history as being one of the most brilliant men to ever live. And yet his experiments in wireless energy ruined his reputation and sent him deeply into debt.

Am I really going to trust him with my life?

4

NOVEMBER 13, 2077

Black water swirled around her slowly moving boat. A cool breeze tickled the back of her neck, messing with her curls.

Dorothy stared into the darkness, watching for movement. She had Roman's dagger in one hand, the weight of it a familiar burden at her side. In her chest, her heart rose and fell like hammer blows.

She was ready. She would never be ready.

The darkness broke open and there, in the near distance, she saw the anil undulating on a blanket of black waves. It was a sharp splinter in the night sky; a soap bubble bouncing gently on the waves; a deep, dark tunnel.

She tore her eyes away, and only then did she see the figure standing in the boat just before the tunnel, waiting for her. He didn't move or wave to her but only stood, waiting for what he knew was about to come.

Dorothy shifted the dagger beneath the folds of her cloak, swallowing. He might know what she came here to do, but she had no intention of making it any harder than it already had to be. She pulled her boat alongside his and stared into the darkness until her eyes adjusted and Ash's face began to take shape.

Lips and nose and mouth. Long eyelashes. Gold eyes.

"You came." Her throat constricted around the words.

"Dorothy," Ash said, and reached for her.

She allowed him to pull her close to him, arms wrapping around her narrow shoulders, and then his lips found hers and they were kissing and everything else fell away.

Oh, how she wished she could stay in this moment.

But the dagger was still there, in her hand. Between them, always.

She pulled back and saw, immediately, how the light seemed to dim from his face. He studied her.

"It doesn't have to be like this," he said.

Dorothy, raising the dagger, said, "Of course it—"

Dorothy jolted awake, her skin burning, sweat coating her forehead and palms. Darkness swirled around her, and for long moments she couldn't remember where she was.

Then, shapes began to take form: tall buildings and trees and sky. She was on the Fairmont roof. She must've fallen asleep.

She closed her eyes, gathering herself. Her hands were trembling. She could still feel the give of Ash's skin and muscle beneath her hands, Roman's dagger sinking into his body with frightening ease, the damp warmth of his blood coating her fingers.

What was that?

It had felt like a memory of some sort. She knew that it was possible to remember things that hadn't happened yet, but she thought that only happened inside of an anil. So, what was this? A dream? A nightmare?

A premonition?

Whatever it had been, it *seemed* real. Like something she'd lived through before.

Dorothy closed her eyes, shaking the remnants of the dream from her head. When she opened them again, she saw that the sky above was tinged with pink. Dawn was approaching. She felt a crick in her neck and stretched, cringing. Perhaps the roof had not been the wisest place to spend the evening. Every muscle in her body was tight, every one of her limbs stiff and creaky.

The sounds of movement and voices drew her attention to some commotion down below. She eased over to the edge of the roof, her boots sending bits of debris tumbling over the side, and peered down.

Cirkus Freaks had filled the docks. Their black cloaks made them look like a swarm of insects, an infestation. Dorothy frowned down at them.

What are they doing? she wondered, creeping closer to the edge of the roof. Mac must've given them some assignment, but what?

She craned her neck out as far as she dared, gripping the side of the roof so tightly her knuckles turned white. The ground spun dizzily below her.

The Freaks appeared to be putting up posters and

handing out flyers. She couldn't read what they said from this distance. She would have to get closer.

She started to back away from the roof's edge when something caught her eye.

It was a woman. Like the Freaks, this woman was dressed all in black. Her black dress had a high neckline and long sleeves, and she wore it with heeled boots, a black hood, and a mask that completely covered her face. It was the mask that drew Dorothy's attention. As far as she knew, she was the only person who wore a mask in New Seattle.

Have I started a trend? she thought wryly. She rather doubted it.

And there was something else about the woman, something . . . disturbing. She had a strangely magnetic quality to her, a gravitational pull. Dorothy couldn't manage to tear her eyes away. She felt a chill move through her as she watched the woman move down the docks before, finally, disappearing around a corner.

Who was that?

Dorothy waited until she was certain the woman had gone and then, making sure that Roman's dagger and the Professor's journal entries were carefully stowed away in her cloak, she crawled over the side of the roof and began the long climb down.

Dorothy kept to the shadows. She watched from around the side of the building as the Freaks hung their mysterious flyers, voices muffled by the sound of the water lapping up against the side of the docks, and the thin, harsh morning wind.

And then, when they began to move on, down the dock and away from her hiding place, Dorothy slipped out into the daylight, quiet as a shadow, to see what the poster was.

Wanted for murder, it read. Below, there was a picture of Ash's face.

Dorothy lifted a trembling finger to the poster, something cold washing over her. It looked like it had been copied from an old magazine clipping. Ash wasn't staring at the camera but grinning at something off in the distance. He was wearing the beaten leather jacket Dorothy knew so well, and his skin was reddened from the sun, wind blowing his blond hair into his eyes.

She looked away, her eyes traveling down the docks. These posters hadn't just been hung on the Fairmont, she saw, but on every building on this block. It was probably safe to assume that the Freaks had papered every building downtown.

A chill went through her. It was one thing when Mac had told the Cirkus Freaks that Ash was responsible for Roman's murder. But now he had the whole city looking for him.

"You certainly picked a good time to disappear," Dorothy muttered, swallowing. If Ash hadn't died in the boat last night, she hoped he had the sense to stay gone. If he stepped foot in New Seattle, he'd be dead within the week.

Feeling a sudden rush of anger, she tore the flyer off the wall, balled it up, and let it drop into the waters below. It wouldn't help, these flyers were everywhere, but she felt some small measure of relief as she watched the ink on the poster bleed, the paper grow soggy. *One down*, she thought. Yanking her hood up over her head, she tried to blend in with the other people on the docks.

She kept her head bent, walking without stopping to think about where, exactly, she planned to go. Every time she thought about those posters, fresh rage bubbled up inside of her. Mac couldn't do this; he couldn't use his lies to turn an entire city against Ash. She wouldn't let him. She had to do something. She had to stop this.

But *what*?

She was helpless. Powerless. Friendless, moneyless.

Oh, how she hated that feeling.

After ten minutes of aimless wandering, she realized she'd unintentionally landed on a destination. In this entire city, she knew of only one place where they wouldn't throw her out immediately.

Taking a deep breath, she turned and headed there now.

Dorothy hid behind a white-trunked tree. Waiting.

Zora was the first to leave. Dorothy watched from her hiding place as Zora pushed a window open and climbed onto the rocking docks below.

She looks terrible, Dorothy thought. Purple circles colored the skin below Zora's eyes, and there was a sickly gray cast to her dark brown skin. She seemed to be muttering something under her breath, an energy bar clutched between her teeth as she hurriedly pulled her black braids into a quick and untidy bun at the base of her neck.

She didn't even glance Dorothy's way but climbed onto her Jet Ski. A roaring sound filled the morning air as she switched on the engine. And then she was gone, an arc of black water spraying the air in her wake.

Willis climbed out the window not three minutes after Zora had left, his eyes moving back and forth, skittishly, as he checked the docks for people. Dorothy frowned. He looked . . . furtive. Like he was doing something he really shouldn't be doing. Like he didn't want to be caught.

Head ducked, he quickly moved down the docks, toward Dante's.

Dorothy exhaled, deep, and moved out from her hiding place. Chandra would be the only person remaining in the library now. That was lucky. She'd been hoping she could manage to catch either Chandra or Willis alone, but, of course, Chandra was her first choice. Chandra had always seemed to like her.

Here goes nothing, she thought.

And she ducked down the docks and over to the library, carefully pushing the doors open.

5

Disco music blared down the library hallway, strings, horns, and electric guitar crashing together like a storm. Dorothy could just make out the rise and fall of Chandra's (off-key) voice as she sang along.

"'You are the *dancing queen*! Young and sweet, only seventeen!'"

Dorothy cringed—she still didn't like modern music—but she supposed she should be glad for the music. It covered the creak of her footsteps as she made her way down the long hall.

She rounded the corner and found Chandra dancing around a crooked stack of mildewed books that was almost as tall as she was. Chandra wiggled her hips and pumped her hands above her head, the kind of dancing someone did when he or she *really* didn't expect anyone to be watching. Dorothy knew she should announce her presence to save the girl from embarrassment, but she couldn't help staying quiet for a few moments longer.

Chandra grabbed an empty bottle off a stack of papers and held it up to her mouth, belting into it like it was a microphone. "'Dancing queen! Feel the beat of the TAMBORINE, OH YEAH.'"

Dorothy stifled a laugh. She couldn't take it any longer. She began to clap, and Chandra released a high-pitched shriek and whirled around, flinging the bottle across the room. It smacked into a pile of papers sitting on an overburdened bookcase, sending them flying to the floor.

"Oh no!" Chandra's hands flew to her mouth. "Zora's going to be so pissed. She spent all morning organizing that."

"I've only been here a minute and I've, somehow, already managed to anger Zora," Dorothy said, kneeling to gather the papers. "That has to be some sort of record, even for me."

Chandra said nothing but hurried over to the ancient cassette player, switching off ABBA. The sudden silence made Dorothy's nerves twitch.

"I'm sorry, I know I shouldn't have snuck up on you," Dorothy said, standing. She placed the messy stack of papers back on the bookshelf. "It's just that I was hoping to talk to you when you were on your own."

"Right," Chandra said. Dorothy couldn't help but notice that her eyes were a touch wider than they'd been a minute before. She glanced at the window and then back at Dorothy, swallowing hard. "That makes sense, I guess."

Dorothy frowned. "I'm not going to *hurt* you, if that's what you're thinking."

"Of course not." Chandra laughed, but it came out sounding a touch nervous. "It's just that we haven't been alone together since you became, well, *her*."

She gestured to Dorothy's white hair and black cloak, and Dorothy felt her heart sink. She'd always thought Chandra liked her. Back when they'd first met, she'd asked question after question about Dorothy's time period, her hair, her clothes. It had seemed like they'd been becoming friends.

But the girl standing in front of her now looked utterly terrified, as though she expected Dorothy to whip a blade out from her sleeve and kill her on the spot. Had she been fooling herself that Chandra might be an ally?

"I'm no different than I was when you knew me," Dorothy said, raising her hands to show that she was unarmed. "I swear."

"Well . . . except for that thing where you eat people now," Chandra pointed out, taking a step backward. "That's new."

"For the love of . . . I don't *eat* people," Dorothy said, in a huff. "They're just rumors. There have been dozens of rumors about me over the last year, but, for some reason, that's the one everyone fixates on."

"Can you blame them?" Chandra asked weakly.

"They're silly," Dorothy said. "Roman and I started them to convince the people of this city I was someone to be feared. There's no truth to any of them, I swear."

Chandra raised an eyebrow.

"Fine," Dorothy snapped. She held up a finger. "I bit *one* guy, and that was only because he attacked me first. Happy?"

Chandra tilted her head, and Dorothy didn't miss the look of grudging approval that crossed her face.

"So," Chandra said, crossing her arms over her chest. "Why are you here?"

"I just want to talk to you." Dorothy kept her hands raised as she stepped forward and lowered herself into a chair. Chandra frowned at her, lips pursed. After a moment she sighed and sunk into the chair beside her, arms crossing over her chest.

"Okay, then," she muttered. "What do you want to talk about?"

Dorothy thought of the look that had crossed Chandra's face when they'd all been talking the night before, that slight frown, like she knew something but wasn't sure whether she should say it out loud. That was why she'd come back here. She needed to know what that look meant.

"Last night," she said carefully, "when we were all talking, it looked like you wanted to say something, but Zora—"

"Zora's not your biggest fan right now," Chandra cut in, glaring. "And I don't blame her." She shoved her glasses up her nose. "Ash's . . . disappearance has us all really freaked out, but Zora's taking it particularly hard."

"So am I," Dorothy murmured.

Chandra's eyes grew wet. She blinked a few times, looking away. "Yeah, me too, but Zora . . . she's obsessed. She won't rest until she figures out where he is." Her eyes cut back to Dorothy's face. "And who put him there."

"We should be on the same side," Dorothy said, leaning forward in her seat. "I know that you all blame me, but I want to get to the bottom of this as much as you do."

Chandra bit her lip. For a moment, it looked like she was having some sort of internal debate with herself. And then, heaving a sigh, she stood and hurried out of the room.

Alone now, Dorothy frowned. Was their conversation over? Did Chandra expect her to leave? To follow her?

Chandra appeared a moment later, carrying a cloudy pitcher and two jelly jars.

"Tea," she explained, seeing the confusion on Dorothy's face. She placed the pitcher and the jars on a bookshelf next to Dorothy's chair. "Willis has a ton of the stuff, so I iced it. I'm not a big fan of hot beverages."

She poured them both a glass. "I just figured that, if Willis were here, he'd offer you a drink," she mumbled, pushing the tea toward Dorothy.

Dorothy lifted an eyebrow. "He would?"

"Don't get me wrong, he doesn't like you very much, either, but the dude has manners, and you are, technically, a guest." Chandra finished pouring and set the pitcher down on the table, slopping a little tea over the side. "So. You said you wanted to talk?"

Dorothy felt a rush of gratitude. She pulled the tea toward her and wrapped both hands around the cool glass. "Thank you—"

"If I find out that you hurt him, I'll kill you myself,"

Chandra said, her voice almost pleasant. She lifted her cup of tea to her lips and took a small sip. "I might not be very strong, and I might not be a good fighter, but I know poisons that can kill in seconds. You'll have to watch what you eat and drink for the rest of your life."

Dorothy had been about to take a sip of her own tea, but now she thought better of it. She placed the glass back down on the table, clearing her throat anxiously.

"I didn't kill him, I swear," she said. She closed her eyes, sighing deeply. "I don't know what really happened that night, but—"

"He's known for weeks that you were the one who was going to kill him, and he didn't even care," Chandra said, her voice bitter. "He loved you that much. Did you know that?"

Dorothy felt the tears gathering behind her eyes, and she blinked, fast, so that they wouldn't fall.

"No," she said, after a long moment. "I didn't know that."

Chandra released a great sigh and stared down into her tea, no longer seeming interested in drinking it. "I thought this last week of secret meetings meant he was trying to figure out a plan, some way to stop it from happening, but—"

"Secret meetings?" Dorothy said, interrupting her. "What are you talking about?"

Chandra's eyes went wide. She took a quick drink of tea, her cheeks coloring. "It was nothing. Never mind."

Dorothy leaned forward in her chair, suddenly alert. "Ash and I have been meeting in private?"

"Well, sort of, but I . . . I really wasn't supposed to tell you about that." Chandra anxiously turned her glass between two fingers, tea sloshing up against the sides. "You see, Zora thinks—"

"I don't care what Zora thinks; Zora isn't here." Dorothy reached out, grasping Chandra's arm. "Chandra, you have to tell me. *When* were we meeting?"

Chandra stared at her for a moment and then, with a sigh, she said, "It's just been a few times over the last week, since the ball." She lifted a hand to her mouth and started gnawing on her thumbnail. "Ash would sneak out to meet you when he thought the rest of us weren't paying attention."

"No," Dorothy said, frowning. "That . . . that can't be right. I saw Ash the night of the ball and once, briefly, at a bar downtown but, otherwise . . ."

Even as the words were leaving her mouth, she remembered a strange conversation she'd had with Eliza on the night that the Black Cirkus revolted. Eliza said that she'd seen Dorothy and Ash, together, outside the Dead Rabbit. Dorothy hadn't thought much of it. Eliza had clearly been trying to frame her, to get the rest of the Black Cirkus to turn on her more quickly.

But, now that she thought about it, why would Eliza bother? Mac had already been well on his way to bribing the Cirkus over to his side. What more could Eliza have gained by making up stories?

"How many times?" Dorothy asked, when she could speak again.

"You've met three times, I think," Chandra said. "Once,

after the ball, and then again at that super-shady bar near the Fairmont, and then, you know, when you saved him."

Saved him, Dorothy thought, a shiver moving through her. Of course. Eliza had accused her of setting Ash free when Mac had been holding him prisoner. Another lie that wasn't a lie after all.

"Why didn't Zora want me to know about this?" Dorothy asked.

"I think she was worried that telling you about the meetings would somehow set the whole chain of events that leads to Ash's death into motion," Chandra said. "But I don't think time travel works that way."

Three meetings, Dorothy thought. She'd seen Ash three times over the last week, she'd spoken to him. About what? What could've been so important that it sent her back in time to find him?

There was a sound in the other room, a window sliding open, and then Zora's voice calling, "Chandra, did you see that book on theoretical physics? I thought it was in the workshop but—"

Chandra leaped to her feet. *Go*, she mouthed to Dorothy, her eyes suddenly wide. She flapped a hand down the hall. "You can get out through the kitchen in the back room, the window leads to the docks on the other side of the building."

Dorothy hesitated. She put her hand on the Professor's journal pages, which were still tucked inside her cloak.

She really should tell Chandra what she'd found. She wasn't sure whether any of them knew that the Professor had been looking into traveling through time without a vessel prior to his disappearance, but she imagined that information would be invaluable to them. Right now, Mac had everything he needed to travel back in time—the last remaining time machine, not to mention all the exotic matter. If there was a way of time traveling without those things, surely they would want to know about it.

But something made Dorothy hesitate. Right now, those pages were her only remaining bargaining chip. She might need them. It seemed foolish to hand them over without asking for something in return. And she could only imagine what Zora might do if she found Dorothy here, interrogating Chandra.

"Thank you," she whispered to Chandra, leaving the pages where they were. And then she slipped down the hall and through the back window before Zora could discover her.

LOG ENTRY—AUGUST 20, 2074
14:20 HOURS
THE WORKSHOP

I've spent the last two days constructing Nikola's device for inserting exotic matter into my person, using the blueprints that he so helpfully laid out in the notes he left for me. I tweaked them a bit—science has come a long way in the last 150 years—but the general idea is his. As such, I've decided to call this little gadget the "Death Ray" since that's what he told the press he was working on in his final years.

Oh God, please let that name remain ironic.

The Death Ray is now complete. It's a handheld device about the size and shape of a small gun, with a long needle where the barrel would normally be. I'm to use this needle to extract exactly ten milliliters of exotic matter and insert it directly into my aorta.

I should pause for a moment to point out that a ruptured abdominal aortic aneurysm can cause life-threatening bleeding.

So, ha ha, I better not mess this up.

Here goes nothing.

Oh God . . . my hand is actually trembling.

UPDATE—
AUGUST 20, 2074
16:05 HOURS

And . . . I'm back! Also, not dead! I've successfully injected myself with exotic matter, and I think it's safe to say that I have *not* caused any life-threatening internal bleeding. A toast to small victories!

As the first man alive to have exotic matter implanted into his person, I also feel it necessary to point out that this stuff feels *weird!* There was a cool, tingly feeling at the injection site, followed by what I can only describe as a *brightness* bursting through my veins. It felt like liquid sunshine spreading through my entire body. Extraordinary.

In any case, this is only step one. Step two is, actually, not as complicated. According to Tesla, there are millions of microscopic anils below the earth's surface. The exotic matter should stabilize my body for travel, so now I just have to harness the power of these tiny wormholes and allow them to transport me back in time. As I will not be in a time machine, navigation will be more difficult. I'm not actually sure how it will work. When I'm in the anil, I look for specific patterns in the tunnel walls.

Tesla has theorized that time travel using the energy of the smaller anils below the earth's surface should work like water moving through stone. In other words, I'll be likely to travel through well-worn territory, revisiting places where I've been recently or often. Very interesting.

If he's correct in his theory, all I need to do is "align myself with the Puget Sound anil." To be perfectly honest, I'm not entirely sure what he means by that. How does one "align himself" with an anomaly of the natural world?

I do know this—the Puget Sound anil opened in the Cascadia subduction zone. I believe it's possible that just being near the subduction zone could be enough to harness the power of the anil.

Which is why I'm sitting in a little rowboat right now, just outside the zone, preparing myself to—to put it scientifically—row forward and see what happens. Here I go.

If Tesla's theory is correct, I should feel a sort of current, which he said should feel like a fishhook in my navel and—

Oh—

6

Dorothy kept to the shadows, following the winding, rickety docks through the city. The sun had come out of hiding, and its crushingly bright light glimmered off the black water, edging the day in gold.

She found herself looking over her shoulder more than she needed to and hunching down in her cloak, like the thin layer of cloth might protect her from a gunshot or the cold slash of a blade. This sort of brightness always put her on edge. It tricked her mind into thinking she was safe. It made her drop her guard. Here, that was practically a death wish. She doubted she'd ever be safe again.

The dock dipped. Water inched past the edges of her boots, bringing a poison-green snake with it. The snake slithered around her ankles, tail flicking in and out of the black. Dorothy kicked it loose, swearing as the pest disappeared below.

Chandra's words tripped through her head:

You've met three times . . . Once, after the ball, and then again at that super-shady bar near the Fairmont, and then, you know, when you saved him. . . .

She ran a hand back through her hair. How could this be true? She knew how to fly a time machine, but she wasn't currently in possession of one. The *Black Crow*—the *last* time machine, as far as she knew—was currently locked up in the Fairmont, guarded by an army of Cirkus Freaks and Mac Murphy himself. There was no way she could get her hands on it without getting herself killed.

Waves lapped against the dock. Wind rustled the white tree branches. Dorothy hunched down in her cloak, trying to quiet the frustration she felt building inside of her. Every time she thought she was on the verge of discovering something new, she seemed to slam into another wall, another obstacle. It was infuriating.

She shook the wet from her boots and kept moving. Dante's bar was just ahead. Freaks didn't drink at Dante's, Dorothy knew, so she might actually be safe there. For a little while, at least. Long enough for a drink, maybe even some food. Her stomach rumbled, reminding her that it had been a full day since she'd eaten anything.

She glanced around to make sure no one was following her. The dock was empty, the water surrounding it still. Satisfied, she found the window that acted as the bar's entrance and climbed inside.

Grease stains crawled up the walls, and the air held the heavy smells of fried fish and beer. Dorothy's stomach rumbled painfully. She pulled her hood low over her face, hoping no one would notice her as she made her way toward the cheery sounds of voices and laughter.

Dante's was a cramped, dirty space filled with mismatched tables and chairs, with strings of half-busted café lights hanging from the low ceiling, and a few vinyl booths shoved up against the walls. A boxy television set from 1985 sat behind the bar but, for now, it remained dark.

Dorothy waited at the bar, her hood pulled low, white hair carefully hidden, until a shortish, youngish guy wearing a baseball hat made his way over to her.

"What can I get you, darling?" he asked.

"Hooch?" Dorothy said, remembering the clear drink Zora had ordered for her the first time she'd come here. "And food, if you have it."

"Kitchen's closed right now," the bartender said apologetically. "But we got a shipment of protein bars from the Center, and a few bags of black-market chips if you're interested."

Dorothy wet her lips. She was interested in anything as long as it was food. "I'll take both, thank you."

The bartender nodded, wiping his hands on a white apron that hung from the waistband of his baggy shorts. He pulled a bottle of clear liquid out from behind the hubcap that served as the bar and filled a glass. Then he found a protein bar and a dusty bag of chips and tossed them onto the bar next to it.

"Thank you," Dorothy murmured, dropping a few bills onto the counter. She took her drink and moved through the crowd, head ducked. She kept imagining that people were sending sideways glances her way, whispering to themselves. She had no way of telling whether the paranoia was in her head.

Finding a seat near the back of the bar, she took a sip of her drink. The hooch burned all the way down her throat and settled in her gut like a tire fire. She swallowed, grimacing, and tore into the protein bar, a brownish, lumpy substance that tasted salty and chocolaty and a little like sawdust. It was the least "food-like" food she'd ever eaten, but it managed to calm the rumbling in her belly, at least a little.

While she ate, she went over everything she knew.

Chandra said she'd been meeting with Ash in the past. She didn't have a time machine, but she did have the Professor's journal pages, and they happened to detail just how one might travel through time *without* a machine.

She tightened her fingers around her sticky glass, thinking. Was that what she'd done? Figured out how to travel through time without a vessel? It seemed unlikely. The Professor's journal pages were helpful, but they weren't exactly an instruction manual. And he'd made quite a point of talking about just how dangerous it was to even attempt such a thing. Dorothy still couldn't get the phrase *skin ripped from his body* out of her head. She shuddered and put the rest of the protein bar down on the table, uneaten. She couldn't imagine a less pleasant way to die.

The boy at the bar suddenly raised a hand, motioning for

the patrons to quiet. He was staring at the television hanging over the bar. The image on the screen had skipped, and then froze.

Dorothy watched, dread pooling in her stomach as the image disappeared completely, replaced by two figures: Mac, and that strange, unfamiliar woman in black she'd seen on the docks that morning.

And now, she felt her anger flare. They were standing in her studio, the one she and Roman had built in the Fairmont's basement. They were using the cameras that Dorothy had stolen from a defunct television station in 2044 and standing in front of the tattered American flag that Roman had hung from the ceiling.

How dare they?

"Friends," Mac said, smiling slightly. He was a toad-like man, stumpy and short with thick lips and perpetually red-rimmed eyes. "Do not attempt to adjust your television set. This broadcast has taken over every channel. It is untraceable."

Dorothy couldn't speak. She knew those words. For heaven's sake . . . she'd *written* them. This broadcast had been a pet project of hers over the last year, a way of telling the citizens of New Seattle the truth about what time travel was capable of, of showing the people that she and Roman were on their side, that they were working to make the city better.

And now *Mac Murphy* was the one standing behind the camera?

It was enough to make bile burn up the back of Dorothy's throat.

Her fingers curled around her glass of hooch. It took every bit of willpower left inside of her not to pick the glass up and hurl it at the television. If Mac himself had been standing before her, she knew she wouldn't be able to resist.

Mac continued, voice solemn, "It is my great misfortune to tell you that our beloved Crow, Roman Estrada, has been murdered."

A tense silence fell over the crowd, everyone turned toward the television screen. Dorothy had a feeling she knew what was coming next. She gripped her glass a little tighter.

By you, she wanted to scream. *He was murdered by you.*

"Roman longed to help the people of this city," Mac said. "He managed the incredible feat of traveling back in time, and he used that power to provide us with electricity, heat, and much-needed medical supplies. Because of him, New Seattle is better off today than it was yesterday.

"Unfortunately, not everyone shared Roman's desire to make this city of ours a better place. Late last night, during a trip to the future, two people plotted and executed Roman's assassination."

Mac and the woman in black suddenly disappeared from the screen, and a photograph of Dorothy and Ash appeared in their place.

Dorothy stared, openmouthed. She'd never seen this photograph before. It seemed to have been taken on the docks

59

outside the Dead Rabbit, late at night. The colors had blurred together, almost as though they'd been rendered in watercolor, a hazy mix of dark purples and blues and blacks. And in the middle of it all, clear as day, she saw herself and Ash, leaning close together, like they were about to kiss. Ash had a hand raised to her face. Her eyes were closed.

Dorothy touched her cheek in the same spot where the Ash in the photograph was touching it. Her mind tripped, trying to figure out when she'd been there, when this could have happened.

But, of course, it *hadn't* happened. Not yet.

Mac was speaking again. "I am, of course, disgusted by the events that have taken place. I've always considered Roman a close friend, an ally to the cause. And, more than that, he was a true asset to our city. There might not be any way to change what happened to him, but I believe in my soul that there's a way we can make things right.

"And now, it's time to put my money where my mouth is. I'll be offering a reward for the capture of the traitors in question, Jonathan Asher and Quinn Fox. If any of the fine citizens of this city were to bring me one or both of these traitors—dead or alive, hell, I'm not picky—I'd make it my personal mission to make sure they're brought to justice and made to pay for their crimes."

Mac paused for a moment, grinning that horrible, toad-like grin. "And, of course," he continued, "I'd make that citizen very, very rich."

Murmurs broke out among the bar patrons. Dorothy felt

a sudden thrill of fear. How stupid it was of her to come here! If anyone realized who she was, she'd be taken to Mac at once. She needed to run, to vanish.

She slid out of her seat, thinking she could sneak out using the window in the women's room, same as she did the first time she came here, when the bartender in the baseball hat suddenly appeared before her.

He looked skittish, nervous. He wouldn't look her in the eye.

"Miss Fox?" he said in a low, urgent voice. "I'm afraid I'm going to have to ask you to come with me."

7

Dorothy felt her heart beat against the back of her throat. Her palms had started to sweat.

Surely this tiny, baseball cap–wearing boy didn't think he could just deliver her to Mac?

Not if she had anything to say about it.

She reached into her cloak, fingers curling around the hilt of Roman's dagger—

"Ah, not so fast, there." The bartender produced a gun from his jacket. This wasn't terribly surprising, bars in New Seattle were rowdy, dangerous places, and Dorothy knew that most of the bartenders were armed. This one at least had the decency to look uncomfortable holding a gun.

Still, it was a *gun*, so Dorothy froze, one hand still clenching Roman's dagger.

"Why don't you hand that over?" the bartender said.

She felt the corners of her lip twitch. "I'm sure we can come to some sort of arrangement."

"The only arrangement I'm interested in is the one where you hand over whatever you have stashed up your sleeve and walk, calmly, down this hallway here, and I don't have to—to shoot you." The bartender motioned toward a back hallway with his gun, his cheeks slowly going pink. "Does that . . . does that sound okay to you?"

Dorothy's fingers twitched. She could see no way out of this that didn't involve a full-on brawl, which would alert everyone in the bar to the fact that she was here and likely lead to at least twenty other people joining to help the bartender take her down. Not odds she loved. It would be better to get this small, twitchy boy on his own and deal with him then.

She removed the dagger from her cloak and held it out to him.

Great. Now she was unarmed.

The bartender made her walk ahead of him, his gun half-concealed beneath his jacket so as not to alert the other patrons to the fact that there was something going on.

He probably doesn't want to risk losing his precious reward, Dorothy thought, smirking. She wondered if her sleight of hand was as good as it used to be. While walking past a table, she carefully slid a butter knife up her sleeve, glancing back over her shoulder to see whether the bartender had noticed.

He had not. He appeared to have had his eyes glued to the back of her head and, when she turned to look at him, he startled and nearly dropped his gun.

Oh dear, Dorothy thought, turning back around. This was

going to be laughably easy. She almost felt bad about it.

The metal was cool against her arm. A butter knife wasn't much of a weapon, but she figured she might be able to jam it into the little bartender's leg, perhaps make her getaway as he howled for his mommy. . . .

He led her through the crowded bar and down a narrow hall. Dorothy, frowning, felt a prickle of familiarity. Hadn't she been down this way before?

She held her breath as the bartender stopped in front of a closed door and turned to her.

"Look," he said, scratching the back of his head. "I got a business to run so . . . well it'd be great if we could keep this on the quiet side."

Dorothy let the knife fall into her palm and wrapped her fingers around the cool metal. "That won't be a problem," she said.

The bartender gave a short nod and pushed the door open.

Dorothy's eyes flickered over the space. For a moment she was too shocked to act. This was the same room she'd woken up in a year ago, when she'd first landed in 2077. Same bed and dresser, same broken mirror. She felt something like nostalgia and, for a fraction of a moment, she could almost pretend that none of the last year had even happened, that it was her first day in the future, and she still had everything ahead of her.

Oh, how many choices she would have made differently!

It was almost too much to think about.

And then the moment passed. Dorothy pulled her eyes away from the room and, instead, eyed the bartender's leg for a good spot to stab. She didn't want to hit an artery. The plan was to distract him, not kill him. No matter what the rumors said, she'd never actually killed anyone before.

She lifted her knife—

A man stepped out of the shadows. He seemed to appear out of the air itself, the darkness moving away from his face like oil from water, leaving only his smooth, pale skin and heavy brow.

Dorothy froze, her heart stuttering. "Willis?"

"It was stupid of you to come here," Willis muttered. His expression was dark, but he didn't look as angry with her as he had the night before, at the library. He moved past her, eyes flicking down the hall to make sure no one had followed them. And then he grabbed her arm and pulled her into the small room, closing the door behind them both.

Only then did he seem to notice the knife she was clutching. He lifted an eyebrow. "Really?"

"Well, I didn't realize he was a friend of yours," Dorothy muttered, placing the knife on the dresser. "He was a bit cryptic."

"I couldn't risk anyone overhearing us." The bartender perched on the edge of the twin bed. Other than the dresser, it was the only piece of furniture inside the small room, but Dorothy happened to know that the mattress was lumpy, so she was perfectly happy to stay standing.

"You can call me Levi," the bartender told her. "I'm a friend of Willis and the others. I don't think you remember me, but I was around when Ash first brought you in a few weeks ago. I was the one who said it was okay for you to rest back here. You were, uh, different then. Not so much with the hair and the . . ."

Levi motioned to his face, then turned red, and let his hand drop back onto his lap.

"Levi's a good guy," Willis explained, in that low, smooth voice of his. "You can trust him."

"*I* can't trust anyone," Dorothy said, frowning at Willis. "Or didn't you hear the broadcast just now? Mac Murphy has turned the whole city against me. I'm on the run."

Levi cleared his throat. "That's actually why we thought you might want to stay back here," he said quickly. "It won't be safe for you out on the docks."

Dorothy looked from him to Willis. "You're helping me, now? Zora gave me the impression that you all were done with me."

"Ah, so this part doesn't actually concern me," Levi said, looking a little embarrassed as he stood. "And I should get back to the bar. Willis? You'll be okay?"

Willis nodded, his eyes never leaving Dorothy. "I think I can take her, if it comes to that."

"Or, you know, the two of you could try to solve this *without* fighting. You might break something." Levi stood up on

66

his tiptoes and planted a kiss on Willis's cheek. Turning back to Dorothy, he added, "You need anything? Another drink, maybe?"

"I'm good," Dorothy quickly answered. And then, blushing, she added, "And thank you."

"Of course. Any friend of Willis, and all that." He handed her the dagger. "Try not to stab anyone, will you?"

"I can't make any promises," Dorothy said, stowing the dagger away.

"Well, I tried." And, with that, Levi stepped into the hall, pulling the door closed behind him.

For the first time, Dorothy noticed that Willis looked a little uncomfortable. He cast his eyes to the floor, like he couldn't quite bring himself to look Dorothy in the eye.

"I'd . . . er . . . . appreciate it if you didn't say anything to Chandra about me and Levi," he said, running a finger over his lower lip. "She's had a thing for Levi for a while now. I'm still hoping she'll move on."

Dorothy raised her eyebrows. "My lips are sealed," she said. "Does Chandra know that you're helping me hide?"

"She told me you stopped by the library earlier. She seemed to think you had a plan for finding out what happened to Ash." Willis scratched his chin. "Is that true?"

Dorothy swallowed. She did *not* have a plan. She had the beginnings of an idea for half a plan, at best. But she didn't want to disappoint Willis after he'd helped her.

"I'm . . . working on it," she said.

Willis was watching her, arms crossed. After a minute, he nodded and said, "Well, then. I'll leave you to it."

It was the kind of thing you said before leaving the room to go spend a little more time with your secret boyfriend. Dorothy waited for him to leave but, instead, Willis licked his lips, cleared his throat.

"Is there something else?" she asked.

He nodded, seeming to come to some decision, and drew himself up to his full height.

Dorothy took a step backward without making the conscious decision to do so, her stomach curdling with fear. In the entire time she'd known Willis, she'd never known him to be frightening before. At least she'd never known him to try to frighten *her*. He'd always had the air of a gentle giant, someone who was large but who never used his size to intimidate.

But, now . . .

He took up the entire doorway, his head practically scraping the ceiling, and he looked at Dorothy with no kindness in his eyes. His mouth was a straight, hard slash in a face like granite and his arms . . . had his arms always been that large? They were the size of dogs. It was as though Willis had two pit bulls strapped to his torso.

For a moment, Dorothy couldn't catch her breath.

"I'm helping you because I think you're here to figure out a way to save Ash's life," Willis said. "If I find out that's not the case, if at any point it seems like you're the reason Ash is dead after all . . . well, then we'll be having a very different conversation."

"U-understood," Dorothy managed to choke out.

Willis stared at her for a beat longer, and then he threw open the door and was gone.

LOG ENTRY—SEPTEMBER 14, 2074
12:21 HOURS
THE WORKSHOP

You'll notice that it's been a few days since I last updated. That's my fault, recovery's taken a bit longer than I expected. But I can sit upright now, and I seem to have regained the full use of my hands, so I can't complain.

Needless to say, my last experiment was not quite the wild success I'd been hoping it would be. I was able to implant the exotic matter inside of my person and align myself with the anil, and I did feel a sort of... pull, for lack of a better word, as though something was dragging me forward...

Unfortunately, that's where everything went terribly wrong. Moments after I felt that telltale pull below my navel my skin began to prickle. The sensation was odd, at first, but not entirely painful. Unpleasant, certainly. It felt as though all my nerves were firing at once. I admit, I'd wondered whether this was some sort of unpleasant side effect to the exotic matter, and so I did not react to the sensation right away but attempted to hold my ground, so to speak. That was a big mistake.

It couldn't have been more than two or three minutes before the unpleasant prickling became a full-out burning. I began to lose the feeling in my extremities, my fingers and toes went numb, and I no longer had control over my hands. It was terrifying.

Most terrifying of all, perhaps, was the fact that I didn't know exactly how to stop it. I was not inside the anil, but "aligned with it" according to Tesla's instructions, which I'd interpreted to mean inside the Cascadia subduction zone. I was getting desperate. My hands were shaking, and my skin felt like it was going to burn off, so I did the only thing I could think to do. I got the hell out of the subduction zone. Luckily, my symptoms stopped progressing immediately, and I was able to get myself back to the workshop without further harm coming to my person. My hands and feet were still badly injured, but after a few weeks rest they seem mostly back to normal.

Over the last few weeks, I've had little to do except think.

How did my experiment go so badly wrong? The only thing I can come up with is that I didn't manage to inject the exotic matter into my person just right. When I was first building the *Second Star*, it was crucial to work the EM into the vessel in such a way that it fused with the overall structure of the machine. That must be true when it comes to injecting the EM into your person, too. When I injected the EM, I must have done so in the wrong place. The exotic matter didn't entirely fuse with my body and, thus, failed to protect me from the energy of the anil.

It seems that I must go back to square one.

8

Dorothy spent the remainder of her evening curled up on the lumpy twin bed. She'd found an old notebook and a stubby pencil in one of the dresser drawers, and she was using them to scribble down everything she could remember of the days between seeing Ash at the Fairmont ball, and finding his blood-spattered boat outside the anil.

There'd been all those trips into the past . . . the meetings she and Roman had taken with Mac Murphy . . . broadcasts to the city . . .

Once she'd written down everything she could think of, she sat back, frowning. She'd been busy these last few weeks. She couldn't have found time for secret rendezvous with Ash, even if she'd wanted to.

Sure you could, said a voice in her head. *You did.*

She gnawed on the end of her pen, her gaze returning to the Professor's journal pages, scattered across the bed around her.

Willis wanted her to come up with a plan. But, so far, the only idea she had involved stealing something priceless and well guarded from a vicious gang of thieves and attempting to perform a deadly scientific experiment that only one—possibly *two*—people have managed to accomplish in all of history.

It was mad. *She* was mad for even thinking of it.

The candle that lit her room was burning low. With a sigh, she got up and blew it out. But she only lay in her bed, staring up at the ceiling, her mind spinning.

Three hours. That was how long Dorothy spent trying to fall asleep. But it was no use, she *knew* it was no use, and so she climbed out of bed and grabbed her cloak. She needed to do something. Anything.

She eased the door to her small room open and peered out into the hallway. Distant voices and nothing else. Being careful to keep the door from creaking behind her, she eased it shut and was off.

Moonlight glimmered off the black water. Dorothy was careful to keep to the back alleys and side docks, her hood pulled low over her face, terrified at every turn that someone might see her. Every boat that passed sent a jitter of fear up her neck, every passerby had her heart racing . . .

All it took was *one*. One person catching a glimpse of her hair. One person recognizing her cloak, her face. She had to be careful, now more than ever.

After a while, the Fairmont rose up above her, bright and glittering as always. Dorothy slowed as she approached, her breath catching in her throat. It was lovely even in its debilitated state, but Dorothy still remembered the way it had looked when she and Roman had seen it in the future, when all of New Seattle had been destroyed.

Then, it had been a black husk protruding from the ice, a skeleton of the building it once was. She couldn't help shivering, thinking of it. If things continued as they were now, New Seattle was going to fall to ruin. The Fairmont, along with everything and everyone else this close to the coast, would be destroyed.

"One problem at a time," she muttered to herself. "You can save the future after you figure out what happened to Ash."

Shuddering, Dorothy hurried forward, through a back door.

During her time in the Black Cirkus, she'd discovered every secret doorway and staircase inside the Fairmont. She used that knowledge now, sneaking like a shadow into the depths of the hotel and down the back stairs to the door that led to the parking garage. She knew, of course, that there was little chance that the Cirkus would keep the *Black Crow* unguarded. Even so, she was unprepared for what she saw when she pushed the garage door open.

Spotlights glared from all four corners of the parking garage, lighting the space up like a carnival. Dorothy blinked and took a step backward. It seemed as though the entire Black Cirkus was surrounding the time machine, shouting and catcalling. The din was enough to make her ears ring.

What is happening here?

She pulled her hood low over her face and did her best to blend in with the crowd as she made her way to the center of the room. Luckily, no one seemed to be paying any attention to her.

The Freaks had surrounded the *Black Crow*, the last time machine in existence. Dorothy watched as one of them separated from the crowd and then turned to face the others, arms lifted overhead in triumph. The crowd cheered.

Dorothy pushed her hood back, just a little. It was Eliza.

Eliza was beautiful, if predators could be beautiful, with eyes like ice, heavy brows, and skin so pale it was nearly white. Dorothy covered her own face with one hand as Eliza strolled past her, climbing up the time machine's short, retractable staircase and into the cockpit.

And now, Dorothy felt a grin touch her lips. She couldn't actually be attempting what Dorothy thought she was attempting. . . .

A hush fell over the crowd as Eliza began fumbling with the dials on the control panel. The time machine made a wheezing sort of noise and lurched forward. A plume of smoke erupted from the tail pipe.

The crowd groaned.

Beneath her hood, Dorothy pressed her lips together, stifling a laugh. *This* was their plan? To try to fly the time machine themselves? Fools. It had taken her the better part of a year to learn, and that was with Roman at her side, slapping her wrist whenever she reached for the wrong lever and pointing out the finer details of the clouds in the anil so that she'd know when to exit. Mac was an idiot if he thought anyone here would manage to so much as get the time machine off the ground.

Eliza remained in the cockpit for several minutes longer. Dorothy couldn't see what she was doing, but she heard swearing and, soon after, Eliza stomped back into the parking garage, slamming the time machine door behind her.

"It's impossible!" she shouted, as boos and hisses erupted from the crowd. "There's some sort of . . . of secret trick to it! I can't even get the key to turn!"

Try turning it the other way, Dorothy thought, smirking. It was such a small thing, but it had been something that confused her, too, how the key needed to be turned toward her instead of away. Roman told her it had been a little trick of the Professor's, designed to slow down anyone who might want to take the time machine without permission. There were dozens of similar fail-safes worked into the machine's design. Dorothy wasn't even sure she knew them all.

Things couldn't be going well, if the Cirkus couldn't even figure out how to turn on the damn thing.

"How hard can this be?" growled a familiar voice, and a cold chill wormed up Dorothy's spine. She turned.

Mac Murphy separated himself from the crowd, the woman in black drifting, silently, behind him. Dorothy felt her eyes drawn to her, curiosity piqued. This was the closest she'd been to the stranger since first seeing her on the docks. Her fingers twitched, wanting to grab her and throw her hood back so that she might catch a glimpse of her face.

The woman in black was small and slight, with a slim mask covering her face, a hood pulled over her hair, and black gloves to her elbows. The only bit of visible skin that Dorothy could see was the white of her neck. Everything else was hidden.

Dorothy felt a shiver of familiarity, studying her. Impossible though it might be, she had the strange, tilting feeling that she was looking at herself.

Was that impossible? She knew that she'd gone back in time. Perhaps she'd stayed, found a way to infiltrate the Cirkus and regain her spot as its leader.

But why? Dorothy frowned as she turned this question over in her head. She didn't actually *want* to lead the gang again, and she certainly didn't want to work alongside Mac Murphy. So why go through all this trouble, the time travel, the disguise, the lies?

Dorothy turned back around, watching a few more Freaks try and fail to get the *Black Crow* airborne. She gritted her teeth, nerves climbing her neck. The novelty of watching them was beginning to wear thin. They showed no intention of leaving the time machine behind, and Dorothy's entire plan revolved around stealing the canister of EM inside of the main cabin. How was she supposed to do that if the *Black Crow* was surrounded?

She chewed her bottom lip, frustrated.

And then she realized . . .

Quinn Fox, assassin, cannibal, leader of the Black Cirkus, might not have a way to get to the EM—but Dorothy, con artist and thief, certainly did.

She lifted a hand to her head and slid a hairpin out of her curls. It was a pin from her original time period, made of solid silver and—so far—strong enough to work any lock without bending or breaking. Dorothy had been careful to keep it with her over the years. It had served her well many, many times in the past.

While the crowd was distracted, she drifted around to the back of the time machine, fingers traveling over the cool metal until she found the crack of a door.

The cargo hold.

She grinned. She was quite familiar with it.

Glancing around to make sure that everyone's eyes were still on Bennett—the latest poor fool to attempt to fly the *Black Crow*—Dorothy pressed her back against the cargo hold door and slid her hairpin into the lock. She gritted her teeth, and turned left, and then right.

It took a moment for the lock to catch—

There. She felt a click and closed her eyes, a smile crossing her lips as she exhaled.

Still got it.

She eased the door open behind her back and slipped inside, pulling the door shut again very quickly. There wasn't much time. She groped along the back of the hold in the darkness until she felt the edges of the panel that separated her from the main cockpit. She pressed her ear to the wall and waited until she heard nothing but silence in the main hold.

Then, barely daring to breathe, she slid the panel away.

The cockpit was empty. She exhaled in relief and slipped forward, kneeling.

The internal control panel was one of the key design elements of the *Black Crow*. The exotic matter was stored in a hidden compartment. Dorothy moved her hands over levers and buttons, until the panel fell open, revealing a glass cylinder filled with liquid sunlight. Then a shadow passed overhead, and the substance turned the color and texture of steel. A moment later, it was a swirling blue mist.

Dorothy's breath caught in her throat. She could easily stay there and watch the strange, ever-changing substance forever, but there wasn't time for that. She needed to get gone before another Freak climbed into the cockpit to try his hand at flying the damn thing.

Moving quickly, she removed the canister of exotic matter from the ship and slipped it inside her cloak, then she went back out the way she'd come, replacing the panel that separated the cockpit from the cargo hold and slipping silently back into the garage.

Here, she paused a moment, looking around. No one was watching her. They were all turned to the front of the garage, waiting to see who the next fool to attempt to fly the time machine would be. She swallowed, hard, trying to still her nerves. The canister of EM seemed to bulge beneath her cloak.

A tall, thin boy separated from the crowd, his hands raised. Dorothy frowned, not recognizing him. Unlike the rest of the Cirkus Freaks, this boy wasn't wearing a black cloak. He wore a bomber jacket, the leather badly beaten and cracked. Recognizing it, Dorothy froze. She felt a chill move through her.

"Ash?" she murmured, voice low. She watched the boy, skin tingling. He had his back to her, and so she saw only the knit hat pulled down low over his head, his shoulders.

Had she and Ash both come back in time to this moment?

No, she told herself immediately. It wasn't possible—Ash could never have walked into a room filled with Cirkus Freaks without being recognized.

And yet Dorothy couldn't pull her eyes away from that boy. She watched as he climbed into the cockpit, easily flipping switches and dials.

There was the low groan of a motor. A flash of lights. The hair on the back of Dorothy's neck stood on end. He was doing it. Somehow, he was making the time machine work.

With a lurch, the time machine lifted from the ground and was airborne. A mix of awe and horror churned through Dorothy's chest as the machine shot off through the parking garage windows, Cirkus Freaks cheering as it took to the sky.

Dorothy stood, dumbstruck, watching the time machine disappear. The pilot wouldn't notice that the exotic matter was gone until he tried to take it into the anil. Then, the time machine would begin shaking and falling apart and—if he didn't act quickly—he would be torn apart by the vicious winds inside of the time tunnel.

If he was just another Cirkus Freak who'd happened to

find Ash's coat, that would be a good thing.

But if . . .

Dorothy shook her head, pushing the thought away. It *couldn't* be Ash, she told herself again. But she didn't know what else to think. Who else would've been able to fly the time machine?

The EM felt suddenly huge and obvious inside her cloak. She had the sense that anyone glancing at her would know that she'd taken it. She had to get out of here.

She wove through the Cirkus Freaks and hurried to the back of the garage. She reached for the door—

Behind her: the click of a gun.

Dorothy felt her heart plummet.

She dropped her hand from the door and turned to see Eliza standing behind her, pistol raised.

"Old friend," Eliza said, a vicious grin on her face. "What brings you back here?"

9

Nerves pricked the back of Dorothy's neck. Her mouth filled with the taste of something sour.

She and Eliza hadn't always hated one another. Or, at least *she* hadn't always hated Eliza. In fact, there'd been a time when Dorothy had hoped Eliza could become something of an ally to her, maybe even a friend. It seemed silly now, but they had been the only two women in the Black Cirkus. Dorothy always thought they should have had each other's backs.

But she'd dismissed such notions months and months ago. Eliza was vicious and cruel and seemed to only want power and more power. And, for reasons that Dorothy had never fully understood, Eliza despised her.

Dorothy pressed her lips together, thinking fast. Despite all of this, there had to be something she could say, some way to get Eliza to see reason.

Her eyes flicked past Eliza's head. The rest of the Cirkus was still gathered near the far wall of windows, watching the time machine grow smaller and smaller in the night sky. They hadn't noticed the commotion going on near the back door. There was still time to get out of this.

"Eliza," Dorothy said, slowly lifting her hands to show that she was unarmed and therefore not a threat to her. "You don't have to do this. You could pretend that you never saw me."

The corner of Eliza's mouth twitched. "And why on earth would I do that, little Fox?"

Dorothy opened her mouth but found that she couldn't come up with an answer. She had no money, no power, nothing to bribe the other girl with.

Eliza, smirking, seemed to realize this at the exact same moment that Dorothy did. She turned and called, over her shoulder, "Mac! Seems we've had an old friend drop in on us."

Dorothy felt a muscle in her jaw tighten as Mac Murphy turned, his eyes lighting with glee at the sight of her. She checked to make sure that the stolen EM was well hidden in her cloak. It was. Thank goodness for small mercies.

Mac took his time making his way to the back of the garage. He'd been shot in the leg not long ago—by Chandra, Dorothy knew now—and, though he no longer needed to use crutches to get around, he still walked with a bit of a limp, his knee not quite bending the way it was supposed to.

He used that disability to his advantage, taking his time and walking slowly across the garage, making her wait. The Cirkus Freaks who'd been distracted by the time machine now turned their attention to Dorothy, curious, she was sure, to see what terrible things Mac had planned for her.

She forced herself to hold her chin high, to keep her shoulders back. Whatever he wanted from her, she would face it head-on.

"Quinn," Mac said, grinning delightedly. "I figured you'd be halfway to the Center by now."

It was a cruel jab. Mac had allies working the borders that separated the Center states from the Western Territories, but he had to know that Dorothy didn't have such resources. Without a time machine, she was trapped here.

She refused to give him the satisfaction of pointing this out. "And miss seeing your smiling face," she said, through a tight smile of her own. "Not likely."

Mac laughed, a deep rumble in his belly that almost seemed genuine. "I should have killed you days ago," he said when he'd finished, wiping a tear from his cheek with his thumb. "But I have to admit, I would've missed these moments together."

The Cirkus Freaks were gathering in a loose circle around them, blocking the doors, making sure there wasn't a way for her to escape. She felt a nerve near her eye twitch as she marked the few exits, all of which had been blocked. *Blast.*

Mac pulled a gun from his waistband and let it dangle, lazily, from one hand. Dorothy knew he meant it as a threat, and so she refused to look at it.

"So why did you?" Mac asked, raising an eyebrow. "Come back, I mean."

The exotic matter seemed to bulge beneath her cloak,

announcing to the entire Black Cirkus what she'd done. She searched her brain for a good lie and came up blank.

"I—I had nowhere else to go." Her voice cracked a little as the words left her mouth, betraying how true they were.

Mac chewed the inside of his cheek. "That so? You expect me to believe you plan on being a faithful ally once more?" He glanced toward the back windows. "I don't need you to fly my machine anymore. So what use are you to me? You've already proven, more than once, that you can't be trusted."

Dorothy's stomach turned over. There was no arguing with that. "What are you going to do with me?"

His smile widened, showing off two rows of cracked, nicotine-stained teeth.

"I have a few ideas," he said. To the Freaks, he added, "Take her upstairs. I'll be up to join you shortly."

Dorothy felt sick as they climbed the stairs, the slow shuffle of their feet over carpet the only sound in the halls. Something musty-smelling rose up from the floor, making her nose twitch. She didn't think she'd ever get over the smell of this city, how the perpetual damp left everything reeking of mold and rot.

Mac Murphy had taken over the hotel's Olympic Suite. At fifteen hundred square feet, it took up the entire top floor of the hotel and was roughly the size of a small house. Unlike the lower floors, the top floor of the Fairmont was bright, lit by sconces holding candles that dripped thick puddles of wax onto the carpet. Freaks stood to either side of the double doors that led to Mac's suite.

Something prickled, uncomfortably, in Dorothy. "I'm to have guards?"

Eliza gave her a look and escorted Dorothy into the room. Dorothy assumed that Eliza would be going, but the other girl just stood there, one eyebrow cocked.

"What?" Dorothy asked. "Are you waiting for a tip?"

Eliza lifted a key from her pocket. "I've been ordered to lock you in."

"Have you?" Dorothy asked, amused.

"Order comes directly from Mac himself."

Dorothy released a sharp laugh. She couldn't remember the last time a simple lock had been enough to hold her anywhere.

Reluctantly, she stepped into the room, standing in silence as Eliza pulled the door shut. And then there was a click of metal hitting metal, and she was alone.

Nerves tingled in her fingers as she turned, taking in the space. Mac had begun hoarding the items she and Roman had brought back from the past, she saw. A baseball from the Cubs' first World Series win had rolled against his dresser. A wineglass from the *Titanic* sat on his bedside table, where it was currently being used as an ashtray. The bass guitar that Dorothy had stolen from the dressing room of the Beatles' first show in Liverpool was lying on the floor near the far wall, in pieces. It hadn't been in pieces when they'd brought it back. Mac must've smashed it.

Grimacing, Dorothy tore her eyes away from the

treasures, telling herself that none of that mattered, now. If she'd left them in the past, they would've been destroyed by the ravages of time anyway. This wasn't any worse.

And she had to work quickly.

She removed the EM from her cloak, fingers trembling as she unscrewed the top of the canister. The EM glittered inside, strange as always. She couldn't risk losing any, not when there was such a limited supply left in the world. And she wasn't sure how much she'd need for this little experiment. The Professor, infuriatingly, hadn't been very specific in his calculations.

Not a good sign, whispered a voice in her head, but she quickly pushed it away. What other options were there? She'd just have to make do.

She hurried into the penthouse bathroom and pushed the door closed behind her, jumping a little as she heard it latch. She fumbled for the light switch—*success*. Electric lights flicked on above her, gleaming off the white marble and black tile. She should've known that Mac would have his private rooms set up with electricity as soon as possible.

Exhaling deeply, she placed the EM canister on the countertop and met her own eyes in the mirror above the sink.

She looked dreadful. Hair mussed from a night spent outdoors and going so long between washings, face smudged with dirt and grime. A nervous smile twitched at her lips. Was this really how she wanted to greet Ash after so long? Unwashed and filthy? Her eyes flicked to the shower stall behind her, and she found herself wishing she had time to bathe.

Footsteps outside the hotel room door made her tense. She didn't know how long she had before Mac came up here to do . . . whatever he planned to do to her. And she didn't know how long this would take to work.

"Here goes nothing," she murmured, on an exhale. She pulled Roman's dagger out from under her cloak and gathered a very small amount of EM on the tip of the blade.

It looked like something dark and dripping. Then, a moment later, it was green goo clinging to the metal. It was gaseous, vanishing into the air. It was solid, like ice.

She blinked and looked away. The constant changing was causing a nerve near her temple to pulse. She pushed her cloak aside, revealing the cool white skin of her abdomen.

The dagger trembled in her hand.

She took a breath—

Over the last few days, I've been going over Tesla's notes again and again to see what I might've missed. I have a few theories, but the most logical is that I simply injected the exotic matter into the wrong place.

Tesla posited that, in order for the EM to fully integrate with your body, you'd need to inject it directly into your aorta. This makes sense, because your aorta is the artery responsible for carrying blood from your heart to the rest of your body, so it connects with every other major artery. Its job is to distribute oxygenated blood throughout, so it would stand to reason that, if you were to inject exotic matter into your aorta, it would spread throughout your entire body in the same way that oxygenated blood does. Right?

Well, that's the theory. I'm not a medical doctor, I'm a physicist, and I'm working well outside my comfort zone here. I know that it's unusual for medication to be injected into arteries instead of veins, but I have to trust that Tesla had reasons for specifying the aorta as the ideal injection site, especially when it's much more difficult to locate than a close-to-the-surface vein. The only choice I have is to try again and see if, this time, I can get it to work.

Tesla included a sort of "map" of the inside of the human body with the rest of his notes but, this time, I'm going to go off the most modern medical illustrations I can find. I borrowed one of Chandra's books and studied the human body until I located the best place to attempt a second injection. Once again, aortic rupture is a concern. But I'm trying not to think about that just now. Here I go.

Okay! The second injection appears to have been success-ful. I experienced the same strange, tingling sensation as I did the first time I attempted this and, so far, no aortic rupture. So that's a good sign.

Now, it's time for me to go back to the Cascadia subduction zone and see if, this time, my mission will be successful.

10

Dorothy's fingers trembled. The dagger she held twitched and then fell with a clatter into the sink below. The exotic matter that had been clinging to the blade disappeared in an iridescent haze that smelled, oddly, of campfire smoke.

Blast. She exhaled, her eyes snapping closed. She didn't think she could do this. It was simply too terrifying, too risky. She'd spent the last day reading through the Professor's journal pages—pages that contained lurid, visceral details of all the ways that experimenting with exotic matter could go wrong.

Skin burning off her body and hands, and feet left numb and useless. Not to mention death . . .

The Professor had come dangerously close to these complications himself, and he'd been using medical illustrations to find the exact location of his aorta, he'd had a special gun that he'd built using schematics from one of the most brilliant scientific minds of all time, while *she* had dagger that hadn't even been sterilized properly.

And he'd *still* missed the first time he'd attempted the injection. She didn't stand a chance.

"Hiding, little Fox?" Mac's voice traveled from the other side of the bathroom door, making Dorothy twitch. She was losing her edge. She hadn't even heard him enter the room. Hands shaking, she quickly replaced the top of the container of EM and stored it, along with Roman's dagger, in the space underneath the bathroom sink. Mac was going to search her, she knew, and hiding these things in his personal bathroom might keep them away from him for long enough to give her time to form a plan. She hoped.

She'd only just closed the cupboard when the bathroom door burst open and two black-clad Cirkus Freaks appeared. She lifted her eyes to the mirror and saw Donovan and Eliza standing behind her.

Her shoulders tensed. She hadn't seen Donovan since the night he'd betrayed her. According to Mac, he'd done it for a *peach*, of all things. Dorothy still couldn't decide whether she was horribly offended by this or if she merely pitied him. How sad must a person's life be if they would betray someone for a piece of fruit?

She fought as they each grabbed one of her arms (more for show than anything else, she couldn't have these two telling the others that the great Quinn Fox had come along easily) but they were two and armed, and she was only one. Before long, they'd managed to drag her back into the main penthouse and shove her to the floor.

Her knees and the palms of her hands scraped against the hard wood, roughly enough that she felt certain she'd have bruises in the morning. From her position, she could see only Mac's boots, which were black and freshly polished. A distorted version of her own face reflected back from the leather.

She pulled her gaze away and, gingerly, pushed herself to her knees. Then, in the most pleasant voice she could manage, she said, "Mac, darling. I was beginning to think you'd forgotten about me."

Mac grunted. His squashed, toad-like face was nearly always twisted into an unpleasant, vaguely constipated expression but, just now, he seemed even more annoyed than usual. He'd probably expected her to cry or beg. It delighted her, that she hadn't given him the pleasure.

"Donovan?" he grunted. "The bag."

The bag? Dorothy felt her nerves tighten. Whatever the bag was, she knew that it couldn't be good. She worked hard to keep the fear from her face as Donovan crossed the hotel room, hauling a duffel onto the hotel bed. Dorothy thought she saw the muscles in his shoulders stiffen as he unzipped the bag and stared down at what was inside.

When Donovan spoke again, his voice was choked. "Sir?"

"Leave it there for now." Turning back to Dorothy, Mac said, "Believe me, princess, I want to use what's in that bag." His thick lips twisted. "In fact, I want to use it very much, but I figured I'd be all gentlemanlike and give you a chance to come clean first." He paused, blinking, before adding, "Is there anything you'd like to share with the rest of the group?"

"Come clean?" She worked hard to keep her expression innocent. He must be talking about the exotic matter. His pilot must've returned once he'd discovered that it was missing.

There was no one holding her anymore, so Dorothy pushed herself to her feet and perched at the very edge of the hotel room bed, trying to look like she was preparing herself for nothing more than an unpleasant chat. The bag hovered at the edge of her vision, but she wouldn't allow herself to look at it directly, she refused to give Mac that satisfaction.

It didn't stop her from wondering what it might contain, though. Some arcane tool he was planning to use to torture her with, perhaps? Or . . .

No, it was almost certainly going to be the torture. Her throat felt suddenly tight.

To Mac, she said, "I have no idea what you're talking about. I missed you all, and so I returned. It's as simple as that."

"I ain't stupid, Fox," Mac said.

"Obviously not," she said, without conviction, letting her eyes travel around the room. Donovan and Eliza flanked the door, and she knew that another two guards stood on the other side. The only other way out was through the window. Which was possible, she knew from experience. But highly unpleasant.

She turned back to Mac and said, her smile tight, "Even so, I'm afraid I have no idea what you're talking about."

Mac studied her, mouth working like he was chewing on

a piece of grass. After a long moment, he spat on the floor.

He said, "You really expect me to believe that the two of you aren't working together?"

Two of you? Dorothy straightened, her interest piqued. She thought of the boy she'd seen climb into the time machine, the one wearing Ash's jacket, the one who'd been able to fly the *Black Crow*.

Ash, she thought again. She waited for the other voice, the one telling her that this was impossible, that Mac would've recognized Ash, even if he'd somehow managed to get past the other Freaks, Mac would have seen his face and known.

This time, that voice was silent. She'd kept her true identity hidden for a year, after all. Ash could've figured out how to do it for a few minutes.

She could feel herself leaning forward, almost as though she could drag the answers from Mac using physical force. She had to work very hard to keep her voice casual, as she said, "Who do you think I'm working with?"

"That kid who stole my time machine." Mac yanked a chair away from the desk in the corner and pulled it across the room. He sat, resting his elbows on his knees. "The two of you were working together, right?"

Dorothy was quiet for a moment, her tongue lightly tracing the backs of her teeth. It wasn't so crazy to think that boy was Ash. There were only so many people in the world who knew how to fly the time machine. Roman was dead and she was, well, *she* was sitting right here. So who did that leave?

Willis knew how to fly it. She'd seen him do it once, back

at Fort Hunter. But Willis was quite a bit larger than the boy she'd seen.

She swallowed and said, all innocence, "Someone stole your time machine?"

Mac sniffed. "You're going to want to watch your tone."

Dorothy knew he meant it as a threat (that bag still hovered at the edge of her eyesight) and yet a smile parted her lips. "I'm afraid I can't think of a thing to help you," she said. "My apologies."

A shadow passed over Mac's face. He swallowed and said, through clenched teeth, "Search her."

Eliza practically leaped at the chance. She crossed the room in two long strides, and then her hands were running over Dorothy's cloak, digging into her pockets.

You won't find anything, Dorothy thought, smug, mere seconds before Eliza withdrew her hand, something white pressed between her fingertips.

"What's this, little Fox?" Eliza asked. She opened her hand, revealing a folded stack of loose pages.

Dorothy felt her stomach plummet. *The Professor's journal pages*. She'd foolishly left them tucked up her sleeve instead of storing them with everything else she hadn't wanted Mac and the others to discover. And now Eliza had them and there was nothing she could do to keep her from reading them, from learning what had arguably been the Professor's greatest discovery.

How could she have been so stupid?

Eliza unfolded the pages, her lips quirking. "Diary entries? Have you been keeping a diary, Quinn? How sweet."

Dorothy had to work hard to keep her smile in place. Her only hope now was that Eliza might not realize how important those pages were.

Throw them away, she prayed, silently. *They're nothing.*

"As a matter of fact, I have been keeping a diary, yes." Dorothy did her best to keep her voice light, trying for a wobbly smile. "Dear Diary, today this horrible girl who I used to work with got a bit mouthy with me, so I slit her—"

Eliza brought the back of her hand down, hard, across Dorothy's face. Knuckles bit into her cheek, smashing the inside of her mouth right up against her teeth. Her head whipped to the side, pain flaring up her neck. For a few minutes, she saw stars.

When her vision cleared, Dorothy stretched her jaw and spat, cringing when she saw blood hit the floor. Eliza had nearly knocked out one of her teeth.

And the diversion hadn't worked, anyway. Eliza was frowning down at the journal pages, now, the skin between her brows creased in concentration.

"This looks like something you might be interested in, sir," she said, waving the journal entries at Mac.

Dorothy felt panic rising inside of her. It was like a bad dream. Things kept getting worse and there was nothing she could do, no way to stop it.

Mac crossed the room and ripped the pages from Eliza's

hands. There was a moment of silence as he read over them, lips moving to help him make sense of the longer, more difficult words.

After several moments, he lifted his eyes to her, one eyebrow cocked. There was a look on his face that Dorothy could only describe as glee. Once again, she'd made this terrible man happy.

"Is this true?" he asked, pointing the pages at her. When Dorothy didn't answer, he came closer and grabbed the collar of her cloak in one meaty hand. His face was close to hers, now, and she could inhale the stink of his breath. Cigarette smoke and whatever he'd had for lunch. Tuna fish, from the smell of it.

He said, "Are you telling me I could've been traveling through time all along, without a bleeding pilot, without a time machine, just by sticking some of this . . . this stuff into my body?"

Dorothy said, through gritted teeth, "Give me a dagger and we can experiment, if you like."

Mac let her go and took a sudden step backward, excitement glinting in his black eyes. "That's how he did it, isn't it? Your friend Asher, that's how he got to the future with us. He figured this thing out, didn't he."

"You'll have to ask him," Dorothy said.

Mac smiled at her. "Ah, okay. I see how it's going to be. You're mad because I figured out your little secret, so now you don't want to talk anymore. I get it. Luckily, I brought a friend with me. I figured she might do a better job at loosening your tongue."

Mac stepped to the side, and Dorothy's attention slid away from him and landed on the woman in black, who was standing in the doorway.

Her breath caught in her throat. "You," she said, numb.

"I thought it was time the two of you meet," said Mac. "Quinn Fox, I'd like you to meet my new associate, Regan Rose."

Regan moved past her, shadowlike. Her feet didn't make a sound as they sunk into the faded carpet, but her coat flapped back with the movement, and the fabric released a soft *whiff.* It was an old-fashioned coat, Dorothy saw, something from before the flood. It was long and made of heavy wool, with drooping sleeves, and a fairy-tale-witch hood to hide her face.

Dorothy eyed Regan. "I don't know you."

"That doesn't surprise me." Regan seemed unconcerned by this admission. There was blood on her hands, Dorothy noticed. She didn't hide it. In fact, she pushed her sleeves up, leaving a slick of red along the pale skin.

So. It was going to be torture then.

Dorothy had to work hard not to shudder.

11

Regan peered into the duffel bag sitting on the hotel room bed. "Would you like to see my collection?"

She didn't wait for an answer before she began pulling ancient-looking tools out of the bag and placing them on the bed. Watching, Dorothy understood that this was part of her torture, the anticipation of what was to come.

First, there was a set of handcuffs. The cuffs themselves were vises attached to thin, metal levers and Dorothy knew, in a glance, how they would work. She could already picture Regan twisting the lever so that the vises would slowly crush the bones in her wrists, rendering her hands useless. She swallowed a shudder.

An iron mask was placed beside the cuffs. Spikes ran along the inside of the mask, made to dig into cheeks and skin and lips.

A leather whip came out of the bag next, and then chains and other tools Dorothy didn't entirely understand—crude, metal objects covered in jagged edges and points. A thin wooden stick. Clamps. Screws.

The fear Dorothy had been fighting against hit her in a wave. She tried to breathe, but her throat closed up and the oxygen shot right into her head, leaving her dizzy.

Stay calm, she told herself, lips pressed tight. She forced herself to breathe steadily through her nose. *Don't let them see your fear.*

Regan examined the tools for a long moment before eventually choosing the stick. It was long and smaller in diameter than a pencil. It was by far the most innocent-looking object she'd removed from her little bag of tricks, but Dorothy still felt a shiver shoot up her spine.

"Do you know what a bastinado is?" Regan held the stick up to the light, and a line of silver appeared along its edge. "It has been used in some of the most ancient forms of torture. You merely remove a person's shoes and socks and whip the bastinado against their bare feet."

Regan demonstrated by cracking the small stick against her own, gloved palm. It made a sound like a whip as it hit the leather.

"So simple," she continued, grinning behind her slim mask. "And yet so effective. In fact, the first documented use of a bastinado in Europe dates back to the year 1537. In China, it's been used since 960."

Dorothy swallowed. One look at that stick and she could practically feel the wood biting into the soft flesh on the bottoms of her feet. She imagined how her skin might rip, how the blood might trickle down between her toes.

She licked her lips to stop them from trembling. "I told you that I don't know anything. Whipping that thing against my feet won't change that."

Regan glanced to where Eliza and Donovan were standing and nodded, once. Some deep, animal instinct inside of Dorothy kicked to life. She no longer cared about looking frightened, she shot off the bed and took a slow step backward, toward the door—

The others were too fast. Eliza's hands clamped down on her shoulders, holding her in place.

Dorothy jerked beneath her grip. "Let go of me!"

But then Donovan was on her, his hands tightening around her wrists. His palms were sweating, Dorothy noted. That sweat, more than anything else, told her how real this was. Even Donovan was scared, and he wasn't the one about to be tortured.

She inhaled, her breath shuddering down her throat like a sob. She'd never been tortured before. She didn't think she would be good at it.

She thought she could pull her hands loose if she caught Donovan off guard, if she jerked her body away fast enough. But then she'd still have to get past Eliza and Regan and Mac. It was no use.

"Take off her shoes," Regan said, still examining the stick, as though looking for flaws.

Dorothy was forced onto the bed, her boots roughly removed. She shivered when the cool air touched her bare skin, but at least she was able to hold it together enough not to beg or cry. She wouldn't give these people the satisfaction.

Regan rested the stick against the arches of Dorothy's feet. Dorothy could feel every splinter of wood against her skin. Her muscles drew tight, waiting for the stick to be drawn back, for it to come cracking down against her feet . . .

Instead, Regan leaned down and murmured, low enough that Dorothy had to strain to hear her, "I'm told you have friends. People you care about."

Dorothy closed her eyes. "Don't."

"Chandra and Willis and Zora. Is that right?" She clicked her tongue. "It would be such a shame if something happened to them."

When Dorothy said nothing, Regan flicked her wrist, bringing the stick down against her foot with a sharp crack. The wood nicked her skin, and Dorothy flinched, releasing a short, terrified yelp. But it didn't hurt as much as she'd expected it to. Regan must be saving the worst of the pain for later.

"Shall I go fetch them?" Regan asked. "Or will you tell me what I want to know?"

She leaned closer, until her masked face was only inches from Dorothy's own. Dorothy could see nothing of her appearance, nothing except for two black, emotionless eyes.

Regan lowered her voice to a purr, like she was speaking to a lover. "Who are you working with, little Fox?"

Dorothy closed her mouth and then opened it again. "I'm working . . . with Princess Mary," she managed to choke out.

Regan's black eyes narrowed behind her mask. She drew her arm back, and Dorothy braced herself for the feel of the harsh wood against her feet—

And then the hotel room door crashed open, and a bullet whizzed past her cheek, close enough that she felt the burn of gunpowder flare across her skin. Donovan and Eliza released their hold on her, swearing as they took cover and reached for their own guns. Dorothy had just enough time to lift one hand to her face before the air filled with gunfire.

Blast. She rolled off the mattress and came to a crouch in the narrow space between the bed and the wall, heart hammering in her chest. There was an initial rush of bullets, and then brittle silence fell over the room like a layer of ash.

Dorothy braced herself, waiting. She didn't know who was on the other side of the wall, or what they wanted from her. To be perfectly honest, she wasn't entirely sure she *wanted* to know. This spot right here, hidden behind the bed, this was perfectly fine with her, thank you very much. She closed her eyes and exhaled, silently, through her mouth. At least down here no one was shooting at her or torturing her.

But one minute became two and then—*damn it to hell*—her curiosity got the better of her. She was Quinn Fox, for God's sake. She couldn't be found crouching behind this bed, hiding like a child.

Exhaling, slowly, she moved out from behind the bed—

The boy from the parking garage stood in the middle of the room, his back to her. From her position on the floor, Dorothy could make out the beaten leather of his jacket and the smooth fabric of his trousers, but nothing else. His hair was dark, much darker than Ash's, and he seemed to be wearing it in braids.

Getting no more information from the boy, Dorothy allowed her eyes to tick off other people in the room. Eliza was crouching behind a chair, and from beneath the bathroom door Dorothy saw the tips of boots that, if she had to guess, she would say belonged to Donovan. Mac and Regan were nowhere to be seen.

Movement caught her eye. She looked up and saw that the boy had turned, and now he was looking at her.

Only it wasn't a boy at all—it was Zora.

Dorothy's eyes fell closed. Of course. Professor Walker was Zora's father. Zora had helped build the time machine. She would know how to fly it.

When she opened her eyes again, Zora was staring at her.

"Duck," she said calmly.

Before Dorothy could react, the floor in front of her exploded. She crawled backward, swearing. There was another crack of a bullet—this one whizzing past her face—and then Dorothy saw Mac crawl out from behind the other side of the bed, trying to make it to the door. He was feet away when Zora flew at him, slamming him to the ground. Mac coughed, hard, and tried to push himself up, but Zora was still on his back, one arm braced against his neck and the base of his skull. Mac threw his head back, his skull connecting with her face. Zora grunted, a spray of blood flying from her mouth.

"Start running, you idiot!" she snarled. She still had an arm angled across Mac's back.

Dorothy leaped to her feet—

Eliza was instantly on her. She curled an arm around Dorothy's neck and tried to drag her backward, but Dorothy hurled herself to the side, sending Eliza rolling across the bed and crashing into the opposite wall. She was seeing stars, and her arms and legs felt like jelly, but she made herself push up to hands and knees, blinking. She needed weapons. She needed—

Oh God. The EM.

Dorothy crawled for the bathroom, ignoring the gunshots crisscrossing over her head. She threw the door open, and Donovan let out a surprised *yelp!*

"How are you doing?" she said, nodding at him. Before he could react, she'd thrown the door beneath the sink open and snatched the EM and Roman's dagger. To Donovan, she added, "Have a pleasant evening."

Zora was suddenly behind her, gripping her arm and dragging her to her feet. "Let's go," she said, "or do you expect me to hold off your enemies forever?"

The two of them crashed into the hall, sparing no time to see whether they were being followed.

"This way!" Dorothy shouted. She thudded down the back stairs as fast as her feet could carry her, and then it was through the hotel kitchens and out a delivery door that she happened to know was no longer in use.

There was a rickety dock out back, she knew, but she felt

her heart sink as she slammed through the door and out into the cold.

It was foggier than she'd prepared for, and a thick cloud cover had crept over the stars and the moon. It wasn't just dark, it was dark as pitch, dark as oil. She couldn't see a thing. Where were they supposed to go now?

A headlight flashed on, breaking up the darkness.

"There's our ride," Zora said, crashing through the door behind her. "Watch your head."

Dorothy ducked a second before a Cirkus Freak she didn't recognize tumbled onto the docks after them. Mac must've called for reinforcements.

Zora fired, sending an explosion of wood and water crashing up around them. Dorothy swallowed and took a step backward. Her grip on Roman's dagger tightened.

The Cirkus Freak stood, drawing his own gun. Zora let another bullet loose, and it hit the Freak in the shoulder, knocking him back. He groaned and dropped to his knees just as three others appeared in the doorway behind him. They were outnumbered.

Zora cracked off three more shots, not hitting anyone but keeping them back. "Where's our boat?"

Dorothy didn't have time to answer. A Freak charged at her, and there was a crash as her dagger met his. The Freak grunted and threw his weight against his weapon, causing Dorothy to stumble back a few steps. Another Freak approached from behind, and Dorothy opened her mouth to yell a warning, but Zora didn't need it. Just as the Freak drew back to strike, Zora whipped around, drawing the butt of her gun against his cheek, and knocking him from the dock. The Freak fell into the water with a splash.

Dorothy peered over her shoulder. That headlight didn't seem to be coming any closer. She grabbed Zora's arm. "Come on!"

Together, they raced down the docks, skidding to a stop at the place where they forked. Here, the distance between the dock and the parking garage was narrowest and—without bothering to stop and think of what might happen if she didn't make it—Dorothy leaped—

Thud! She hit the ground still running and stumbled, pain shooting up through her knees. But she could see the boat now, bobbing in the black water, Chandra crouched inside.

"Sorry!" Chandra shouted. She appeared to be fumbling with something. Dorothy heard a growl, and then a whine as the motor died. "I can't get this damn thing started."

Another *thud* and Zora tumbled onto the dock after them. She pushed herself back to her feet and let a few bullets loose at the surrounding Freaks.

"What's taking so long?" she demanded.

"The motor," Dorothy said, as a bullet whizzed past her face. She swore, one hand flying to her cheek.

Zora didn't look down, didn't even pause in her shooting, just grabbed the motor's cord out of Chandra's hand and gave it a single, hard yank. Chandra yelped as the motor growled to life.

"How did you *do* that?" she demanded.

Dorothy didn't wait for Zora to answer. She jumped into the boat, ducking as another bullet whizzed over her head. Zora climbed in behind her.

"Whatever you do, don't let me fall in!" Zora told her. She crouched at the back of the boat, facing toward the docks so she could aim her gun at the still-approaching Freaks. Dorothy grabbed a handful of leather and held tight, as the boat zoomed forward.

Dorothy heard the sound of gunshots in the distance, the cackle of laughter. But they were fading, growing distant as they sped away. Until, finally, there was nothing.

12

Dorothy peered out over the black water. The Cirkus Freaks were long behind them and, in the darkness, all she could see were the shapes of rooftops jutting out of the waves like icebergs. She reached out to touch the side of one as they floated past and found it hard and grainy beneath her fingers, covered in a layer of moss. Only the ghostly white trees broke up the darkness. Their white branches stretched into a canopy above their heads, and the bark appeared to be glowing.

Dorothy had always thought those dead white trees looked like cobwebs. In fact, the whole of New Seattle had always given her the impression of something alive growing over the bones of a long-dead corpse.

She swallowed and curled her fingers around the edge of the boat, pushing the morbid thought from her mind.

Zora's voice rumbled behind her. "I think we finally lost them."

"Good," huffed Chandra. She glanced behind her, eyes

flicking from Dorothy to Zora as though looking for support. "Come on, it's a good thing, right? We celebrate now?"

"Hardly," Dorothy murmured, absently touching the locket hanging from her neck. "We might've lost them, but they're going to turn the city upside down looking for us. It's not like anywhere we go now is actually safe."

To Chandra, Zora said, "I think that what she meant to say was thank you both so much for saving my ass." Then, turning back to Dorothy with a smirk, she added, "It was nothing, really."

"I'm grateful, of course," Dorothy murmured, lowering her eyes. The words seemed insufficient to describe what she was feeling. How, exactly, was she to make it clear how touched she'd been that Zora had come for her? Zora didn't trust her, and Dorothy knew she was still half convinced that she'd killed her best friend, and yet she'd taken on Mac and the Black Cirkus just to break her free. It was loyalty beyond anything Dorothy had ever known. Not that *that* was saying much, but still.

"Don't mention it," Zora said, gruff as always. Dorothy's gratitude seemed to make her uncomfortable, and she became, suddenly, very interested in a loose cuticle near her thumbnail. "What were you trying to do back there, anyway?" she asked. "Because, from the outside, it looked like you were committing suicide by way of psychotic gang."

"Not exactly." Dorothy hesitated a moment, trying to figure out how much to reveal. At any other time in her life, she would have lied. The exotic matter and the Professor's discovery were valuable bargaining chips. Who knew how useful they might be later, if she needed a little leverage?

But Chandra and Zora had just risked their lives to break her out of the Fairmont. It had softened her. She couldn't imagine trying to manipulate or blackmail them now. They deserved the truth.

And so, exhaling, she found herself telling them everything. "I was in Roman's room early this morning, looking for . . . well, looking for money, if I'm being perfectly honest. I'm broke and, as I'm anticipating being on the run, I figured I'd need everything I could get my hands on."

She waited, eyes shifting from Zora to Chandra, to see whether either of them would pass judgment on her, but they stayed silent.

"I didn't find any money," she continued, after a moment, "but he had these . . . these papers hidden in his bedside table."

Zora, blinking, said, "Papers?"

"Journal entries," Dorothy clarified. "They're from the Professor's journal. I recognized the handwriting from the last time."

A year ago, to Dorothy, and just a few weeks ago to Chandra and Zora, Dorothy had found the Professor's journal among Roman's things. She'd handed it over to Ash, but only after making a bargain. She wasn't particularly proud of that moment, now.

Clearing her throat, she continued. "Roman must've torn the pages out before he left the journal for me to find. He didn't want us knowing about them, for some reason."

"You read them, though," Chandra said, frowning. "What did they say?"

"Well . . . among other things, they seemed to indicate that it was possible to travel through time without a time machine."

"No." Zora's brow furrowed. "My father would have told me if he were working on something like that."

But Dorothy thought she detected some hesitation in her words. Did Zora know Ash had already done it? He must've told her.

"I . . . wouldn't know," Dorothy admitted, lowering her eyes. "I broke into the Fairmont so I could steal the exotic matter from the *Black Crow* and attempt it myself, but I . . . well, I chickened out. And then Mac found me and, as I had the journal entries on me . . ." Dorothy let her sentence trail off, hoping Zora and Chandra would fill in the rest.

"*Mac* has the journal pages?" Chandra said, frowning. "That's . . . that can't be good."

Zora added, gently, "There's not much he can do without any EM."

"It was stupid of me not to hide them when I had the chance," Dorothy said. "It's enough that he even knows it's possible to travel through time without a vessel. You and I both know that he won't rest until we've shown him how to do it. Even if it means—"

A light appeared in the darkness, and Dorothy closed her mouth, biting back the last of her words. Chandra had gone silent, too, and Zora crouched at the back of the boat, one hand resting on the gun in her waistband.

The light glimmered in and out of focus, passing behind distant trees. Dorothy heard voices, shouting and talking, and then a series of sharp cracks broke through the night. As the boat drew nearer, she could make out black-clad figures inside. A boy holding a lantern, another holding a short, shiny pistol.

The boat zoomed past them and then vanished into the white trees just as quickly as it had appeared. Dorothy watched the light grow smaller and smaller, hardly daring to believe that it was gone.

Zora and Chandra relaxed, but Dorothy still didn't move. Cold fear gripped her chest, and her knees had gone watery.

They wouldn't stop looking for them, she knew. There was nowhere in New Seattle where they would be safe.

"I need to leave," she said, turning back to Zora. "Tonight. Right now, actually." She thought of Regan's terrible threat. *I'm told you have friends. People you care about.* A lump formed in her throat and she added, in a low voice, "None of you are safe while I'm here."

Chandra snorted a laugh, possibly amused by the idea that they had ever been safe.

"He cares about Ash, not the rest of you," Dorothy pointed out.

"Flattering," Chandra sniffed.

Zora shook her head and said, to Dorothy, "Where are you planning on going? You just said that the city isn't safe. And the borders—"

"I don't want to cross the borders. I want to go back in time."

Zora stared at her for a beat and then said, her voice low, "That's not possible."

"What are you talking about? Of course it's possible. Mac told me that you stole the *Black Crow*, and *I* have the exotic matter, and I know how to fly a time machine—"

"I didn't say it's not *physically* possible," Zora said, cutting her off. "I said it's not possible. As in *I* won't let it happen."

Zora crossed her arms over her chest, eyes narrowing to slits. Dorothy felt the backs of her teeth grit together, a muscle in her jaw tightening. Of all the foolish things to be stubborn about.

"Can I ask why not?" she asked, as calmly as she could manage.

"If I let you go back in time, you'll kill Ash," Zora said. "Neither of us may know why, but we know that it happens."

"It's already happened," Dorothy snapped. "Zora . . . Ash is *gone*. If we do nothing, he's going to *stay* gone. Can't you see that?"

"You can't know that for sure."

"I *can*," Dorothy insisted. "Time is a circle. Meaning that whatever we do has already affected the world as it is now. I have to go back in time because I've already gone back in time. Chandra told me that Ash and I met in secret over the past week. Three times."

Zora shot Chandra a furious look.

"And Willis backed her up," Dorothy added, lest Chandra

get into too much trouble. "I already went back, Zora. Ash and I spoke, and somehow, somewhere in the midst of all that something happened, those meetings resulted in him being gone. I'm not going to be able to rest until I find out why. Will you?"

Zora was staring at her very intently now, chewing on the inside of her cheek. After a while, she swore and looked away.

"Fine," she said. "Come on."

After what felt like an eternity, they drew up alongside a dock and pulled to a stop. Zora cut the engine, but the sound of a rumbling motor ghosted around them, not quite willing to die.

"Where are we?" Dorothy asked. As far as she could tell they were still entirely surrounded by black water and white trees.

"Hiding place," Zora said. "Or, the best I could come up with on short notice. This area used to be Volunteer Park, but now it's nothing, just water. I figured, what better hiding place than in the middle of a bunch of nothing?"

Dorothy still couldn't see a thing beyond the pulsing darkness, but she felt the boat tip below her and then rock as Zora climbed out. There was a sound like a key being fit into a lock, and then a light flicked on, illuminating gleaming aluminum siding, a finned tail, the dark glass of the *Black Crow*'s windshield.

"The *Black Crow*," Dorothy exhaled, relieved to have the time machine in her possession once more. Roman had built it using Professor Walker's own schematics, and it was perfect, made in the exact image of another time machine, the *Dark Star.*

Dorothy wasn't sure how close a model it was. She'd seen the real *Dark Star* once, a year ago, but *this* was the only time machine she'd ever flown, and the one that she'd spent the most time in. It felt like a small piece of home to her.

She climbed out of the boat and came to stand next to Zora on the dock, already itching to climb into the cockpit, to feel the cold leather of the pilot's seat envelop her, to experience that strangely thrilling drop in her stomach when the time machine lifted from the black water and became airborne. Her fingers twitched.

"I can try to get my father's pages back from that maniac," Zora said. "And you . . . well, Willis told me you had a plan."

She turned to her with a raised eyebrow, as though to say *please have a plan.* Dorothy hated to disappoint her.

"I have . . . the beginning of a plan," she admitted.

"That's not terribly comforting," Zora muttered, turning back to the boat. After a moment, her hand shot out, fingers curling around Dorothy's arm. She pinned her in place with her dark eyes, silent for a few seconds before saying, "Find him. Bring him home." She swallowed, and Dorothy saw a flash of pain on her face, gone a moment later. Her voice was choked as she added, "Promise me."

It wasn't a promise Dorothy could make. She had no idea what was going to happen when she climbed inside that time machine, no idea what had happened to lead her to the moment when she'd lured Ash out to the anil and thrust Roman's dagger into his chest.

And yet, she found herself saying, "I promise."

The anil appeared in the distance. In the darkness it was like a thick gathering of swirling clouds, or the beginnings of a tornado. Lightning flashed deep inside the tunnel, its faint reflection bouncing off the water.

Dorothy brought the *Black Crow* to the mouth of the tunnel and set the ship to hover. She'd never been spooked by the anil before. She felt more at home in the crack in space than she ever had wandering the country with her mother, pulling cons. She knew exactly who she was inside that tunnel.

She was Dorothy Densmore, con artist.

But she was also Quinn Fox, assassin, cannibal, time traveler.

She was a monster. But she could be a hero, too.

She ran a hand back through her white hair and found that it was damp with sweat. She glanced at the EM gauge. Full capacity.

"Find him," Dorothy whispered to herself. She thought of the golden-haired pilot who smelled of campfire smoke, and couldn't help smiling. "Bring him home."

She pushed the throttle to 2,000 RPMs.

The *Black Crow* shot forward, disappearing into the crack in time.

LOG ENTRY—SEPTEMBER 22, 2074
APPROXIMATELY 12:00 HOURS
LOCATION—CASCADIA SUBDUCTION ZONE

Take two.

Crazy though it may seem, I am currently sitting inside of my trusty old rowboat, floating just outside the limits of the Cascadia subduction zone. I have reinjected myself with exotic matter and I'm confident that, this time, I've managed to do it correctly.

Relatively confident. I'd say I'm working at about 80 percent confidence here.

Woah. Okay. I didn't realize I would be so nervous. Let's just say that I don't want to deal with the skin-burning sensation, again. That was unpleasant, as was the fact that I wasn't able to move my hands or feet for several weeks afterward. I would very much like to avoid going through that again.

I'd like to avoid it so much that I almost don't want to do this.

Oh to hell with it all—I'm a scientist, aren't I? It's time to do this. Fear be damned!

Wish me luck. I'm certain I'll need it.

PART TWO

People like us, who believe in physics, know that the distinction between past, present, and future is only a stubbornly persistent illusion.

— Albert Einstein

PART TWO

LOG ENTRY—UNKNOWN
TIME—UNKNOWN
LOCATION—UNDETERMINED

I've only just regained consciousness. It appears that I've landed in a secluded field somewhere outside of Seattle.

Or, I suppose I should say that I *believe* I'm somewhere outside of Seattle. From where I sit, all I can see are pine trees and wild grass; flat, gray sky; and the distant, burning sun. I'll need to hike a bit before I can make out the city skyline. Until then, I'm taking it on faith that I'm still on the West Coast at all. And I have no way of knowing *when* I've landed. Or how to get back.

But at least I still have my skin attached to my body (unlike some other, less lucky, would-be time travelers I can name . . .). I suppose I should consider myself thankful for small mercies.

I shall update soon.

UPDATE: TIME STILL UNDETERMINED

I've successfully hiked to the area that was once known as Lower Queen Anne. For those of you reading who are familiar with the city of Seattle as it existed in the year 2074, this neighborhood is where the Space Needle stood.

Stands, as of my current timeline. In the future, the floods caused by the mega-quake leave the Space Needle almost entirely underwater. You can see the saucer-shaped top of the structure, if you get close enough, but otherwise it's entirely submerged. In this current timeline, however, the Space Needle is still where it's supposed to be, and the city remains unflooded. And so, I can clearly deduce that I'm in Seattle, preflood. From the look of the technology I've seen on the people around town, I think it's also fair to say that we're in the mid-twenty-first century, likely not too far from the time of the earthquakes. That's probably why I'm having so much trouble finding a damn newspaper.

Unfortunately, I think I'm going to have to do the thing. You know, the cheesy time traveler thing. Stop someone on the street, ask them what year it is, pretend I don't notice the deeply suspicious look they give me.

Hold on . . . I think I have an idea!

UPDATE—
DATE: OCTOBER 10, 2073
19:10 HOURS

Success! Rather than stopping a stranger to ask them to tell me the year, I stopped a stranger and asked to borrow his *phone*. Time and date were right there on the home screen. It's October 10, 2073, right around seven p.m. Why did I come here, now?

Let's see . . . what was I doing in October of 2073, at around seven o'clock at night? 2073 was before I started working at NASA, so I must've been . . .

Oh right—of course.

I know where I'm going now.

UPDATE: 20:45 HOURS

And I made it! I'm currently standing outside my old office at WCAAT, staring up at my window, watching my past self work.

In, oh, about two hours from now, I will officially discover time travel.

That's why I came back here. Because this is *it*, the beginning of everything.

I should be attempting to get back now, but there's a part of me that wants to stay here a while and watch my past self work. In just two short hours, I will be at the happiest point in my entire life (short of my wedding day and the birth of my daughter, of course). Is it really so bad to want to experience that moment again?

UPDATE: 23:13 HOURS

Oh dear . . . I had forgotten that, back in 2073, my ingenious solution for testing my theory of time travel was to travel back in time myself, come to this exact spot, and wave.

I only just remembered and managed to duck behind a tree before my past self strolled out onto the sidewalk right where I'd been standing and waved up at yet another past self of mine.

Three selves! All in one timeline. I'm fairly certain I'm breaking some law of physics here.

In any case, I think it's time I head back home.

If I can get back home, that is.

13

The prememories slammed into Dorothy's head, coming so fast and hard they left her dizzy—

There was the black sky of a ruined world, ashes and dust floating through the air around her. Roman was there. She heard a gunshot, and then a bullet slammed into his chest, jerking him back—

Then she was on a boat surrounded by black water. Ash was standing before her, his face lit up by the ever-changing lights of the anil.

"It doesn't have to end like this," he said.

Adrenaline surged within her as she curled her fingers around a dagger—

And now she was in the church on the day of her wedding, racing up the aisle, Avery standing before her—

No. She wasn't in the church at all, she was running through an empty hallway, following a dark figure. Through the door, into a stairwell.

"Professor?" she shouted—

* * *

And then she was out of the anil, the *Black Crow* skidding wildly across the surface of the Puget Sound. She was going to crash.

She yanked back on the yoke, pulling the ship to a hard stop, waves and wind slamming up against the windows around her. The ship shook for a moment and then went still.

Breathless, Dorothy collapsed back against her seat, breathing hard. It took a long time for her mind to stop spinning. She tried to grasp hold of the images that had been flying through her head, to make sense of them, but they dissolved like sugar in coffee, leaving her feeling light-headed and sick to her stomach. Groaning, she opened her eyes.

The world on the other side of her windshield looked very much like the one she'd just left behind. Black waves lapping against the sides of half-submerged buildings, ghostly white trees growing straight out of the water, like weeds. In the distance, she could make out the dark shape of her city, a labyrinth of complicated bridges and docks weaving between open windows and rooftops. With effort, she pushed the last of the prememories from her mind and focused on getting the *Black Crow* airborne again. Wing flaps up, throttle back up to 2,000 RPMs. She hovered low over the waters, sending ripples over the surface, and squinted through the windshield.

This city was quiet tonight, she saw, with little light to illuminate the darkness. No boats on the water, no people on the docks. A prickle of excitement went through her as she remembered why.

Of course. Tonight, everyone in the city would be at the ball.

She steered her time machine toward downtown New Seattle, her heart thudding steadily in her throat. It had taken her and Roman *months* to plan this ball, but it had been so worth it, in the end. The night had turned out beautifully, one of the best of her life. A small smile twitched at her lips, as she thought of it now. There was a part of her that wanted to experience the night all over again. Was there time?

She glanced at the clock on the ship's dashboard. At this exact moment, her past self would be putting the final touches on her outfit for the evening. The floaty blue dress, her hair in intricate braids. Soon, she would stand in front of the Fairmont ballroom, Roman beside her, and the two of them would reveal their great plan to save the city. She could still remember how it had felt to look out on all those excited faces, the whole of New Seattle staring up at her with rapt attention, *trusting* her.

And then she would see Ash in the crowd. And—

Heat rose in her face. Ash had followed her to the hotel bathroom that night. They'd argued, and then they'd kissed. . . .

She blinked, surprised to find tears gathering in the corners of her eyes. She would give anything to live that night all over again, but she couldn't see how she could risk it just now. She hadn't seen any sign of her future self wandering around the ball. In fact, it would probably be best if she avoided the

Fairmont ballroom entirely. So she must spend her evening elsewhere . . .

She flew the *Black Crow* on autopilot, muscle memory taking her to the Fairmont parking garage, where she brought the time machine to land beside an identical *Black Crow*, this one from the past. It unnerved her, a little, to see two versions of the same ship parked side by side.

She flipped off the machine's engine and sat in the gathering chill of the cockpit.

Where to go?

It had been clear when Ash approached her in the bathroom that evening that it had been his first time seeing her as Quinn Fox. So she must not speak to him again until after that confrontation.

She climbed out of the time machine and made her way outside, around the side of the hotel, to the back docks that led just below the bathrooms where she'd met Ash. It was cool but not unpleasantly so, and the shadows hid her well. She waited.

A few moments passed. And then the bathroom window slid open and a man's torso appeared in the darkness.

Dorothy stood in silence, a hand pressed to her mouth as Ash's dusty-blond head exited the window, followed by his shoulders, his torso.

Watching him, she felt her breath catch in her throat. He was here, *alive* and looking very much as he had the first time she ever saw him. Thickly muscled arms that hinted at days performing hard labor, skin reddened from spending so long in the sun, and that leather jacket that seemed to fit him like a second skin. Warmth spread through her chest and climbed her neck. It took every bit of willpower she had to keep herself from reaching out for him.

Ash grunted as he wriggled through the small space, not once looking her way. Once he'd pulled himself all the way through, he hesitated, still crouched on the sill just below the window and staring down at the black water below. Dorothy took a deep breath. This was it. She needed to announce her presence, say something.

But, when she opened her mouth, she found that she couldn't quite find her voice. It was funny, she'd spoken to Ash only a few days ago, and yet it felt like she hadn't seen him in years.

And now here he was, close enough that she could reach out and touch his shoulder, and she found that she couldn't utter a single word.

A moment later, Ash jumped, spraying the dock where she stood with dirty black water.

Dorothy shook her head, cursing herself. This was *Ash*, after all. And, according to Chandra, she'd already spoken to him. What had her so nervous? She moved away from the shadows and came to stand at the edge of the dock, waiting for him.

Ash surfaced a moment later, spitting up a mouthful of water. It took him a moment to wipe the water from his eyes, and then he was blinking up at her, frowning slightly.

"You got out here quick," he said, grasping the edge of the dock to pull himself up.

Dorothy's throat felt suddenly dry.

Ash crawled onto the dock and pushed the wet hair back from his forehead. "Did you change your mind?" he asked.

The question caught her off guard, and Dorothy found herself blinking at him, confused. She searched her memory, trying to remember what they'd been talking about the night of the ball, but she came up blank.

"Change my mind?" she managed.

Ash took a step closer to her, water dripping from his hair, his jacket. He still smelled like smoke, even soaking wet, and she could just make out the gold of his eyes in the darkness.

She couldn't help herself. She lifted a hand to his face, pressed her fingers to his cheek. His skin was wet and rough with stubble. He leaned into her touch, then covered her hand with his own.

"About coming with me?" he said, voice low.

Dorothy closed her eyes, the memory coming back to her in a rush. *Ah yes.* When they'd seen each other in the bathroom the night of the ball, Ash had asked her to run away with him and the rest of the Chronology Protection Agency. It had seemed impossible at the time. She and Roman had been on the verge of enacting their plan to save the city, and the idea of leaving and starting over somewhere else had been ludicrous. Now, though, she felt an ache, remembering.

She'd been so cruel, blowing him off the way she did, telling him that she didn't want to go with him, that she'd found her own place, here, at the Fairmont and she didn't need him or his friends anymore. She wanted to climb through the window Ash had just jumped out of and slap her past self. Why had she thought that working with Mac was a better idea? She should've left when Ash had given her the chance. If she had, Roman might still be alive. *Ash* might still be alive. Her chest clenched.

Stupid, stupid . . .

"I—I didn't," she said, swallowing. Her skin burned. "I just wanted to see you again. To tell you that I . . . I've missed you, too."

Ash stared at her for a moment. *What is he thinking?* Dorothy wondered. Was he remembering their kiss?

"I imagined this going differently," he said, instead.

Dorothy blinked very quickly. It seemed *she* was the only one thinking about that kiss. "Um, you did?"

His eyes moved over her face, something dark flickering through them. "Call me crazy, but I didn't figure I'd be doing a lot of kissing when I found the girl who's gonna kill me. 'Course, I didn't realize it was going to be you."

Dorothy caught her breath, her heart beating very hard inside her chest. She hadn't expected him to come out with that so bluntly. *The girl who's gonna kill me.* Despite what Willis had told her about Ash's prememories, she'd still been holding on to some hope that there'd been a mistake, that Ash had seen someone he only thought was her, that all of this could be explained away, somehow.

She swallowed and said, very carefully, "You know that

for sure, do you? That I'm going to kill you?"

Ash gave a little shrug. "Prememories are never wrong."

"But how do you know it's me?" she asked. "Did you see my face?"

"Nope. I saw this." Ash twirled a strand of her hair around his finger and pulled it, like a bell. "White hair. The girl in my prememory has white hair. I realized it was Quinn Fox when I saw you running around the halls back at Fort Hunter. That's when I finally put two and two together."

Dorothy felt a flicker of something deep in her chest. Wait a minute . . . she *hadn't* been to Fort Hunter—not as Quinn Fox, anyway. Roman had gone back in time to complete that mission on his own.

"But you didn't see my face," she murmured, thinking.

Ash cocked his head. "What?"

"You said that you saw Quinn Fox at Fort Hunter. But did you actually see my face? Or just the white hair?"

"Dorothy, I might not have seen your face, but I saw your scar, your cloak. It was you."

Dorothy pressed her lips together, considering this. Each new piece of this puzzle seemed to point to yet *another* place in history that she'd traveled back in time to visit. So far, she'd taken it for granted that it was always *her*. But, now, she wondered.

Could someone else have gone back instead?

Someone pretending to be her?

For some reason, she thought of the woman in black, *Regan Rose*.

"Hair can be dyed," she said, more to herself than to Ash. She took a measured breath and added, "What about in this prememory? Did you see my face, then?"

Ash let her hair unravel from his finger. "I didn't want to believe it, either," he murmured, tucking it back behind her ear. "But I'm trying to make my peace with it. Prememories are memories, there's no way to stop them—"

"Just tell me," Dorothy interrupted him. "Did you see my face?"

"Why this sudden interest in my death?" Ash frowned, studying her. "Unless . . ."

Zora's voice suddenly reached out of the darkness. "Asher!"

Dorothy turned, squinting. She could make out the shape of someone standing on a dock in the distance, the long, thin silhouette that was, unmistakably, Zora.

"I have to go," Ash said. He, too, was looking at Zora, and his shoulders had gone rigid. "Will I see you again?"

There were two more secret meetings that Dorothy knew about, the next occurring the very next night.

"You will," she said. "Soon."

He touched her cheek, briefly. "Take care of yourself."

And before she could ask him anything else, he was off, diving into the black water, swimming toward Zora.

Dorothy remained long enough to make sure he made it safely onto the dock. And then, numb, she made her way back to the *Black Crow.*

14

It started to rain as Dorothy flew the *Black Crow* back to the anil, heavy splatters of water smacking against her windshield, making it impossible to see anything in the inky darkness. Wind howled and battered into the sides of the ship, sending her sliding back and forth on the pilot's seat.

She gritted her teeth. Roman could've thought to include windshield wipers in his design. Or, at the very least, a *seat belt*.

A moment later, the thought turned bitter because Roman wasn't here to tease about it.

She took a deep, steadying breath and tightened her grip around the yoke. *One down*, she thought, trying to ignore the knot forming in her stomach. Two more to go.

She still had so many questions. Was *she* really the one Ash had been seeing in his prememory? Was she deluding herself, thinking there was a chance that someone else had been posing as her, trying to trick him?

Perhaps. But she couldn't waste these last two meetings asking the same questions over and over again, hoping for a different answer. There were other questions she needed to get to the bottom of.

The Professor's experiments through time without a vessel, for instance. Other than the Professor himself, Ash was the only one who'd managed to figure out the secret. Perhaps he could teach Dorothy what he'd learned.

She pressed down on the gas, and the sudden acceleration sent her rocketing backward so that her body felt glued to the chair behind her.

The time machine leaped forward, into the future—

NOVEMBER 7, 2077

Dorothy landed the *Black Crow* in the tangle of docks behind the Dead Rabbit and cut the engine. She hadn't needed Chandra to tell her about this meeting. She'd seen Ash inside the Dead Rabbit herself. She remembered how he'd motioned for her to meet him.

She hadn't. She'd followed Roman to his room and confronted him about what they'd seen when they'd traveled to the future. But, later, Eliza mentioned spotting the Ash and Dorothy on the docks. And there was that photograph of the two of them about to kiss . . . her cheeks burned just thinking about it.

She made her way around to the back of the bar and waited beside the back door, one hand tucked inside of her coat, fingers curled around the hilt of Roman's dagger. The

Dead Rabbit was known to have some unsavory clientele. There was no telling who else might be wandering around back here. She couldn't be too careful.

Some time passed. Dorothy saw no one and, eventually, her grip on the dagger loosened. The air outside was cold and wet, and she shivered, letting go of the dagger altogether so that she could hug her arms around her body, holding in what remaining warmth she had left. The dock tilted beneath her, making her feel a little seasick. She would never get used to the way that this damned city was always moving, how nothing felt steady.

She was just starting to wonder if she'd gotten it wrong, if they hadn't met after all, when the bar's back door creaked open and Ash stepped outside.

"You're already here," he said, letting the door fall shut behind him.

"I thought you . . . wanted me to come," Dorothy said, suddenly awkward. All this time out here and she couldn't have come up with a better line? Her cheeks flushed.

"I just meant that you got back here quicker than I expected," Ash said.

Dorothy nodded, and began twisting her fingers around her braided hair, so that she had something to do with her hands. She felt more nervous than she'd expected, maybe because of that photograph, because she knew what was coming next.

"I know a shortcut," she murmured. "I used to come out here a lot."

Ash appeared to be waiting for her to say more and, when she didn't, he crossed the dock, and rested his hands on the wooden banister just beside her, close enough that his hand grazed her hip. She felt a trail of warmth where he'd touched her.

This was it. He was going to kiss her now. Heat rose in her chest.

"I looked for you this morning," Ash said.

Dorothy blinked at him. Her thoughts felt slow and confused. *You*, he'd said. But which "you" did he mean?

The bride who'd stowed away on his time machine? The woman with white hair destined to kill him? The bloodthirsty leader of the Black Cirkus?

I don't even know who you are, Zora had told her. *Are you Quinn? Or are you Dorothy?*

"You looked for Dorothy," she said carefully. "I'm not Dorothy anymore."

What she'd meant to say was: *What if I'm not Dorothy anymore? Would you still like me? Or would everything be different?* But Ash drew back before she could correct herself, his brow furrowing.

"A new name doesn't make you a new person," he said.

"It's . . . not just the new name, though, is it?" Dorothy shook her head, frustrated. She was explaining this wrong. How could Ash want to be with her if she didn't even know who she was? *That's* what she wanted to say.

"You mean . . ." Ash brought his hand to her face and she inhaled, sharp, a second before he touched her, already anticipating the feel of those rough hands on her skin. He froze, fingers hovering over the line of her scar. "Is this. . . okay?"

She closed her eyes and was quiet for a long moment. No one had ever touched her scar before. She even tried not to touch it. The feel of the mangled skin beneath her fingers disgusted her. It seemed to represent every horrible thing that she'd ever done, all the ways she'd failed. If Ash touched it, she was certain he'd see how different she was from the girl he knew.

And yet she said, almost without realizing she was speaking, "Yes."

Ash lowered his hand to her scar, and every nerve in her face flared so that all she felt was spark and heat. She'd been holding herself stiffly, but now she released a breath that was almost a sigh. "Ash."

He lowered his forehead to hers and, for a moment, she felt only the warmth of his skin, the softness of his hair.

"Come back with me," he said, his voice urgent. "Please, you don't belong here."

Was it possible? Could she leave now and never ever look back? For a moment she considered it, to hell with time-travel logic and the future and all the people who were counting on her.

It was Ash himself who stopped her. It was the fact that he'd touched her scar, that he knew about her past, her sins, and he wanted her anyway.

Maybe I could be better, she thought. Maybe all was not yet lost.

"I wish I could." She pressed a hand to his chest, frowning.

"But that's not why I came. There's something I need to ask you."

"Can it wait?" he murmured into her hair. God, he still smelled the same, like engines and fire and oil. She wanted to inhale him.

"It's important," she said, and pulled away. She didn't know how long they had before Eliza stumbled upon them. She needed to be quick.

"I need you to think back," she said carefully. "Did the Professor ever mention Nikola Tesla?"

Ash frowned and leaned away from her, clearly caught off guard. "What?"

"The Professor was doing experiments with Nikola Tesla." Dorothy cast an anxious glance at the door behind Ash and then shifted her gaze back to his face. No sign of Eliza yet. "Did he ever say anything about that to you? Anything at all?"

"I don't think so." Ash frowned. "What—"

"They would've had to do with traveling through time without a vessel. Does that sound familiar?"

Ash scratched the back of his neck, frowning. "It isn't possible to travel through time without a vessel. A few people tried, back before the Professor built his time machines, but the anil is too volatile, and they were all badly injured."

"Yes, but the Professor went on experimenting with it, to see whether he could find a way." Dorothy fiddled with the locket hanging from her neck, her fingers anxious. "Think.

Maybe he wrote something in that journal of his? Have you read the whole thing?"

Ash was already shaking his head, then stopped. "Wait a minute," he said, almost to himself. "There were entries missing. I don't know where they went, but—"

He was interrupted by the sound of wood creaking, a footstep on the other side of the door.

Blast, Dorothy thought, her heart leaping into her throat. *Eliza*.

She shifted back, into the shadows, a moment before Eliza stepped onto the dock. The other girl made a show of pulling a pack of cigarettes and a book of matches out of her pocket, and then slowly lighting the cigarette as her eyes traveled over the shadows, searching.

Dorothy glowered back at her. She wasn't fooled. Everything that was happening on the docks could be heard through the thin door that separated them from the Dead Rabbit's halls. Eliza came out here to show Dorothy she'd been made.

Eliza's eyes moved over the shadows gathered thickly around the dock, casually, as though she were only glancing around her surroundings.

I don't see you, she seemed to say, *but I know you're there.*

Cursing her misstep, Dorothy slipped back into the shadows, turned down the docks—

Almost instantly, someone grabbed her from behind.

LOG ENTRY—SEPTEMBER 22, 2074
22:07 HOURS
THE WORKSHOP

I've only just returned to my present timeline, and I'm currently alone in my workshop, where I might finally let myself ruminate on all that I have seen.

Getting back wasn't nearly as difficult as I imagined it might be. Once I made my way back to the Cascadia subduction zone, I felt that same tug, just below my naval, where I'd injected the EM. A current, Tesla had called it. I found that I could resist by tensing the muscles in my body. But if I let myself go loose—not just physically, but mentally as well—the world sort of floated away and I was able to . . .

Well, following Tesla's river metaphor, I suppose that *drift* is the best word I can come up with to describe the sensation. It felt almost exactly like lying in the water and allowing the current to pull you along.

I was lucky. The current of time took me right back to where I'd left. Navigating to a specific point in history or to a *new* point in history or the future is completely outside of my realm of abilities right now.

This new mode of travel will require quite a bit more research before it is as capable as the standard form of time travel.

I shall experiment further in the morning.

For now—sleep.

15

Dorothy was dragged into the darkness, one arm wrapped around her torso, holding her own arms to her side, while the other gripped her face, a hand pressed against her mouth to keep her from screaming. Fear roared up inside of her, blotting out everything else.

Had Mac found her? Or one of the Cirkus Freaks? Or . . .

Oh God, was it Regan Rose?

She felt like her legs might go out beneath her. She couldn't face torture again. She couldn't. She gathered what remained of her strength and tried to twist out of the grip—

A voice hissed in her ear. "Knock it *off*, will you?"

She froze.

That voice. She *knew* that voice.

Her captor dragged her down the docks and around a corner before, finally, releasing his grip. Dorothy whirled around, squinting in the dim light. It took a long moment for the familiar features to separate from the shadows.

Pale skin and a tangle of dark hair. Cleft chin. Wicked smile.

"Roman." Dorothy threw her arms around her old friend, hugging him hard. He stiffened beneath her embrace—they'd never been the hugging type—but she couldn't help it. Just a few days ago (Two? Three?) she'd watched him die. She'd cried for him, grieved him, and now he was here, breathing and moving and talking like none of that had happened.

Because it *hadn't* happened. Not yet.

"God, you're bad at this," Roman said, patting her once on the back before pulling away.

"What do you mean?" Dorothy brushed a tear from her cheek, trying to pretend she was just scratching an itch. Roman lifted an eyebrow. He seemed to be trying very hard not to roll his eyes.

"Come on. You are clearly here from the future, and you're hardly keeping a low profile." He dragged a hand back through his hair, sighing. "Are you *trying* to get caught? Is that part of whatever plan you've come up with?"

Dorothy's mouth felt very dry. "How did you—"

"How did I know? You're kidding, right? The Dorothy from *this* timeline was just outside of my room, dressed in a completely different outfit, listening at my door."

Dorothy felt her cheeks grow warm, remembering how he'd caught her listening outside his door less than a week ago. And she'd thought she was being sneaky . . .

"I was following you," Roman continued, dark eyes narrowing. "Or, at least, I was trying to. Before I could catch up,

I found future you out here making googly eyes at your ex-boyfriend." He flapped a hand at her, nose wrinkling. "Not exactly what I would call keeping a low profile."

"I was hardly making googly eyes," Dorothy muttered.

"And then there's the way you attacked me just now, and how you're looking at me like I'm Lazarus risen from the dead." Roman made an attempt at his normally charming smile, but he wasn't quite able to pull it off. There was a troubled look in his eyes, and the corner of his mouth twitched. "So, then. Have I died? Is that why you seem so happy to see me?"

Oh, he was good. Dorothy hadn't been expecting him to come out and ask so boldly. She opened her mouth but found that she couldn't come up with the words to answer him.

Should she tell him the truth? According to the note he'd left for her, he'd already seen his own death, so he knew it was coming. Her fingers twitched as she pictured him lying in the dirt, eyes wide and unseeing.

"As a matter of fact . . . don't." Roman had been studying her very carefully and now his eyes narrowed. "I think I can live without knowing whatever is happening inside your head to make your face look like that. Come on, let's get you somewhere safe."

The night was moonless and blurred at the edges. The distant sound of a motor cut through the air and then faded into nothing. Milky, gray fog clung to the surface of the water, making Dorothy feel like she was floating on a cloud.

Roman led her down the docks and around to the back

of the Fairmont. "When are you from?" he asked when they reached the back door.

"A few days from now," Dorothy said. Wind picked at her hair as Roman opened the door and ushered her inside. She counted the days back in her head and said, "Six, I think?"

"Six days," Roman murmured, and Dorothy knew he was wondering what could've happened in less than a week that was so terrible it had sent her traveling back in time to fix it. He flashed a cautious, nervy smile. "So, I suppose it's not going to be a very good week, is it?"

"Don't be silly, it's fabulous." Dorothy had to work hard to keep her voice light. "I only came back to tell you that we save the city. Electricity for all, new medications, an end to disease. We're being hailed as heroes. Parties every night, that sort of thing."

Roman lifted an eyebrow. "And do I finally meet a nice girl and settle down?"

"Indeed you do. *Eliza*, would you believe it? It's all anyone can talk about."

"God, I hope you're joking about that," Roman said, grimacing.

"You don't think Eliza's pretty?"

"She's pretty all right just . . . prickly. I think she'd sooner arm wrestle me than kiss me."

"Aw, young romance."

They'd reached Roman's floor. He poked his head out of the stairwell and, seeing that it was empty, ushered her down the hall and into his room.

146

As soon as Dorothy stepped inside, she felt a rush of déjà vu. There were Roman's books, haphazardly stacked on top of his dresser just as they'd been this morning, when she'd come in here looking for cash. There were his spare boots, kicked off and forgotten in the corner, and there was the dirty shirt he'd tossed over the back of his desk chair.

She felt a strange twist in her gut, looking at that shirt. He wouldn't put it away before he'd died.

"What are you here to do, really?" Roman asked, closing the door firmly behind him.

Dorothy blinked, looking away from the abandoned shirt. She didn't want to give Roman any more reason to worry about the next six days, so she decided not to mention his death or Mac Murphy's takeover of the Black Cirkus, or Regan and her terrible bag of toys.

"Ash is . . . missing," she said, instead. "Everyone is certain that I've killed him. Including Ash himself, apparently. I came back to see if I could figure out what really happened. And stop it, if possible."

It was an abridged version of the truth, but it was still the truth, more or less. It would have to do.

Roman leaned against the door, head tilted, a funny look on his face. "You're here trying to stop *Ash* from disappearing? You don't honestly expect me to help you with that."

"Oh, stop," Dorothy snapped, frustration rising inside of her. With everything that's going on, this was what he wanted to focus on? "Your little vendetta against Ash is played out. You don't know this yet, but you're going to forgive him, like, tomorrow, so can we *please* just get on with it?"

Roman, to his credit, looked chastened. "Was I this annoying when I went back in time to see you?"

"Are you joking?" Dorothy huffed. "All that *time is a circle* nonsense. I wanted to murder you."

"Touché," he murmured, studying his hands. After a moment, he sighed and looked back up at her. "So, if I'm to understand you right, you've come back in time to figure out if you really did kill Ash, correct?"

"I actually have a theory that someone disguised as me might've killed him," Dorothy admitted. But, as the words left her mouth, she had to admit that they sounded . . . unlikely.

Roman only lifted an eyebrow. After a moment, he said, "When you came up here before, in the past, you were hoping to convince me to do something to change the future. Do you remember?"

Dorothy was quiet a moment. Of course she remembered. Before Roman and Ash had been murdered, Roman had taken her into the future and shown her a bleak, terrifying vision: their city, abandoned and destroyed. Buildings had toppled, and all the people who lived here had either died or disappeared. She still felt sick, thinking about it.

She hadn't given that terrible vision of the future much thought over the last few days. She'd been too busy trying to save Ash, trying to save herself. It bothered her now, that she'd forgotten everything that had happened so easily.

"You asked me if I had any idea what might have happened

to lead to that," Roman continued. "And I told you that I didn't."

"I remember," Dorothy said, frowning.

Roman, sheepish, said, "That's not entirely true."

Dorothy felt a chill down the back of her neck. Part of her wanted to tell Roman to leave it. She didn't think she was strong enough to take anything else just now. She could deal with the future when she'd saved Ash and stopped Mac and convinced her friends to trust her, again.

But she'd always been curious, and she couldn't stop herself from saying, "You know why our world falls apart?"

Roman gazed back at her. "Before I started researching time travel with the Professor, I was working on a computer program," he said. "It was supposed to help predict upcoming earthquakes. My research was ultimately inconclusive, but the data seemed to indicate that there was a relationship between travel through an anil and the movement of tectonic plates."

"I don't understand," Dorothy said, blinking at him. She had a sudden memory, Zora and Ash and the others gathered together in the schoolhouse where they all used to live, trying to explain earthquakes to her. "Tectonic plates? That's something to do with earthquakes, isn't it?"

Roman didn't seem to register her interruption. "I'd been paying particular attention to the earthquakes we've experienced over the last year. They've become more frequent. Can you think of any reason why that might be happening?" He paused and looked up, as though waiting for Dorothy to catch on. When she said nothing, he added, "Dorothy, the earth-quakes are caused by time travel."

Dorothy felt the edge of her lip twitch. It was a tick, smiling to cover her nerves. "That's not possible."

"I keep going over the data and it remains, stubbornly, consistent. The dates and the times and the Richter scale numbers, they all add up to one clear conclusion." Roman released a short, bitter laugh. "It's honestly amazing to me that no one else has put it together."

"Roman, you hear what you're saying, don't you?" The smile had dropped from Dorothy's mouth. She licked her lips. "If the earthquakes were caused by time travel, that would mean that *we* caused them. You and me."

Roman stared back at her, not blinking.

"That's not possible!" she said again. Her heart was beating very fast inside her chest.

"I wanted to be wrong. But the numbers don't lie."

Dorothy shook her head as cold fear oozed through her, leaving her numb. She thought of the neighborhood they'd gone back in time to loot, that little old woman and her dog, Pumpkin. Roman's sister.

The earthquake that had occurred after they'd left that time had killed all of them.

Oh God . . .

She sunk to Roman's bed, her entire body feeling, suddenly, very heavy. She lifted a hand to her mouth, thinking of all the times they'd traveled back into the past, all the silly, frivolous things they'd done.

How many lives had been lost because of them?

"Why didn't you tell me sooner?" she asked.

"Why indeed." Roman lowered himself to the bed beside her, sighing deeply. "To be perfectly honest, I only accepted it myself a few hours ago. It was after you and I went to the future with Mac and saw what was going to happen to our city. I realized then that my hypothesis was correct. If humans keep traveling through time, we're going to destroy everything. We have to stop."

Dorothy closed her eyes. She felt a sort of nagging sensation as several ideas that had seemed so separate attempted to come together.

The Professor said it was possible to travel through time without a vessel.

Mac wanted to travel through time.

Time travel was going to bring about the end of the world.

And she had, apparently, killed Ash.

Were they connected, somehow? She just couldn't tell, it was like looking at a jigsaw puzzle without half its pieces. She was still missing something.

Out loud, she said, "Ash knows how to travel through time without a vessel. We see him tomorrow, when we go back for the medical supplies."

Roman frowned. "The only way that would be possible is if there was a very small piece of exotic matter lodged inside of his body."

Dorothy cut her eyes at him. "You've read the Professor's missing journal pages? His experiments with Tesla?" Of course he did. She found the pages in his room, after all.

"And, apparently, so have you," Roman added, eyebrows raised. But he didn't sound altogether surprised. "I considered attempting the experiment myself, but it seemed . . ."

"Utterly terrifying?" Dorothy filled in.

"Exactly."

"I had the same experience," Dorothy admitted. "I think I actually might've tried it, but Mac interrupted me before I could work up the nerve. He has the journal pages now."

Roman cut his eyes at her. "Mac knows it's possible to travel through time without an anil?"

Dorothy nodded. "You said that the only way to stop the city from being destroyed is to stop traveling through time, but Mac won't stop, not ever. Now that he knows it's possible to time travel without a ship, he'll be even more desperate to do it himself."

Roman frowned, and there was a moment of quiet while he appeared to be turning this new information over in his head.

"Time travel without a ship might be possible, but he still needs exotic matter. So we'll just have to destroy the exotic matter." Roman paused, giving Dorothy a meaningful look. "*All* of it."

Dorothy studied Roman's face for a long moment, certain that she had misunderstood. "You mean that I need to destroy the exotic matter inside of Ash," she said. "I need to kill him."

Roman gazed back at her. "To save the world."

16

"You think that's why I kill Ash?" Dorothy asked, numb. She felt her heart fluttering inside her rib cage like a trapped bird and pressed a hand to her chest, willing it to stop.

This is a mistake, she told herself. *Just some big mistake.*

"If you don't kill him, time travel will continue and, eventually, bring about an earthquake that will destroy us all," Roman said. "I don't think you have any other choice."

Dorothy stared at Roman. When he said it like that it all sounded so simple. It left her feeling cold.

"No." She started shaking her head. She wouldn't believe this. She *couldn't*. "This is Ash we're talking about. Ash doesn't want the world destroyed any more than you or I do! If we were to find him, talk to him—"

"I'm sure we could convince Ash to stop traveling through time, sure." Roman sounded frustrated, like he couldn't believe that he had to explain something so obvious. "But what happens when Mac gets to him? You said New Seattle is crawling with Cirkus Freaks whose only job is to bring Ash in. And that was before Mac found out that your boy's capable of traveling through time without a vessel. Gives him a bit more incentive to figure out where he's gone, doesn't it?"

Dorothy said nothing. She didn't want to give Roman the pleasure of letting him know that he'd made a fair point.

"Consider this," Roman continued. "Once you destroy the rest of the EM and Mac realizes that he has to actually live in this shithole he's created, how long do you think it'll take before he realizes Ash is his only chance of traveling through time? The entire city's already out looking for him! It's only a matter of time before someone finds him."

"Even if that's true, Ash has no idea why he's able to travel through time without a vessel. If you and I are too terrified to experiment with exotic matter, what makes you think Mac won't be?"

"How much of that journal did you read before Mac took it off your hands?" Roman asked, frowning.

"Enough. Almost all of it."

Roman cocked an eyebrow. "Did you get to the part where the Professor starts experimenting with whether a single person with EM in their body can transport others?"

Dorothy felt suddenly cold. "No."

"It's complicated, but not impossible. Which means Mac doesn't need Ash to understand how he's going through time, he just needs him to give him a ride. Do you honestly think there's a chance in hell he'll ever stop looking for him once he reads that?"

Roman steadied Dorothy with a look. She swallowed, hard. "No, I suppose not."

"No," Roman agreed. "And, after a while, he's not going to be satisfied with tagging along with Ash every time he wants to travel through time. Eventually, he's going to cut Ash open and dig the remaining EM out of his body so he can take it for himself. Ash is only safe as long as he's gone. And the future is only safe if he never comes back."

"Stop." Dorothy pressed her hands to her ears, wanting to block out everything Roman was saying. "You can't be serious. You can't actually believe that *this* is the only way to save the world." She felt the taste of something bitter fill her mouth as the reality of what he was proposing settled over her.

She couldn't have killed Ash. She didn't believe it.

"If you look at the bigger picture, all of this starts to makes sense," Roman said gently.

"No." Something deep inside of her started to ache. "There must be something else we can do. This can't be the only way. *It can't be.*"

Roman was leaning against the far wall of his hotel room, arms crossed over his chest. He pinned her in place with a look and said, very calmly, "I thought that's why you were here? To figure out why you killed Ash?"

"I'm here to figure out how *not* to kill him!" Dorothy snapped.

All at once this was too much for her. She felt energy coursing through her veins, nervous, jittery energy that made her want to move, to do something. She stood and started to pace the length of the small room.

Roman, from his position beside the wall, said, "You know as well as I do that's not how time travel works."

Dorothy huffed, and only paced faster.

She didn't want to accept this. Not *any* of it. Roman couldn't actually be suggesting that the only way to save the world was for Ash to die. It was cruel . . . it was *ridiculous*. She had a time machine, didn't she? She could simply take Ash and disappear back in time. They could go somewhere fun. 1960s London or 2050s Seoul, somewhere filled with food and fashion and parties . . .

But, even as this plan was taking shape in her head, she thought of the horrible future she'd seen.

New Seattle in ruins. An entire city reduced to ashes and ice.

Could she really live with herself, knowing she had let that happen? That she'd let all those people die even though she'd known how to stop it?

She stopped pacing. She kept telling herself that she wasn't a monster, but walking away, leaving an entire city to its fate when she knew how to fix things, that was monstrous.

There had to be another way. There *had* to be . . .

"Look," Roman said, in a slightly kinder tone of voice. "You said yourself that he's seen his death, right? He's had a prememory?"

"Yes," Dorothy said. She felt a sudden sinking in her gut.

"Well if he's *seen* his death that means it's already happened. A prememory is a memory. There's no way to change it."

Time is a circle, Dorothy thought. She suddenly wanted to scream.

"I don't believe that," she said, turning on Roman. "The future isn't fixed, yet. You said it yourself—"

"Some things are fixed, no matter whether you want to believe in them or not," Roman told her.

"You're only saying that because of your stupid vendetta," Dorothy shot back, suddenly furious. "If it were anyone else . . ."

In her anger, she couldn't think of how to finish that thought, so she only shook her head, leaving the rest of the sentence hanging. She needed to be alone. She needed to think.

She headed for the door—

"Before you go," Roman asked, stopping her just as her fingers were wrapping around the doorknob. "Do you mind telling me exactly how long I have left?"

Dorothy looked up. His voice had been painfully casual, but Dorothy wasn't fooled. Roman was at his most vulnerable when he was pretending he didn't have a care in the world. This must be killing him.

"Do you really want to know?" she asked.

"I've been seeing visions of my own death for the last year, little Fox." Roman stared down at his own hand, studying his cuticles with a soft smile on his face. "I may as well know when it's going to happen."

Dorothy swallowed. She didn't know how to talk about her best friend's death without breaking down, but she could try, if that's what he needed.

Her mouth was dry. "It's been four days for me," she said. "For you it happens in two."

Roman's face shadowed. He turned his back to her. She got the feeling that he wanted to be alone, but she couldn't quite bring herself to leave.

"See," Roman said, after a moment. "I told you there are some things you can't change."

The halls were dark, but Dorothy knew that didn't mean she was alone. She climbed down the stairs to the Fairmont's main floor, eyes peeled for movement. All the while, Roman's words echoed in her head.

Some things are fixed, no matter whether you want to believe in them or not.

Not this, she told herself, gritting her teeth. She wouldn't be the one to kill Ash, no matter what it meant. She would find another way.

The floors in this part of the hotel were perpetually damp, slicked with the sludgy water people carried in from the docks on the soles of their boots. The furniture was all black with mold.

Dorothy hoped she might manage to sneak back outside and to her time machine. But, almost as soon as she stepped into the main hall, she heard voices.

"This the woman you were telling me about?"

Dorothy froze, her skin creeping. That was Mac.

She hid behind a bit of moldy wallpaper and ducked her head around to see what was going on.

A group of Cirkus Freaks had gathered a few feet away, near the very door that she'd been planning to slip through. One of them was Eliza, Dorothy saw, her nose wrinkling. They weren't looking her way, and so she breathed a little easier. They must not have heard her on the stairs. A small bit of luck.

"It is," Eliza said, her shark's smile glinting in the dim light. "Mac, meet Regan Rose."

Dorothy hadn't noticed the woman in black standing among them until she took a step forward, separating herself from the crowd. She looked exactly as she did in Dorothy's present timeline: small frame, black cloak, and mask and gloves. Studying her, Dorothy felt a little ripple of hysteria move through her body.

She forced herself to stay quiet as she listened.

"Charmed," Mac Murphy was saying, his voice gruff. He didn't let even a hint of a smile invade his face as he took one of Regan's small, gloved hands into his own meaty one. "Tell me why I haven't heard of you before now."

He seemed to be trying his best to intimidate her, but Regan was poised and calm behind her black mask. "A woman in my line of work does best to keep her reputation under wraps," she said in a low, husky voice.

Mac considered her for a long moment. He sniffed. "And you know what we're looking for?"

Regan inclined her head in a slight nod. "I've heard that Quinn Fox will soon be out of employ. It seems you'll need a replacement."

Mac raised his eyebrows, pausing to exam her more closely. "You tell her that?" he asked Eliza.

Eliza shook her head.

Mac said, to Regan now, "All right, love, where are you getting your information?"

"You can hardly expect me to answer that," said Regan.

Mac's nostrils twitched.

In her hiding place, Dorothy bristled. So this was what he'd been doing while she and Roman were messing about in the past. She'd known for a while that Mac had been working against them, but it felt like another thing entirely to witness it, to hear evidence of his treachery and her gang's disloyalty with her own ears. It made her want to scream.

Mac rubbed his chin as he studied Regan, his lips twisting: almost a smile. "And would you be interested in an arrangement like that?"

"That would depend. What are your plans for after?"

"Let's just say I've seen the future of this city," Mac said with a shrug. "It ain't what I'd call pleasant. The best thing any of us can do is get the hell out of Dodge, leave this damn city to its ruin."

Regan tilted her head. "And my payment?"

"I might be compelled to take someone who helped me

out along with me to the past." Mac's toad-like eyes narrowed. "*Life*, girl, would be your payment."

"An intriguing offer," Regan said, head tilting. She took a moment to consider before saying, "I accept. *Sir.*"

She held out her hand. The two of them shook.

Mac let out a bark of a laugh. "I'm sure we'll be an excellent team."

Dorothy took a step backward, so that she was entirely enveloped in shadows once more. For a moment she stayed still, barely daring to breathe.

Even after everything else he'd done, Dorothy had assumed Mac felt some small loyalty to his city. Oh how wrong she'd been. Mac cared for nothing but himself. He really was going to let the city fall to ruin.

Unless . . .

If you don't kill him, time travel will continue, and, eventually, bring about an earthquake that will destroy us all, Roman had said.

Dorothy pictured bloody water. An empty rowboat. *Pre-memories are memories*, she thought. *They've already happened.*

There's nothing you can do to stop them.

LOG ENTRY—OCTOBER 1, 2074
20:34 HOURS
THE WORKSHOP

Now that I've determined that Tesla's theory for time travel without a vessel actually works, I'd like to begin the complex process of breaking down exactly *how* it works.

Initially, I posited that Tesla had figured out a way to travel through time without exotic matter, access to an anil, or a vessel to travel in, but that's not quite the case. I used exotic matter, I just inserted it directly into my body. And I may not have needed to physically travel into the Puget Sound anil, but I *did* end up utilizing the power of the smaller, microscopic anils that exist within the earth's crust to pull me along the currents of time.

So, really, the only thing that I no longer need is a vessel. My body, essentially, became the vessel.

This, naturally, leads me to wonder how far the exotic matter extends beyond my physical body. For instance, when I traveled back in time, I was able to take my clothes and my glasses with me. I did not show up in the past blind as a bat, wearing nothing but my birthday suit (thank God, no one wants to see *that*). No, I'd been lucky enough to appear wearing the exact same faded jeans and T-shirt that I'd been wearing in my original timeline. And they were in good shape, too! No rips or tears, a little ripe around the armpits, but I'm afraid that's because I've been wearing them for a few days, not because traveling years into the past caused my shirt to stink. Everything was just as it was in my present timeline.

Which means that the exotic matter extended beyond my physical person to protect the things closest to my skin.

But how far beyond myself does that power extend? Could I, for instance, take an object with me?

A small animal?

Another person?

The only way to know for certain whether that's possible is, of course, to experiment. Best start with something that's not actually living, shall I? Like, for instance, a potato? No one can be angry at me for injuring a potato.

This, actually, is a tad nerve-racking. It reminds me of that old Jeff Goldblum movie, *The Fly*. For those of you who aren't familiar with 1980s horror, our boy Jeff experiments with teleportation and accidentally crosses chromosomes with a fly. He then starts turning into a fly, which is a horrifying thought to say the least.

Will attempting to take a potato back in time cause me to start turning into a potato?

I'm only half joking.

In any case, without further delay, I bring you:

Mission: Goldblum 1

Objective: Attempt to extend the EM's protection beyond my physical person.

Simplicity is key for this experiment, I think, and so I will keep it all fairly basic: my plan is merely to travel back in time, just an hour will do, while holding a potato.

Wish me luck.

Goldblum 1 was a success! I'm actually a little shocked at how easy it was. I simply rowed out to the Cascadia subduction zone, just as I had done during my first vessel-less voyage back in time (try saying that five times fast). Only, *this* time, I was holding my lucky potato.

I felt the familiar pull of the time tunnel. The world sort of dropped away, and there I was. In the past.

With my potato. It wasn't bruised or anything. It was perfect.

I'm really flying high right now. I sort of don't want to let this feeling go, so I'm going to move on to the next stage of my experimentation: living subject.

In other words, I caught a mouse.

I'll let you fill in the rest.

Here we go:

Mission: Goldblum 2

Objective: Attempt to extend the EM's protection to another living subject.

Let's do this.

UPDATE—

OCTOBER 1, 2074

22:45 HOURS

I almost don't want to write this. I know I'm a scientist, and I really should be impartial here, but I'm also an animal lover and this . . .

164

Well this is hard to get out.

Okay, here goes: I'm afraid that Little Jeff didn't make it through the last experiment.

Right—Little Jeff is what I named the mouse. As a scientist, I really shouldn't name test subjects, but I couldn't help it. He looked like a little Jeff Goldblum.

And now he's gone. I'd prefer not to get into the specifics of how he was killed but will say, only, that the exotic matter did not extend its properties beyond my physical person to keep him safe inside the anil. It seems, for some reason, that it couldn't protect a living creature like it could an object.

I really wonder why this is. I have some theories, but I'm afraid each is less likely than the next.

17

Dorothy spent the rest of the day following Mac, watching as he turned first her gang, and then the city, against her.

It was heartbreaking. Devastating. Dorothy had stayed hidden, peering out from behind the half-crumbling columns and dark corners of the hotel, her heart sinking deeper and deeper as she watched how easily Mac turned her closest allies against her.

It was like watching a lion seeking out prey. He would wait until he found a Freak on his own, and then he would hobble up to him, all smiles and promises.

Would the Freak like a new set of weapons? A warmer pair of boots? Some expensive food or drink that could only be found in the Center? Mac would snap his fingers to show how easy it would be for him to obtain such things. That terrible smile would grow wider and wider, as he promised the Freak everything he wanted and more.

And, all the while, Regan Rose was a shadow behind him.

Silent, menacing, her presence a clear message.

Quinn Fox isn't in charge anymore.

It made Dorothy seethe.

By midday, Mac had won over half the Freaks, and Dorothy could see that he'd have the rest on his side by nightfall. They were already whispering among themselves, spreading the news that Mac Murphy was willing to give them everything that Quinn and Roman could not—or *would* not.

Dorothy expected Mac to remain around the hotel, to continue his campaign to turn her gang, but just when he seemed to have them all in his grasp, he just . . .

He *left*.

He took a boat downtown, Dorothy following as close as she dared. He hit the small-business owners first, always offering them something in exchange for their loyalty. A larger space for their store. An introduction to someone in the Center who could make facilitating trade easier. Then he made his way into the few remaining wealthy neighborhoods in town, always with some bribe. Fresh strawberries and expensive bourbon, a crate of wine, medicine, a few solar panels, so the rich could have working lights again.

Something, something. There was always something.

Dorothy's blood boiled as she watched him work. By nightfall, it seemed as though he had the entire city of New Seattle believing that she was evil, treacherous. She had no idea how far and wide his reach extended. But she should've. She never should've trusted him.

I did this, she thought, horror washing over her. Mac never would have gotten to where he was if it hadn't been for her, for their alliance. She'd practically handed the city over to him, silver platter and all.

Roman didn't return to his room that night. Dorothy waited around for hours and then, remembering that this was the time they'd missed their exit coming back from the past, she curled up on his bed, wondering what on earth she was supposed to do now.

It had gotten dark, but she didn't feel like getting up to light a candle. She buried her face into Roman's pillow, breathing hard. She couldn't remember the last time she'd felt so lost.

Maybe it was the day of her wedding, realizing that she'd tried everything she could think of to get away and nothing had worked, that she might have to marry Avery after all.

Or perhaps it was the moment she'd woken up on the docks a year earlier than she'd meant to, alone and friendless, wondering how she was going to survive in this strange new world.

She sighed, frustration roaring up inside of her. If she were being honest with herself, neither of those moments compared to how she felt now. As desperate as she'd been, she'd always had some backup plan, some way of regaining control even as everything seemed to get harder and more complicated. And she'd had people she could turn to. Ash and Roman, even her mother.

But now . . .

She'd joined the Black Cirkus because she'd honestly believed in their message. *The past is our right!* It had been the question that had plagued her ever since she traveled a hundred years into the future and found the world very, very different from what she expected.

What sort of problem *couldn't* be solved with time travel?

It turns out, only one.

When Dorothy finally fell asleep, she dreamed up a world of perfect dark. There were no stars to illuminate the ghostly white tree trunks, no distant oil lamps flickering through the black like fireflies, no far-off buzz of electricity, no moon.

And then a light cut through the darkness like a knife, revealing that the sky was dark as oil and the city was gone. In its place, a single jagged structure rose from the waters, covered in layers of craggy black rock and ash.

It was the Fairmont, only it no longer had a roof, and a gaping hole had opened up in the middle of its walls. It had been beautiful, once. Now, it was only a ruin of burnt bricks, broken glass—

Dorothy awoke, gasping, memories of the terrible future still flickering through her head.

That was what awaited her if she didn't stop Mac. That blackened, burned-up city. It was getting harder and harder to tell herself that there was an alternative to Roman's plan. Mac wouldn't stop, and now that he had the entire city on his side, it was seeming less and less likely that he would fail. She was going to have to destroy the remaining EM.

All of it.

Cursing under her breath, she crawled out of bed. She wouldn't sleep again after that.

She needed a drink.

The city was black as pitch. The dock rocked beneath Dorothy's feet, following the gentle rise and fall of the waves.

She wouldn't go to the Dead Rabbit, she decided. There was too much of a chance of being recognized by some Cirkus Freak out for a late drink. Instead, she hurried deeper into the heart of the city, toward Dante's. She was only a few doors down when she heard voices.

"You're wrong, anyway . . . went through an anil . . . a time machine . . . survived . . ."

Ash, Dorothy thought, grinning. It was only now, hearing his voice, that she realized she'd hoped she would find him here, that it was the reason she'd chosen Dante's out of the dozens of bars in the city.

She took a step closer—

"True," said a second voice. Zora.

Dorothy stopped hard, her grin faltering. She wished she knew whether Zora would be happy to see her, but, if Ash was already aware of her role in his death, she had little doubt that Zora would be, too.

Don't think of her, she told herself. *Think of Ash.*

The fog was thick, but Dorothy's eyesight was beginning to adjust. She could make out the shape of Ash kneeling on the edge of the dock, his body barely more than an outline in the darkness. Zora appeared to be hovering over him, helping him up, but Dorothy could see little else. She took a step forward, intending to call out to them—

"But she was holding the container of exotic matter," Zora was saying. "And her hair turned white. All of us got white streaks in our hair after we fell through the anil without a vessel. But your hair isn't white."

White hair.

They were talking about her, Dorothy realized. She closed her mouth, no longer sure whether she wanted to make her presence known. Not before she heard what they had to say.

"It's not?" Ash was frowning, trying to pull his hair far enough away from his scalp to see it.

Zora said, "Nope, dirt blond, as usual."

"Hey!"

Zora barely seemed to hear him. "Okay, say you *did* travel back in time," she was saying. "Somehow. How did you end up in the *exact* time that Dorothy and Roman went back to?"

Dorothy thought back, attempting to work through the timeline in her head. She and Roman had just gone back to get medical supplies. Ash had followed them, surprising them all by showing up in the past, the first time he'd traveled without an anil. It seemed that he'd only just returned.

Ash, sighing, said, "I don't know."

Something moved through the trees, drawing Dorothy's attention. She narrowed her eyes, but now the shape was still.

Listening, she thought she could hear a motor, low and rumbling. The fog was heavy enough that she couldn't see the boat, though.

She glanced back at Zora and Ash. They were still talking, and they didn't seem to have noticed anything amiss. It would be dangerous for someone to overhear this conversation. She opened her mouth to warn them—

Ash lifted his hand. "We shouldn't be talking about this out here."

Dorothy's heartbeat sped up. She looked back at the trees and could see, instantly, that he was too late. The shape was moving again, a boat separating from the shadows, drawing up alongside the dock.

And now, finally, Ash and Zora seemed to notice that they weren't alone. Ash reached for his gun, but, at that same moment, a shape leaped out of the boat and grabbed him, wrenching his arm behind his back. His gun slipped from his fingers, clattering as it hit the dock. Useless.

Dorothy felt every muscle in her body draw tight. This was how Mac must've captured Ash and gotten him back to the hotel, she realized, this ambush.

She reached into her cloak, fingers brushing against Roman's dagger. Every muscle in her body wanted to race forward and help them, but she knew how this ended. Ash would be captured. Zora would be fine. If she showed herself now, she could be hurt or captured herself. And that would help no one.

"Easy now," came Eliza's cool voice. She knelt to pick

Ash's gun up off the dock and pointed it at his temple.

Dorothy's hand was clenched so tightly around her dagger that her fingers ached.

"We haven't been introduced," Eliza said. "My name is Eliza. And that there is Donovan."

Dorothy turned slightly and saw a shadowy shape that she could only assume was Donovan wrestling with the shadowy shape she thought was Zora.

"Can't say it's nice to meet you," Zora breathed, and Dorothy could picture her clenched teeth and the tip of a smile on her lips. She didn't sound scared but, then, Zora never sounded scared.

A creak of the dock and Mac separated from the shadows. Dorothy squinted. It looked like five . . . no *six* more Cirkus Freaks surrounded him.

She nearly burst forward right then, to hell with time-travel logic. The only thing that stopped her was the knowledge that, even with her help, it would be nine against three. They were outnumbered.

Dorothy swallowed, hard, and stayed hidden. She'd done plenty of terrible things in her lifetime and none of them kept her awake at night. But this one lodged itself beneath her rib cage, making it difficult for her to breathe. She knew in that moment that she would remember, forever, how she'd hidden in the shadows and done nothing while Ash was taken.

She curled her hands into fists, damning herself for being unable to help, to stop this.

"Boom," Eliza whispered into Ash's ear, laughing.

Dorothy saw Eliza's final blow coming and flinched a second before it landed. She heard something crack—*bone*. Ash hit the docks, unconscious. Zora released an angry scream of rage that cut off in a sound like flesh hitting flesh. There was another *thud*, and Dorothy knew that Donovan must've knocked her out as well. The Freaks left her where she was, grabbed Ash by the arms, and dragged him off the dock.

Dorothy pressed a fist to her mouth to keep from screaming. In that moment, she felt like she was back home, performing another of her mother's confidence games. It was as though she were reciting lines she hadn't come up with, acting out a scene instead of making her own choices, all of it an elaborate performance she had no real control over.

More, she thought, remembering her old wish, the reason she'd run away from home in the first place. She'd wanted more than a half-life, more than a fake marriage, more than a long con. But this . . . this was just more of the same.

She closed her eyes, tears gathering below the lids. She hated that there were things she still couldn't change, hated that the only real power she had was in her own mind.

She hated time travel.

18

Dorothy made sure Zora was still breathing, and then she dragged her away from the edge of the dock.

"Sorry to leave you like this," she muttered, pushing one of Zora's braids off her face. "But you're not going to be happy to see me when you wake up, anyway."

Zora groaned and started to stir. Dorothy could hear voices in the distance now, then approaching footsteps. Someone would be down this way soon, and Zora would be found. In the meantime, Dorothy had work to do.

She retraced her steps back to the Fairmont, carefully, carefully, making sure to stick to the shadows, as always. Now, more than ever, she couldn't allow herself to be caught.

She knew where Mac was taking Ash, and so it was no surprise when she caught up with the boat again outside the old Fairmont parking garage. She waited in the shadows until she was certain the Cirkus Freaks had gotten Ash up the stairs and into an empty hotel room. A few moments later, when she made her way up after them, there was no one else in the dank, dreary hallway.

She remembered the next few hours going like this: Mac would come up the stairs, and he would torture Ash until she and Roman came to call him away. Then—and only then—she could break into his room and set him free. That's how this was supposed to happen, she knew. It's what she'd seen.

And so Dorothy waited, staring at the peeling wallpaper. She couldn't help thinking of blood. The blood Mac was going to beat out of Ash in just a few minutes. The blood she would spill when she killed him later tonight. The blood of all the people left in the city, thousands and thousands of people, all dead if she did nothing.

So much blood. Too much. Her future was soaked in it.

She thought, again, about pulling a con with her mother. How many hours had she spent just like this, waiting for a mark to walk down the street or into a restaurant, rehearsing lines in her head and knowing that, if she said even one *word* out of order, it could ruin everything.

No chance of that happening now, she thought idly. According to everything she knew of time travel, it didn't matter what she did. The outcome would be the same.

She frowned, turning this over in her head. She'd never thought of it quite like that before. In a con, she had to control every variable of an interaction in order to get the desired outcome. But time travel wasn't like that . . . it was the *outcome* that was certain, no matter what she did leading up to it. Right?

Thinking about this hurt her brain. With time travel, she'd found, it was easier to sort out the logic by doing and then analyze the facts of what she'd discovered later.

"No time like the present," she muttered to herself. A glance around the corner showed no one coming. The hall was empty, quiet. She couldn't even hear the distant rise and fall of voices, the thud of footsteps.

If her theory was correct, then it wouldn't matter whether she hid behind this wall or tried to break Ash free or performed a waltz up and down the hall. She wouldn't be caught because she *hadn't* been caught.

She slipped down the hall like a shadow and knelt in front of Ash's door, examining the lock. She had barely dropped to her knees when she heard a door open and close somewhere deeper inside the hotel.

She froze, ears pricked.

There—footsteps on the staircase, coming closer.

She ducked back behind the corner where she'd been hiding, frustrated.

What did that just prove? she wondered. If she had tried to break Ash out a minute earlier, would the footsteps have come a minute earlier, too? Were her own thoughts and actions catalysts that triggered other actions, and so on, forever?

She felt like she was on the verge of grasping some new idea, something that no one had thought of yet, but every time she came too close it burrowed itself deeper into her mind and was lost.

Mac appeared at the staircase before she could work this

out one way or another, flanked by two Freaks whose faces Dorothy couldn't see from her position around the corner. She held her breath, waiting for him to look her way, to hobble over to where she was hiding, but, of course, he did neither. He wouldn't, she knew, because he hadn't seen her the first time all this had happened. How far could she push this? she wondered. Would he still be unable to see her if she ran down the hallway screaming? Or would she be unable to do that *because* he hadn't seen her?

It was enough to make her feel like her head might explode.

She watched silently as Mac dug a key out of his pocket and threw the door to Ash's room open, and then she let her breath out in a rush. She leaned a little farther out into the hall, ears pricked.

Ash said something she couldn't hear, and Mac responded with "I aim to please."

A moment later, he and the Freaks stepped inside the room, pulling the door closed behind them.

Dorothy stayed crouched around the corner, alert, listening for any sounds or movement from the other side of the door. She heard muffled thumps, voices. And then— screaming. She closed her eyes the moment it began and forced herself to breathe through her nose.

Time was endless. It seemed that hours were passing, even though Dorothy knew it was only minutes. After a while, she sunk from her crouch to the floor, and leaned against the wall, legs stretched out before her. Waiting, waiting. With every minute that passed she thought that now, finally, Mac would grow bored, would leave. And yet he did not.

You save him, Dorothy reminded herself, when the sound of Ash's screaming became too much to bear. You take him away from here.

Patience.

And then, finally—footsteps. Dorothy sat up straighter, pulling her legs to her chest so she wouldn't be seen. She didn't dare breathe, didn't dare move.

There was a knock on the door. And then hinges creaking and the sound of Eliza's voice. "Mac is busy right now. What do you need?"

Dorothy rose to her hands and knees and peered around the corner. She saw herself, as she'd been four days ago, standing in the hallway next to Roman.

Dorothy tilted her head, unable to look away. She was shorter than she realized. She barely came up to Roman's shoulders. Her hair was tangled and limp, and her boots and cloak were splattered with mud. Dorothy knew this was because she and Roman had spent the day going back in time again and again, in the rain, trying to save his sister's life. A lump formed in her throat at the memory. It had been a difficult day, and it was only going to get worse. In just a few hours, Roman would die. Mac would take her hostage. Her gang would turn on her, and she would learn that Ash had gone missing.

The outcome couldn't be changed, but everything leading up to it could be, she thought.

Did that matter? She didn't know.

Her own voice echoed down the hall, interrupting her thoughts.

"Those are new," she said. Dorothy watched as her past self eyed Eliza's boots suspiciously.

Eliza only grinned. "Mac asked me to do him a favor."

"You're working for Mac now?" Roman asked.

"Don't look so surprised. You were the one who gave me the idea," Eliza said. "Or don't you remember our conversation back at the Dead Rabbit?"

A choked scream issued from inside the hotel room. Dorothy dug her fingers into the hotel carpet.

The outcome can't be changed, she thought. There had to be some way to use that to her advantage.

Her past self was staring at the door, suspicious. "Who's in there?"

"No one you need concern yourself with," snapped Eliza.

The Dorothy of four days ago removed a long, thin dagger from her sleeve and held it up to the light.

"Do you know how much pressure it takes to rupture an eardrum?" she asked. "I don't know, myself, but I hear people used to do it by accident, with hairpins and cotton swabs. Imagine the damage *this* could do."

Eliza stared at the blade and licked her lips. Watching from around the corner, Dorothy smiled. That moment had been fun.

Her past self said, "Tell Mac I need to speak with him now."

Dorothy rose to a crouch, replaying the rest of the scene in her mind as it unfolded in front of her.

Mac demanded to be taken to the future. She and Roman refused, and then he opened the door to the hotel room, showed them Ash, and she'd caved at once.

She felt heat rise in her cheeks as she watched herself, remembering how hard she'd worked to keep the emotion from her face, to appear as though Ash's torture didn't bother her.

I'd been a fool, she thought now, staring back at herself. She could see each emotion play out as clearly as if it'd been written in black marker on her forehead. The horror, the pain, the desperation. Anyone looking at her would've known what she'd felt. How embarrassing, that she thought she'd managed to keep it secret.

Roman said, "He should have a public death, don't you think?"

Mac lowered his knife and said, "That's not a bad idea." Over his shoulder, he added, "Keep him alive until I get back."

And he left with them. Dorothy released a low sigh of relief, grateful that Mac, at least, wouldn't be able to hurt Ash any more than he had already.

She counted to twenty in her head, and then the hotel room door swung open and the rest of the Cirkus Freaks spilled into the hall, grumbling about being hungry and wanting a drink as they stumbled toward the staircase. Dorothy watched them go, and then she blinked several times, quickly, like she was waking up.

Now, finally, was her time to act. Ash alone. She had to save him.

She slipped around the corner and knelt before his hotel room door once again. It had taken her most of the last year to figure out how to work these fancy, newfangled locks. They couldn't be broken into using one of her hairpins, as nearly every other lock she encountered could. They were electronic, and so she'd needed something else.

She pulled a card out of her pocket. She'd had Roman configure it especially so that it opened every hotel room in the building. She swiped it through the key lock . . .

The green light blinked on.

She pushed the door open.

The smell of blood hit her first. It was overwhelming, so strong that she wanted to gag. Choking in a breath, she quickly crossed the room and knelt at Ash's side. He didn't look conscious.

"Ash . . . ," she murmured, pushing the sweaty hair back from his forehead. "Come on now, time to wake up."

Ash seemed to struggle to raise his heavy lids. "Dorothy?" he murmured, seeming confused.

Dorothy brought her hand to his cheek. "Hurry," she said. "You don't have a lot of time."

Ash still didn't open his eyes. There was blood crusted in his eyelashes, holding them shut. It hurt her to look at them.

"You aren't here," Ash murmured.

"You have to get out of here," she said urgently, looking over her shoulder. She had no idea how much time they had.

"Mac won't be long and if you're still here when he returns, he'll kill you."

"I don't die today," Ash muttered. "I know when I die."

So do I, Dorothy thought. "Lucky you," she said. "Now *go*."

She didn't wait for him to get up. She didn't need to, she knew that he would. She knew everything that was going to happen next.

Ash was going to follow her and Roman into the future. She would try to kill Mac, and she would fail. Ash and Roman were going to fight, and then Roman was going to die.

Her heart gave a violent tug. She knew it was going to happen like this, because she'd seen it. There was no other way.

The outcome can't be changed, she thought again. Maybe she was fooling herself, thinking there was some loophole to be exploited. Maybe she really was powerless.

She pulled Ash's gun out of her cloak and placed it on the floor in front of him. And then she stood and slipped back out into the hallway, leaving the door wide open behind her.

Her heart was heavy and cold. It felt like a cruel kind of torture, to watch the same things happen over and over again. To know there was nothing she could do to stop them.

I've spent the last few days thinking about my latest experiment. The heartbreaking death of Little Jeff the mouse.

The thing is, I just can't figure out why he died. He was smaller than the potato I brought back, so it wasn't that the exotic matter didn't extend far enough beyond my physical body. It must have something to do with the biochemical makeup of the organisms. The mouse, unlike the potato, had a heartbeat.

So the question becomes: How can I protect the heartbeat?

When I built my time machine, I was able to integrate the exotic properties of the matter into the structure of the vessel itself, thus extending its protection. I did this by utilizing a technique I actually stole from Tesla.

You see, a Tesla coil consists of two parts: a primary coil and secondary coil, each with its own capacitator. (Capacitators are basically just batteries made to store electrical energy.) The two coils and capacitators are connected by a spark gap—a gap of air between two electrodes that generates the spark of electricity. An outside source hooked up to a transformer powers the whole system. Essentially, the Tesla coil is two open electric circuits connected to a spark gap.

The primary coil must be able to withstand the massive charge and huge surges of current, so it's usually made out of copper, because copper is a very good conductor of electricity. I was careful to use copper plates in the structure of all my time machines for that very purpose.

When you have a time machine to play with, creating this kind of circuit is easy. Without one, it gets trickier. I would, essentially, need to use a piece of copper to connect the person with the electronic matter inside their body, to the person without any exotic matter inside their body. Unfortunately, I can't think of a way to accomplish that that doesn't, quite literally, involve knives and stabbing.

Which, obviously, won't work.

19

Three visits down.

Dorothy sighed, deeply, as she climbed back into the *Black Crow*. It was cold in the time machine, and her breath ghosted in the night air, hanging before her lips like a silver cloud. The leather seats felt icy beneath her thin cloak, and her fingers were stiff and awkward with cold. She had to open and close her fists a few times before she began the process of flipping switches and checking dials, to get the blood in her hands moving.

She didn't know how much time had passed since she'd come back. Had she spent a full twenty-four hours chasing after Ash, tiptoeing around in the past? Had it been longer?

Her eyes blinked closed as these thoughts circled her head. All she knew was that she was tired, tired down to her bones. Weight tugged at her, her entire body begging for sleep, and yet she forced her eyes back open and gave her cheek a soft pat.

She couldn't sleep yet. There was still one more visit to go. *The* visit. The one she'd been dreading.

She set the time machine to hover, feeling a slight drop in her gut as the ship lifted off the waves and vibrated in midair. For a moment, she couldn't manage to catch her breath.

She thought of Ash's empty boat, illuminated by the ever-changing light of the anil.

She thought of the veil of blood floating on the water and the abandoned gun at the bottom of his boat.

A sob clawed its way up her throat, but she swallowed it back down. No tears, not yet.

NOVEMBER 11, 2077

The world was just as it had been. Same frighteningly still black water, rippling in the wind, same dark and distant sky. If Dorothy tilted her head and listened very carefully she could hear the hoots and shouts of the Cirkus Freaks leaving the Fairmont and boarding their motorboats. Soon, she knew, the waters would be filled with them. It felt like she'd been gone for years, but it had been only moments. She doubted anyone had even noticed her missing.

She checked the clock on the time machine's dashboard: there was still an hour until midnight. Which meant that she and Mac had just left Roman's body behind in the future, they'd just returned, and Mac had just informed the Black Cirkus that Jonathan Asher was responsible for their beloved Crow's death. Dorothy could still hear his voice, promising the gang of Freaks a great reward in exchange for Ash's body, dead or alive. Right now, it was just the Cirkus hunting for Ash, but Dorothy knew that, soon, it would be the entire city. She would need to act quickly.

She flew to the schoolhouse where Ash and the others lived and landed the *Black Crow* on the water outside. She checked that she still had Roman's dagger safely tucked inside of her cloak. She did. With a low exhale, she climbed onto the docks and wove her way around the side of the school building, counting dark windows until she reached the one that belonged to Ash.

He kept it locked, of course, but the locks in New Seattle were sort of a joke. Dorothy slotted Roman's dagger between the window frame and the sill, wiggling the blade around until she felt a catch. Then, using the dagger like a crowbar, she pushed the window up and up, groaning a bit when the wood finally gave, and a sliver of space appeared between the frame and the sill. Dorothy pocketed Roman's dagger and slid her fingers around the frame, groaning as the window shuddered the rest of the way open.

The room was empty, dark. Ash hadn't returned from the future yet, but he couldn't be too far behind. Dorothy found a spare scrap of paper on his desk, and an old pen and wrote the note:

Outside the anil. Midnight.

She paused when she was done, a shiver moving through her as she studied the message. It hadn't been that long ago that Zora had thrust this exact note in her face and demanded to know why she'd written it and what she'd done with Ash. At the time, Dorothy had insisted it hadn't been her. She felt a sinking feeling now, as she realized she was turning herself into a liar.

That's not the worst thing you'll become tonight, she told herself. A sour taste rose in her throat. She swallowed it down, making her way back to the window.

It was time to get this over with.

Forty-five minutes left until they were to meet. Dorothy flew the *Black Crow* out to a desolate part of the city and did her best to hide it in the trees, even using some spare brush and branches to camouflage it further. She couldn't fly it to her meeting with Ash. With the Cirkus out in full force, she was sure to be spotted. She would have to come back for it later, after . . . after it was all done. Once she was satisfied that no one would stumble onto the time machine by accident, she began the long trek back to the Fairmont.

The hotel was dark when she reached it, Mac and the rest of the Black Cirkus already out looking for their traitor. Her past self, she knew, would be on the fifth floor, in Roman's hotel room, trying to make sense of everything that had happened. There was little risk of anyone seeing her. Still, she pulled her hood over her face, and made her way to the parking garage quickly. There, she found a boat that she doubted anyone would notice missing and climbed inside.

She used the paddle until she'd left the Fairmont behind

her, not wanting to draw anyone's attention with the sound of a motor. When she was far enough out, she turned on the motor, taking some comfort in the sound of the gears chewing through the air. The sound made it all that more difficult to focus on her own thoughts, which was fine with her. Her thoughts weren't entirely pleasant just now.

White trees flew past her, reminding her of fireflies in the dark. She paid them little attention. In her head, she was counting down to midnight, trying to figure out just how much time she had left before she had to do this terrible thing.

Was it fifteen minutes? Ten?

Her breathing grew shallower.

Roman's dagger hung heavily in the pocket of her cloak, weighted down with the expectations of what she was supposed to do with it. She pushed her hand into the fabric and gripped it, her palms quickly growing sweaty around the cool metal handle. She found herself wondering, idly, what kind of dagger had a handle made out of metal instead of bone or wood. Had Roman found this thing in the past? She had no memory of him ever stealing a dagger from the past during one of their journeys through time, but she supposed that didn't mean much. Roman had always been secretive.

She pulled the dagger out and studied it in the dim glow of the boat's headlight.

It looked expensive, she saw, but not old. It was heavy and plain, the blade nearly as thick around as her wrist. And, yes, it's handle was indeed fashioned out of some sort of metal. In the dull light the metal looked brownish, like brass or—

Dorothy blinked. A passage from the Professor's entries flashed through her head:

I would, essentially, need to use a piece of copper to connect the person with the electronic matter inside their body.

The motor shuddered beneath her, spitting up a stream of water that drew her attention back to the boat. She'd been studying the dagger instead of steering and now she shoved it back into her pocket. She needed to concentrate. This would all be over soon.

She saw Ash's boat in the distance. And she saw Ash standing inside, his body silhouetted in the ever-changing light of the anil. She dropped her hand in her cloak and gripped the handle of her dagger tightly between trembling fingers.

Metal handle, she thought. *Copper handle.*

Her mind snagged on something she couldn't quite catch.

It was strange, but she felt a sense of calm in knowing what was going to happen next. She'd tried to change things. Over and over again, she'd tried but, in the end, she'd been unsuccessful. Now there was only the thing that had to be done and an odd, shallow sort of comfort that came from realizing she'd never be able to alter it. Time was a circle. This had already happened. It had been foolish of her to think she had a choice one way or another.

Ash stood in the small boat, black water lapping at the sides. The trees seemed to glow in the darkness around him. Ghost trees. Dead trees. Water pressed against their hollow, white trunks, moving with the wind.

Dorothy pulled her hood up over her hair, breathing hard.

The wind blew a few strands loose, sending them dancing in the darkness. She reached up, pushed those white strands of hair back under her hood with a flick of her hand, and then started the engine on her motor and sailed up next to the man she loved.

He looked like he had when they'd first met: that rugged sunburned skin and eyes that were such a light hazel they were practically gold.

Those lovely eyes fixed on Dorothy and, for a moment, she couldn't speak.

"I . . . didn't think you'd come," she said. What she'd meant was *I hoped you wouldn't come*. But she couldn't say that. Her hopes didn't matter anymore.

Ash looked at her, pleading. She saw in his face that he knew exactly what was going to happen, and, yet, he still didn't believe it. It made her ache that he thought this could all be different.

"It doesn't have to end like this," he said.

Dorothy opened her mouth. *How to explain?* If she didn't do this, Mac would find Ash again. He would dig the EM out of his body. He would use time travel over and over and over again, not caring that it would turn the rest of the world to dust. This was the only way. The outcome couldn't be changed.

Dorothy curled her fingers around Roman's dagger. "Of course it does," she said.

Unless, she thought.

Unfortunately, I can't think of a way to accomplish that that doesn't, quite literally, involve knives and stabbing.

Dorothy hesitated, thinking. An idea was occurring to her. The outcome couldn't be changed, but everything leading up to it could be.

Was it an idea? Yes, yes it was. *Her* actions could change. She could do this differently.

Headlights glimmered in the darkness. Every nerve in Dorothy's body sparked. She heard distant voices, followed by a series of sharp cracks.

Gunshots.

She turned back to Ash. The Freaks were circling closer. Soon, they would be spotted. If she was going to attempt to do this crazy thing, she would need to do it now.

She pulled Roman's dagger loose. Ash's eyes followed the movement, something flashing through them. Not fear; disappointment.

"Dorothy—"

She leaned forward, gripping his shoulder. Ash brought his eyes up to hers, frowning.

"Do you trust me?" she asked urgently.

A look of confusion clouded Ash's face. "What? I don't—"

"Close enough." She plunged the dagger into his abdomen, just below his ribs, where she knew the exotic matter was lodged. She didn't stop until she felt the tip of the blade catch.

I would, essentially, need to use a piece of copper to connect the person with the electronic matter inside their body.

Something sparked—sending energy up her arm. *Please*

work, she thought, and pulled Ash close, her blade still connected with that tiny piece of exotic matter. She dragged both of them over the side of the boat and into the black water below.

The anil swirled angrily, pulling them into its center.

PART THREE

PART
THREE

20

ASH

Heat and pain.

The pain was worse than the heat; it reminded Ash of waves. It would crash into him, over him, and then he'd be sinking.

Down

and down

and down . . .

And, just when he thought he could take no more, the pain would ease, just a little, just enough for him to hear her voice.

"Ash? Ash, can you hear me? Open your eyes . . ."

Dorothy. He opened his mouth and tried to force words out through his lips, but then the pain hit, and it all started over again.

Was this what dying felt like?

He didn't know.

He'd never died before.

21

DOROTHY

JUNE 7, 1913

Smoke and spinning. Flashing lights.

And then she was drifting, drifting . . .

The first thing Dorothy was certain of was the packed earth beneath her knees, the slight damp seeping through her cloak. She was kneeling . . . and then she was doubled over, one hand propped against the ground. She could feel the moist dirt beneath her palm, now. She curled her fingers into the ground and the dirt crumbled between them, which was good. That was exactly how dirt was supposed to behave. It was a strange thing to think, but her head felt swimmy, her chest full and hot, and she wasn't entirely sure that matter would act the way it was supposed to.

She opened her eyes, but the air was thick with a gray haze that might've been smoke or might've been clouds dropped down from the sky.

Where am I? she wondered.

And when?

She began to choke, deep, hacking coughs that felt like they were pulling up bits of her lungs. Thoughts began to form in the haziness of her mind:

Ash. The dagger. The Professor's theory.

"Ash," Dorothy choked out, when she could breathe again. In her hand there was something warm and wet and firm. *Roman's dagger.* She couldn't see through the smoke but, if that's what she was holding, it was almost certainly covered in blood. *Ash's blood.*

Her stomach turned over.

Oh God . . . What had she done?

She began to panic, trying to wave away the thick gray smoke, trying to see anything. "Ash? Are you alive?"

She thought she heard a groan, but she could hardly make it out through the roaring sound that filled her ears. God, what *was* that sound? She'd thought it was her own heartbeat, adrenaline causing her blood to pump hard and fast, blocking out all other noise but, now, she could tell that the sound wasn't coming from inside her at all. It was something else, something close and loud.

There was movement in the smoke. Blinking, Dorothy thought that she saw something, some animal flying through the sky. She squinted . . .

No, what she saw was moving too smoothly to be an animal. It was a machine of some sort. The smoke billowed and cleared around it. Light flared behind distant clouds, illuminating an object, sleek and metallic against the black.

An airplane, Dorothy thought, with a twist of déjà vu.

And now she looked around her, taking in her surroundings. Gnarled branches and flattened grass and the heavy smell of campfire smoke. She was in the wooded area just behind the church where she was to marry Dr. Charles Avery back in 1913.

A small smile curled her lip. She had no way of knowing the exact day or the time, but she could guess that it was the morning of her wedding, and that the machine she'd just seen take to the sky wasn't an airplane at all but a *time machine*, and, in fact, it was the *Second Star*, disappearing into the future with her and Ash on board.

The last thing she remembered with any clarity was standing in her rickety boat outside the anil in New Seattle, 2077, staring into Ash's golden eyes as she slid a dagger into his body and praying to whoever would listen that her foolish idea might actually work.

She released a small, sharp laugh. *Remarkable.* It had happened just as the Professor wrote that it would. Of course, neither the Professor nor she had known that the anil would spit them out here and now, of all the times and places throughout history she could've gone, but she couldn't think about that. Time, as always, was slipping away.

"Ash?" She turned her full attention to the body splayed across the earth in front of her. Now that the time machine had gone and the smoke had begun to fade, she could see him more clearly.

Oh, he looked like death. He was lying on his back, his eyes closed, his arms splayed to either side of his frightfully still body. His skin was gray and sallow, and blood clung thickly to his shirt, the color much too red and garish in the early morning light. Staring down at him, Dorothy felt fear roar up inside of her.

No, she thought, gritting her teeth. He couldn't be dead. That wasn't the plan.

It wasn't going to end like this.

With a grunt, she pulled Ash's head and shoulders off the ground and maneuvered them onto her lap. She lightly slapped his cheek. "Ash? Jonathan Asher, can you hear me? Wake up. *Please*."

He didn't move, didn't make a sound. His eyelashes didn't even flutter. Dorothy felt her fear turn cold.

Oh God, what have I done?

She groped along his neck, desperately searching for a pulse. Nothing and more nothing and more nothing after that . . .

And then . . . *there*. Just below Ash's skin she'd felt something, a slight *bomp bomp bomp*, so faint that she could barely make out the vibration against her finger. It wasn't strong, but it was still a heartbeat, which meant there was hope, if only she could figure out what to do now.

Think, damn you, she thought, looking up. Oh, this was bad. They were in the middle of nowhere, surrounded by trees and woods, a few yards from the old church and a mile or so from the train station. The nearest hospital was in Seattle proper, and it would take them ages to get there.

"Blast," Dorothy muttered, beneath her breath. "All of

history at our fingertips and we couldn't have landed some-where with a bleeding doctor—"

She stopped talking at once. They *had* landed some-where with a doctor. Her fiancé, Dr. Charles Avery, was a surgeon. And not just any surgeon, but a good one. He was the surgeon-in-*chief* at Seattle's Providence Medical Center.

And he was just inside.

Dorothy's heart leaped inside of her. There was a chance. If she hurried, there was still a chance.

She leaned close to Ash, bringing a hand to his face. His skin was cold to the touch, shockingly so. It caused an uncom-fortable shiver to move down her spine, making her shoulders clench. *There was still time; there had to be time. . . .*

"Hold on," she told Ash, her voice a whisper. "I'll be right back. Just . . . please, please stay alive until then."

The church was smaller than Dorothy remembered, a squat, two-story building made of crumbling bricks, with tall, arched doorways and intricately stained-glass windows.

She was breathless when she reached the doors, and she struggled a moment with the heavy wood, hinges screech-ing when she finally managed to haul it open. Inside, the air was thick with dust and the smell of incense. She could hear music playing in another room, something with strings. A cello, maybe, or a violin. Funny, she had no memory of any-one arranging for a cellist or a violinist to play at her wedding.

"Hello?" she called, turning in place. Her footsteps were impossibly loud, and her voice echoed off the stone walls, but that was okay, she wanted to be heard. "Charles—"

The church door thudded heavily behind her, drowning her out.

"Can I help you?" came a voice. Dorothy spun in place, heart hammering as her eyes landed on the petite, impeccably dressed older woman who was just descending the stone staircase.

And now Dorothy pressed her teeth together so tightly that her jaw began to ache. The woman had thick dark hair piled on top of her head in an intricate-looking bun and she studied Dorothy with her head slightly tilted, her black eyes narrowed in confusion.

"I'm terribly sorry, but this is a closed service." She spoke in the sort of coldly polite voice someone might use with an annoying, distant relative. She gestured toward the door. "I'm going to have to ask you to—"

"Mother," Dorothy interrupted, nearly choking on the word. Her mouth felt dry and sticky. She wet her lips and added, attempting a smile, "Don't you recognize me?"

The woman turned her body toward Dorothy and looked at her fully, starting to speak before she registered what she was seeing. "I do not wish to call the authorities, miss, but you see, this is . . ."

She blinked, trailing off. The skin between her brows pinched together. "What . . ."

She took a step closer to Dorothy, her eyes narrowing even further. Her thin lips parted, but she did not speak. For a long, terrible moment, there was only silence.

Dorothy sucked a breath in through her teeth and allowed herself to be scrutinized. She tried to imagine how she must look right now, with her white hair and scarred face, the dirt and blood smudged across her skin, her *trousers*.

Her mother finally released a huff of air through her lips and said only, "I—I don't understand."

How could you? Dorothy thought. But she didn't say that out loud. Her mother deserved an explanation, but she couldn't think of where she might even begin. With her hair? Her scar? The fact that time travel was real?

And that was if she had time to get into any of this, which she most certainly did not.

"Mother," Dorothy said, as calmly as she could manage, "I know this must be a terrible shock for you, but I'm afraid there's no time to explain what's going on. I need to find Charles at once."

"Charles," her mother repeated, looking dazed. She shook her head, half turning back toward the staircase. "I just saw—"

"Charles, Mother," Dorothy cut in, frustrated now. "Where is he?"

But her mother didn't seem to be in contact with the part of her brain capable of answering that question just now. She opened her mouth and closed it again, the lines on her forehead deepening.

Dorothy pinched her nose between two fingers. *Think*, she told herself. It was only a few minutes before the wedding. *She* was meant to be upstairs, sitting very still in her dressing room, so as not to mess up her hair or her dress as she waited for the bridal party to come fetch her.

So Charles would be . . .

Dorothy lifted her head, finding her gaze drawn down a short hallway that ended in a pair of heavy doors. Those doors led to the chapel, she knew. They'd been open while the guests were arriving, but they were closed now, which could only mean that all the guests were already here. And if the guests were all here, then Avery was . . .

Oh no, Dorothy thought, understanding crashing over her. Avery was standing at the front of the chapel next to a bleeding *priest*, with his entire family and all his friends seated in the pews before him. She felt her heart thrumming inside her chest and, for a moment, she thought she might be sick. If she was going to convince him to help Ash, she'd first have to walk down the aisle and fetch him. How horribly ironic.

Her mother suddenly grabbed her by the wrist. "Miss, I don't know what sort of game you're playing, but if you don't leave at once, I'm afraid that I'll have to call the authorities."

"Oh *please*, Mother, you and I both know that you'll do no such thing." Dorothy twisted her hand out of her mother's grip. "You have a rap sheet longer than my arm. You don't want the police showing up any more than I do."

"But, how did . . ." Loretta was clearly trying to sound calm, but her breath caught, making her voice hitch. Her gaze was on Dorothy's face again, and she seemed to be having some internal struggle with herself over what she was seeing.

She muttered, under her breath, "This just isn't possible."

Dorothy took a step toward the chapel. Loretta shifted in front of her, blocking her path, and Dorothy said, with an exasperated sigh, "Mother, please—"

"Stop *calling* me that," Loretta snapped.

"Then, please, just get out of my way." Dorothy side-stepped her mother and hurried forward, throwing the chapel doors open. Music swelled, not just violins and cellos but a full string quartet.

How lovely, Dorothy thought. *Avery certainly went all out.*

And then the music was drowned out by the sound of wood creaking and bodies shifting as seventy-five people swiveled around in their seats to stare at her.

22

ASH

And, sometimes, the pain faded for longer stretches, leaving Ash alone in the nothingness.

Or, not so much nothingness as darkness. Like night layered over more night layered over even more night and on and on forever.

And then, after what seemed like a very long time . . . something that wasn't darkness. The black looked different, somehow. Richer. Ash reached through the haze of his brain, struggling to remember the word.

Blue. That's what it was. And not just blue, but purple, too, and deep, bloody flashes of red. The colors swirled around each other. The longer Ash stared, the more color seemed to be woven in the whorls and tendrils of darkness that was his entire existence.

Here, there was a flash of orange. And, there, a curl of pink. Pinpricks of light flashed deep within the black and, for a moment, they made Ash think of stars. Dozens, and then hundreds, and then an entire galaxy waiting for him.

A deep rumbling echoed from somewhere inside of his mind, and then the stars all winked out at once, like they'd never been there in the first place.

Time tunnel, Ash thought, relaxing. That's what this reminded him of, of being inside the anil. If he was inside the anil, then everything was going to be okay. He'd always felt most at home inside the anil.

He relaxed and, as he relaxed, images of his life began to appear in his mind, there and then gone again, like the flash of a camera:

He was young, small, and running. He could feel the blood pumping through his chest and down into his legs, his lungs expanding and contracting beneath his ribs. The sun was hot on his shoulders, and, all around him, there was the swaying brown and yellow and green of corn. He was racing through the cornfields behind his parents' house, and it was summer.

On days like this, he always felt like he could run forever. . . .

And then the memory changed: *He was sixteen, and it was his first day at flight camp, and he was standing before a group of soldiers, all of them older than he was, scowling and confident. They made him nervous. He figured they must've grown up around planes instead of corn and dirt. He pictured them climbing into the cockpits of their jets like young princes mounting fine steads, coaxing them forward so easily he'd think the planes were living, breathing things. He felt shame climb his cheeks. They were all laughing at him, he knew, joking that he treated the fighter jets like they might bite. . . .*

And, again, the memory changed. *It was night now, and Ash was asleep, but a man had grabbed his arm, shaking him awake.*

"My name is Professor Zacharias Walker," the man said in a deep, vibrating whisper. "I'm a time traveler from the year 2075. If you'll accompany me for a moment, I can show you my time machine."

And again.

Ash was in a dirt clearing, surrounded by trees, the air filled with the sound of church bells. A girl stood in front of him, barefoot, wearing a wedding gown with a hem stained with mud. She was the most beautiful girl Ash had ever seen, with skin like porcelain, a small, rosebud-shaped mouth, and brown curls cascading around her shoulders.

The church bells stopped, and the girl forced her mouth into a practiced smile.

"Actually, I was hoping you might be able to help me," she said, tilting her head. "I appear to be lost."

Ash felt his lips move. "Excuse me for saying so, miss, but it looks like you meant to get lost."

The girl smothered a grin.

And then the images were fading, swirling and disappearing into purple and blue walls and distantly twinkling stars. . . .

23

DOROTHY

JUNE 7, 1913

Dorothy stood, frozen, at the back of the chapel, nerves crawling up her skin. There were a dozen pews before her, all of them filled with people who had turned around in their seats to stare. They'd been expecting pretty dresses, flowers, a *bride*. Not the dirty girl who stood before them, with her white hair and scarred face. She watched as brows furrowed and lips twitched into frowns, confusion breaking out across seventy-five faces at once. Whispers erupted like tiny wildfires, first one person leaning over to her neighbor and then five people, all speaking in hushed undertones, and then, not a minute after she'd thrown the doors open, the whole chapel was talking at once.

"Who *is* that?"

"—could possibly be doing here . . ."

"Anyone recognize her?"

An anxious smile jerked across Dorothy's face. *Move*, she told herself. She took a single step forward, her legs so stiff she thought she might trip over her own feet. *Go on, it's easy. Just put one foot in front of the other.*

One step became two, and then three, and now she was walking down the aisle, her eyes straight ahead, pretending that nothing was wrong.

Charles waited at the front of the chapel, a quizzical expression on his charmless face. Dorothy had forgotten that he looked like this, not unattractive so much as terribly, almost frightfully boring. All his features were just where you'd expect them to be, his nose nose-shaped, his eyes a particularly flat shade of brown and set just exactly the right distance apart from one another, his hair was not too long and not too short and parted in the center. It was the sort of face you started forgetting before you'd even managed to look away.

He didn't seem to recognize Dorothy until she was standing directly in front of him, and then he blinked, twice, and said, only, "Oh."

"Charles," Dorothy said, in a rush, "I'm afraid there's isn't time to explain—"

"You look so . . . so different," Charles managed to say. He tilted his head, studying her like he couldn't quite place what about her appearance had changed. He removed a handkerchief from his pocket and lightly dabbed at his upper lip. "What on earth has happened?"

Dorothy was suddenly, painfully aware of the priest and the groomsmen standing nearby, listening to her every word. In the background, the string quartet played on, bravely. The whispers had died down somewhat, everyone waiting to see what was going to happen next.

Dorothy leaned a little closer to Charles and said, in a low, urgent voice, "Charles, there's a boy in the clearing just outside. He desperately needs your help . . . he's dying."

Charles blinked, frown lines appearing between his eyebrows. He looked like he didn't know for sure what to say. He tried for a smile, then seemed to realize that it wasn't entirely appropriate and pressed his lips together instead.

"My dear," he said finally. "It's our *wedding day*."

"This boy will die if you don't help him."

"We're supposed to be married . . ." His eyes lingered on her scar, a rather distressed expression flashing across his face. Clearing his throat, he added, "Everyone's watching."

"Please, Charles," Dorothy said, grabbing his arm. "He needs you."

There must've been something in her voice, some hint of the deep pain that she felt because, after a moment, Charles nodded and said, rather stiffly, "Of course. Lead the way."

Dorothy took Charles and two of his groomsmen out back, to the flattened clearing where she'd left Ash lying in the dirt. She was still feet away, but, even so, she could see that his skin was paler than it'd been when she'd left him here, and nearly green. She couldn't tell if he was breathing.

She stopped walking, her chest seizing. Was it already too late? Was he—

Charles pushed past her and came to kneel beside Ash's body. He leaned close, checking for a pulse.

"It's there, just barely," he said, after a moment, and Dorothy felt some tension inside of her release.

Oh, thank God.

Charles straightened and began rolling up his sleeves. "I'll need my kit. It's in my dressing room—"

Dorothy turned to run for it, but a groomsman was already racing across the grass. Instead, she crouched beside Charles's shoulder.

"What else?" she asked, anxious. "How can I help?"

Charles looked up at her like he'd forgotten she was there. He was in surgeon mode, she could see, his only goal to save the life before him.

"Hold your hand just here," he said, and took her hand, pressing her palm to the wound below Ash's ribs. "We have to stop the bleeding."

They worked for hours. The wedding guests hovered for a while, watching in awe and murmuring to themselves, until Loretta said something about refreshments and space and ushered them back to the church. Dorothy supposed she was placating them with food before breaking the news that they could go home, that there would be no wedding after all. But, truthfully, she didn't know or care. She only had eyes for Ash.

Dorothy had no idea what Charles was doing, but she was good at following directions. She mopped his brow and fetched him tools from his kit and, all the while, she felt like she was seeing him for the first time. By the time he started stitching Ash up, Dorothy's legs were numb, and her shoulders were knotted around her ears, but she barely noticed the discomfort. Charles was like a master tailor, each stitch he placed into Ash's body so tiny and perfectly even that it was practically a work of art.

When he was finished, he sat back on his heels, sweating. "We'll take him back to the house," he said, dragging a hand over his brow. "I'll need to monitor his progress over the next few days, to make sure he stays stable."

"Thank you," Dorothy said, breathless. "Charles . . . I can't . . . thank you."

Dorothy wasn't entirely sure how long she spent crouched over Ash's bedside. Hours? Longer?

She hadn't slept or eaten since they'd arrived at Avery's house, and she took little notice of the people who flitted in and out of the room, usually Charles, come to check on Ash's progress, or one of the housekeepers come to bring food that Dorothy didn't touch or even look at. None of them interested Dorothy enough to convince her to pull her eyes away from Ash's face.

Was there a little more color in his skin, perhaps? Had his breathing steadied? Was that a flicker of his eyelashes?

She held her breath, leaning closer.

She barely heard the creak behind her that signaled a door opening, or the light footsteps that trailed across the floor, but she couldn't help but notice the sudden heaviness that filled the room, like a change in the temperature. Frowning, she looked up.

Her mother stood behind the chair just next to Dorothy's, fingers wrapped firmly around the back of the seat, her eyes straight ahead. Dorothy felt every muscle in her body tighten.

"Mother," she said, sitting up straighter. "What are you doing here?"

"What am I doing here?" Loretta gave a stiff laugh. She sat, straightening her skirts with a flick of her hand. "You have the audacity to ask?"

"I can explain," Dorothy rushed to say.

"Explain?" Loretta lifted a thin eyebrow, looking amused. "Go on then. *Explain.*"

She tilted her head, waiting. Dorothy felt her teeth clench together. She'd nearly forgotten how good her mother was at making her feel small, like she was still a naughty child begging forgiveness for clumsily knocking over a water glass or speaking out of turn. It was a talent, really.

You ran gangs and took over cities, Dorothy reminded herself silently. *You stole jewels from kings.*

You have no reason to fear your mother.

"Mother," Dorothy said. "I—"

Loretta clucked her tongue, cutting her off. "Perhaps you'd like to start with how you managed to ruin our chances at gaining more wealth and power than you or I have ever seen in our short, difficult lives?" Loretta's upper lip curled ever so slightly as she leaned forward, picking at one of Dorothy's white curls.

"Or, maybe, you'd care to explain *this*. Or . . . *this*." She gestured to the scar cutting across Dorothy's once-beautiful face, her expression crumpling with disappointment, as though Dorothy had just destroyed a precious family heirloom. Which, Dorothy supposed, wasn't too far from the truth.

Her mouth felt dry. She didn't know where to begin.

She understood her mother's rage, certainly. None of their guests had stuck around the chapel for the several hours it had taken Charles to save Ash's life. After, Charles had suggested that they postpone their nuptials considering the . . . well, "extenuating circumstances" were the words he'd used, and Dorothy hadn't bothered asking him to elaborate. She'd known from day one that Avery had wanted a trophy on his arm, a pretty, quiet wife who would smile at the appropriate times and laugh at his colleagues' jokes. Now that Dorothy was . . . different, she was of no interest to him.

Which suited her just fine. She had never wanted Charles. As long as he allowed her to stay next to Ash's side while he recovered, she was perfectly happy.

Her mother, on the other hand . . .

"How did this happen?" Loretta asked her now, her voice low and filled with fury. Her eyes flicked to Ash, still lying motionless on the bed, his skin still pale but remarkably less green than it had been. Loretta's lips twisted in disgust. "*Who is this boy? Where did you find him?*"

Dorothy opened her mouth and then closed it again. Heat burned up her cheeks. She could see no way out of it. Her mother deserved an explanation for all that had happened and yet *this* explanation was so strange, so farfetched . . .

Loretta blinked at her daughter. "Well?" she snapped. "I'm waiting."

Here goes nothing, Dorothy thought.

"Mother," she said slowly. "This boy is a pilot named Jonathan Asher. He's a time traveler from the year·2077."

There was a beat of silence once Dorothy had finished her story. The edge of Loretta's lip twitched. For a moment, the two women just stared at one another, saying nothing.

And then, Loretta released a low, thin breath from between her lips. "What game are you running?" she asked.

"Game?" Dorothy blinked. "Mother, this isn't a con."

"Don't be smart with me, girl, I know a con when I see one." Loretta lifted her bad hand and made quite a show of cleaning a piece of lint out from beneath one of her long, yellow fingernails. "Tell me your angle. You want out of the engagement? Fine, there's nothing I can do to repair that relationship anyway, but if you think for a second that you're getting money—"

"Mother, look at me." Dorothy motioned to the wreck of her face. "How could I have faked this? You saw me moments before I disappeared, but this scar is long healed."

Loretta looked up, her eyes settling on Dorothy's face. Until now, she'd only cast her daughter passing glances, as though it physically pained her to look any closer, but now her eyes narrowed, studying her.

She seemed to be having some internal battle with herself before, finally, she lifted a hand and brought her finger to Dorothy's scar.

Dorothy felt the lightest brush of pressure. Her mother hesitated, her breath sucking inward, and then she dropped her hand, quickly, like she'd been burned.

"I don't know how you did that," Loretta said stiffly.

"It isn't fake, Mother," Dorothy said softly. "I'm telling you the truth."

Loretta shook her head, still unconvinced. She stood and began to make her way to the door. "I'm going to attempt to smooth things over with Avery. If he throws us out now, we'll have no choice but to take to the streets."

Dorothy had to work hard not to roll her eyes. Her mother was exaggerating, as usual. There was always a plan B, a hotel that didn't lock its back door, or a bar filled with business-men whose pockets were heavy and brains were empty, or else there was an old friend who'd let them sleep on the couch. But she didn't want to argue, and so all she said was, *"Thank you, Mother."*

Loretta pulled the door open but paused before leaving the room. "I did all of this for you, you know," she said, in a very different tone of voice. "To keep you safe and fed, to give you a different sort of life from my own. It may not have always appeared that way, but it's true."

Dorothy stared at her mother, taken aback. In all these years of cons and lies, it had never once occurred to her that her mother might be trying to give her a better life. Her chest clenched.

"Mother—" she started.

But Loretta had already stepped into the hallway, letting the door fall shut behind her.

24

ASH

Ash's eyes fluttered in his sleep, images playing below his lids:

He was in the Professor's workshop, standing before the Second Star, *his time machine. He unlatched the door to the cargo hold and threw it open, grunting. "Back in the war, we had a word for—"*

The rest of his sentence got caught in his throat. There, crouched in the Second Star's *cargo hold, was the girl from 1913, her wedding gown creased and muddy around her.*

She pushed the sweaty hair off her face. "I think I'm going to be sick," she said.

And then she vomited on Ash's boots.

The memory faded. In its place, Ash saw a rowboat surrounded by black water . . . *Ghost trees glowing white in the darkness . . . A woman with a hood covering her head . . . White hair fluttering in the wind . . . A kiss . . . A knife . . .*

The image changed again. *Ash was in Fort Hunter complex, watching a girl on a video feed.*

The girl shifted toward the camera, and Ash caught the sketchy, white curve of a foxtail painted over the front of her dark coat.

Quinn Fox. Ash stared, uneasy. If Quinn was here that meant they'd really done it. The Black Cirkus had found a way to travel through time without exotic matter.

Quinn lifted her hands, pushing away the hood covering her face.

She was turned away from the camera and, at first, all he saw was her scar. It carved up half her face, a misshapen, gnarled thing that made it difficult to focus on the rest of her. Ash cringed at the sight of it. It wasn't unusual to see bad scars and deformities in New Seattle—medical care wasn't what it used to be. But now Ash understood why Quinn hid her face. Her hair came out of the hood next, tumbling around her shoulders in a tangled mess of curls.

Ash's heart stopped beating. Somewhere deep inside his body, his veins were leaking acid.

He'd never seen Quinn's hair before. It had always been hidden under her hood, and now he felt stupid for not putting two and two together.

White. *Quinn Fox's hair was white.*

On the screen, a black-and-white Quinn Fox tugged long fingers through her hair, pulling the last few strands loose of her coat. She wasn't looking at the camera anymore, so Ash stared at her hand, studying every detail he could make out on the grainy screen. Her short fingernails. The creases of her knuckles. A small black smudge that looked like a tattoo.

He raised a hand to his cheek, premembering the brush of her fingers on his skin, seconds before she slid a blade between his ribs.

"Quinn," he muttered in his sleep.

25

DOROTHY

Dorothy sat up a little straighter, ears pricked. Ash had spoken. He'd said her name—or, well, he'd said her *other* name. He'd said *Quinn*.

She frowned as she leaned over his sleeping body, brushing a strand of sweaty, blond hair away from his brow. He didn't seem to be getting any better, as far as she could tell. He'd hardly moved, and his breathing seemed just as shallow and labored as it had been when they'd first brought him here. There was still that horrible green cast to his skin that made her think of an outbreak of yellow fever she'd seen in New Orleans ages ago, when she and her mother were passing through the city.

"Shh . . . ," she murmured, pressing the palm of her hand to his forehead. Despite the sweat, he was cool to the touch, alarmingly so. "You need to sleep, Ash. You need your strength."

Ash twitched, shaking her hand away. "Where'd you go, Quinn?" he murmured.

Dorothy frowned. She felt like she was overhearing bits and pieces of a much longer conversation. It was frustrating, like starting a story halfway through. But she and Ash had never had this conversation. So, what was going on? Was it a dream? A fantasy?

"You stay here," Ash murmured, the skin on his brow creasing. "I'll . . . go . . . I'm . . . I can probably convince them I was alone up here. Then you . . . get somewhere safe."

Dorothy leaned closed. These words felt familiar. She'd heard Ash say them to her before.

She said, automatically, her brain supplying the words before she could remember where they'd come from, "You think I'm going to stay behind?"

With that, the memory came flooding back to her: she and Ash were standing in the *Dark Star*, armed soldiers surrounding them. They'd just kissed for the first time, and now Ash was telling her to stay with the time machine so that she wouldn't get captured.

Why had he mentioned Quinn?

Her frown deepened. This wasn't the first time he'd mentioned seeing her at Fort Hunter. When she first went back in time to see him, he'd mentioned spotting Quinn Fox running through the halls with the Professor. At the time, she'd been so overwhelmed by everything else that was going on to give it much thought. Now, it bothered her.

Roman had gone back to Fort Hunter on his own. They'd agreed that it would be much too confusing if she were there, too, and neither wanted to risk her past and current selves accidentally discovering one another. Quinn Fox had never stepped foot inside of Fort Hunter.

And, yet, Ash said that he'd seen her there.

And . . . hadn't she premembered something like this? Something about chasing the Professor through the halls of Fort Hunter? She frowned deeply. It certainly *felt* familiar.

"What did the Professor want with a weapon?" Ash was murmuring, thrashing a little in his sleep. Dorothy chewed on her lip. He didn't look good. She looked over her shoulder, wondering if she should call Avery.

But if she called Avery, Ash might stop talking. And then she'd never know what he'd seen at Fort Hunter.

Making up her mind, Dorothy turned back around and touched Ash's shoulder, rocking him gently. "Ash?" she said. "Where did you see me? What was I doing?"

Ash's brow cleared, his breathing steadied. Dorothy suspected that whatever memory he'd been reliving had passed, that he was somewhere else now, somewhere new. She sat back in her seat, exhaling hard.

How had she gotten back to Fort Hunter? And when?

Any *why*?

None of it made any sense.

Dorothy slipped out of Ash's room and made her way down the hall. Electric lights flickered from sconces on the walls, making the shadows twitch. Her boots echoed off the tile floors and, somewhere deeper in the house, she heard voices that might have belonged to Avery, or might have belonged to her mother. They were too far away for her to know, for sure, whether they were male or female, all she could hear for certain was the cadence of speech, that familiar rise and fall.

Heart hammering, she slipped into her own room and pushed the door closed with a soft click.

This had been the room where she'd stayed in the weeks leading up to her wedding, when it would have been unseemly for her to stay with Avery. She hadn't been here since she'd gotten back, preferring, instead, to curl up in the chair beside Ash's bed, but now she could see that it was exactly as she'd left it. Plush, four-post bed and fussy furniture, expensive dresses left to wilt on the backs of chairs or else kicked into the corners where they would be out of the way.

Dorothy closed her eyes and leaned her head back against her heavy, oak door. She forced herself to focus on her breathing, trying to match her inhale to her exhale. She needed to focus. What did she know? What did it mean?

According to Ash, she'd gone back in time, to Fort Hunter, in 1980, the same day the rest of them had broken into the base to . . . what, exactly? Follow the Professor? Talk to him, perhaps? But *why*?

"Blast, this is giving me a headache," she muttered out loud, lowering her face to her hands. *Think you silly nit, think.* What possible reason could she have for talking to the Professor?

It was true, now that she thought of it, that she wouldn't

mind having a word with the man. She'd never met him, but he was supposed to be the most brilliant scientist who'd ever existed. He could explain these earthquakes that were going to end the world, for one thing, and whether they were, actually, caused by time travel and, if that was true, what were they supposed to even do about them now. She could ask him if there was any chance of saving Ash. And oh, he could explain those damn journal entries. Traveling through time without any EM . . .

She lifted her head, blinking into the darkness of her room.

Traveling through time without any EM.

Dorothy wasn't sure what time it was, but the sky outside was already darkening, so it must be late. She'd left the lights in her bedroom off, too, and the only light that she could see came from Roman's dagger. It sat on her bedside table, the teensy tiny bit of EM still clinging to the blade sparking and twitching in the darkness.

It was purple lightning. It was pale, red liquid. It was hard and metallic.

Dorothy chewed on her lip. That EM had come from inside Ash's body when she'd stabbed him. It had brought her here, to 1913. She'd read the Professor's instructions for how to put it inside her own body to form a circuit.

Her skin pricked. Could she do it?

Had she done it already?

Her skin buzzing, Dorothy crossed the room and picked up Roman's dagger. It felt heavy in her hand, and warm, and she couldn't help shuddering, remembering the last time she'd held this weapon, how she'd plunged it into Ash's gut.

Dazed, as though she were walking through a dream, Dorothy moved across the room, and into the attached bathroom, where she flipped a switch. The lights buzzed to life, filling the room with a dull, artificial glow.

She lifted her head, considering herself in the mirror. Was she really going to do this? According to the Professor's own journals, the ramifications for inserting the EM incorrectly were quite serious. Internal bleeding. Skin flayed from your body. Death.

She swallowed hard. But . . . but she knew that wouldn't happen to her, right? Ash had seen her at Fort Hunter. She must've been successful.

Make a choice, she thought. *Should be easy. Die jumping or die staying.*

The memory caused the corner of her lip to twitch. This had been the thought that had gone through her head moments before she'd leaped out of an eighth-story window. She'd never been one to shy away from something because it was frightening. Why start now?

She lifted the edge of her black T-shirt, considering her pale white skin. She brought the blade to the space just below her ribs, cringing as the cool metal kissed her belly.

All she had to do was add a little pressure. A single prick . . .

She breathed in through her nose and out through her mouth. She added the slightest bit of pressure, making a shallow cut in her skin.

Pain rushed through her. Every nerve in her body flared, begging her to stop. It went against every instinct inside her to keep cutting, to move the dagger into the pain. The room tilted, and she felt like she might pass out. She had to stop . . . she *had* to . . .

She placed Roman's knife on the bathroom counter, breathing hard. Blood dripped down her waist and pooled on the floor, scattering across the white porcelain.

Dorothy blinked down at it, trying to regain her strength. Dimly, she remembered hiding something here. What had it been? Chocolate? Her mother had never let her eat sweets, terrified she might ruin her figure. Perhaps a little sugar would help now.

Dorothy dropped to her knees and fumbled beneath the sink. She didn't find chocolate, but something better: a small glass bottle. A smile broke out across her face. *Gin.*

"Thank the Lord in heaven," she murmured, uncorking the bottle. She downed half in a single swallow. The liquor spread through her like medicine.

She stood and took up Roman's knife for a second time. She gripped the handle tightly and sucked down a deep breath, willing herself to hold it steady.

Die jumping or die staying.

"Our world has no place for cowards," she said out loud. Gritting her teeth, she pressed the blade to her open wound, sliding the remaining EM into her body.

26

ASH

JUNE 10, 1913

A burst of light, too bright to look at directly.

Ash groaned and closed his eyes again. Much, much too bright. What was he thinking, opening his damn eyes like a fool? He was going to need to take this slow.

He focused on his breathing at first. *In and out*. His lungs pushed against his rib cage and something sharp and painful shot through his lower belly.

Well, he thought, grimacing. That was concerning.

Eyes first.

This time, he was careful. He opened his eyes enough to allow a needle-thin shard of light to hit his pupils, and then he stopped. When he was used to the light, he opened his lids a little more, and a little more after that. Eventually he was staring up at a ceiling.

Huh, he thought, blinking. It was quite an . . . *ornate* ceiling. The plaster was shaped like a starburst, radiating away from a light fixture at the center, the glass domed and cloudy, the actual light dim and flickering a bit. It was unlike anything he'd seen, either in his own time or in the future.

Which begged the question: What time was it, exactly?

He started to turn, and then thought better of it. There was quite a lot of pain humming through his body. He could place the primary source—the spot below his ribs where he'd been injured by a piece of his old time machine—but the ache he felt now seemed so much bigger than what he was used to. He'd need to go slow, then, just like with opening his eyes.

Head first, he thought, with a groan. He turned to the left and squinted. He was in a bedroom. Nice furniture, ornate, like the ceiling, and brand-new, even though it was all old-fashioned-looking. Persian rugs on the floor—new, like the furniture—and there was intricate wallpaper covering the walls. So, he was in the past. Fairly far in the past, from the look of those carpets and rugs. Ornate went out of fashion in the fifties.

With a groan, he turned his head to the other side—

And found a woman dressed all in black sitting beside him, staring.

"Oh," he breathed. His voice was a claw raking at his throat. It made him start to cough.

"You're awake," the woman said, one eyebrow lifting. She had a strange air about her, this woman. It bothered him for reasons he couldn't quite put his finger on. She seemed . . .

Tricky. He would have to tread lightly.

"I am," Ash managed to choke out, his voice thin. Very slowly, he eased himself into a sitting position, propping himself back against some pillows. Clearing his throat, he added, "Is that . . . surprising?"

The woman tilted her head, considering his question. "It seemed unlikely, for a while, that you would wake at all. If I were a betting woman, I would have put my money on a slow and painful death. It seems I was wrong."

She said all of this as though she were commenting on the weather and not Ash's mortality. Ash swallowed.

"Lucky for me, I suppose," he choked out.

The woman lifted an eyebrow, as though to say, *is it?* But, out loud, all she said was, "I'm not often wrong."

Yeah, Ash thought. *I could have figured that out for myself.*

"Where am I?" he asked.

"Seattle," the woman told him, voice crisp. She lifted a hand, examining her cuticles for a moment before adding, "Although, if my daughter is telling me the truth, you'd probably rather know the date than the city, is that correct?"

"Daughter?" Ash said. All at once, everything made sense. "You're Dorothy's mother?"

That, at least, explained why she was so terrifying. Dorothy had implied that her mother was . . . intense.

"I am." The woman blinked, slowly. "And you are Jonathan Asher. The pilot she brought back from the future."

She said this with a tightness to her voice, making it clear what she thought about the idea of bringing someone back from the future. But Ash noticed that there was a glint to her eye. She was testing him.

"She told you about that?" he asked.

"She told me a farfetched little story, yes." Again, that glint. She was trying to decide whether she bought it. "In any case, she would have me believe that you don't care a whit where we are. You're more interested in when."

"That would be nice to know ma'am."

The woman nodded. She folded her hands in her lap and sat back in her seat. "The date is June 10, 1913. My daughter was supposed to be married last week."

"Right," Ash murmured, feeling guilty for reasons he couldn't quite explain. "She told me about that."

"Did she?" The woman sniffed. "We can discuss your role in that whole affair in a moment. For now, I was hoping you could tell me what it is you're after, exactly. Money?" She flashed a smile that was utterly devoid of warmth. "Because I don't have any. Every penny we had came from my daughter's former fiancé, Charles. For reasons that should be obvious, he's not exactly keen to fund our lifestyle any longer."

"I don't have much use for money where I'm from, ma'am," Ash said.

"Enough with the ma'ams." The woman shook her head, irritated. "You can call me Loretta."

Ash tried his best to nod despite the waves of pain crashing around his skull. "It's nice to meet you ma—Loretta."

Loretta narrowed her eyes. "Where do you come from, exactly?" she asked.

"Dorothy didn't tell you?"

"We didn't get that far."

"I'm from here, Seattle," Ash explained. "Only the year is 2077."

"2077?" Loretta smiled. "Do women ever get the vote?"

"They do."

"Small mercies." She examined her fingernails and then stretched her hand out straight across her lap. "Well then. If you aren't after money, what are you after? Love?"

She said the word *love* as though it were a silly little joke they were in on together. For a moment, Ash felt as though his voice were caught in his throat.

"As a matter of fact, yes, I am," he said slowly. He was careful to look Loretta straight in the eye. He knew she would be searching for something in his expression, and he didn't want to disappoint her. Even in these odd circumstances, it seemed important to make a good impression on Dorothy's mother. "If Dorothy will have me, of course."

Loretta lifted her chin, her mouth forming a thin line. She didn't say anything, but Ash felt a flicker of triumph, like he'd won some battle he didn't even realize he'd been engaged in. It was possible, he thought, that this woman might have a tiny bit of respect for him.

"Speaking of Dorothy," Ash added, sitting up a little straighter. "Is she . . . here?"

"Oh, no." And now Loretta smiled fully, her mouth full of sharp, white teeth. "It appears that my daughter has just left."

27

DOROTHY

The moon hung full and silver in the night sky, its pale light doing little to break up the shadows of the woods.

Dorothy was huddled behind a gnarled tree, the wind pulling at her hair. Through the dim light, she could just make out the hunched shape of Ash ahead, head bent as he cut a jerky hole into the barbed-wire-topped security gate. Beyond the gate, a great metal tunnel protruded from the side of the mountain, and armed soldiers waited at attention: the entrance to Fort Hunter.

Dorothy held her breath, waiting. She remembered this part from the first time they'd snuck onto the base. How she and the others had hidden behind a tree while Ash pretended to break in, in clear view of the security cameras.

Any moment now—

There. Dorothy caught movement from the corner of her eye and turned as a soldier appeared in the trees. He crept up behind Ash without a sound, withdrew his gun from his holster and calmly pressed the barrel to Ash's neck. Very slowly, Ash stood, lifting his arms. The soldier said something, but Dorothy couldn't hear what it was over the sound of the wind rustling the tree branches. *That was okay*, she told herself. She didn't need to hear their conversation. She'd heard it the first time around.

A moment later, another soldier appeared, along with a slightly younger, still-brunette Dorothy, Chandra, Willis, and Zora. Moments later, a large truck rumbled out of the trees, and the soldiers ushered them inside.

Dorothy exhaled. This was good. Everything was playing out exactly as she remembered it had. She crept forward, picking over twigs and rocks, careful not to make a sound as she ducked down behind the truck. While the soldiers were distracted, she tried the truck's back door.

It wasn't even locked. They were making it easy for her.

No one spoke as the truck lumbered through the trees. The only sounds were the rocks and brush crunching beneath the truck's massive tires, and one of the soldiers clearing his throat again and again, like he needed a lozenge.

Dorothy was careful to remain hunched down in the back, and she kept her breathing soft and shallow, so she wouldn't draw anyone's attention. The woods were a green-and-black blur and rain slanted past her window, speckling the glass. If she craned her neck, just a little, she could watch their progress through the trees.

The truck followed a dirt path that curved out of the trees and deposited them onto a paved road lined by barbed-wire fences. Ahead, a line of soldiers stood guard in front of the Fort Hunter entrance, guns at the ready. Spotlights shone above them. The truck pulled to a stop, and Dorothy heard the slow rise and fall of voices. A moment later, the soldiers shifted aside, and the truck rumbled through.

Dorothy was just able to make out the words WEL-COME TO FORT HUNTER COMPLEX on a far wall before the truck lumbered down a dark tunnel, the sound of its engine echoing off grimy brick as it slowed. Several more long minutes passed, and then they rolled to a stop in front of a white station that looked like an oversize tollbooth. The soldier guarding the station ambled over to their truck, gun at the ready.

Dorothy pressed her lips together. She didn't remember the soldier searching the truck the first time she'd come through here but, still, she couldn't help being nervous.

The driver rolled down the truck window, and he and the soldier talked for a bit before, finally, he nodded, stepping aside so they could drive past.

Dorothy exhaled through her teeth. She was in. Again.

She didn't get out at the holding cell with the others but stayed huddled at the back of the truck until, finally, it rolled to a stop near a mess hall and parked. There was a rumble of voices and footsteps, and then the driver and the other soldiers climbed out, leaving her alone.

She counted to a hundred in her head and then, peeking over the top of the seat to make sure no one would see her, she climbed out herself.

Now, to find the Professor.

After an eternal trek through the dark, dank tunnel, Dorothy was certain she was lost. She'd been walking through the darkness for what seemed like hours, the overhead lights growing a shade dimmer with each step she took farther into the tunnel.

She didn't have a map and, even if she *did* have one, she hadn't any clue where the Professor was headed, and even if she *did* have a clue where the Professor was going, her two choices, at the moment, were to keep following this dark tunnel or head back in the opposite direction, toward the mess hall, where she would almost certainly be seen.

She shoved her hands into her trouser pockets. Her heart was sputtering faster and faster with each passing moment. But, on the outside, she kept calm. Like her mother taught her. She couldn't risk being caught and thrown in a holding cell before she could find him, so down the tunnel it was. The Professor had to be here, somewhere. He had to be.

Something in the tunnel was dripping; the steady beat of water hitting brick was like a metronome. After Dorothy made it to one hundred, she counted back down to zero. *Drip. Drip. Drip.* She said the alphabet next—both frontward and backward. She'd just started trying to remember all the words to a nursery rhyme about a sheep when she reached a solid brick wall.

"Blast," she murmured. Dead end. She turned in a circle, fighting the sudden urge to hit something.

Desperate, she pressed her hands to the wall in front of her, fingers moving anxiously over a brick. There had to be a door. She couldn't be trapped. There had to be something—

After two minutes of searching through the dark, she felt the rough edge of wood. Her breathing began to steady, somewhat. She *knew* it. She followed the edges, until she found something cool and metallic. A doorknob. She tried to turn it, and, there, her luck ran out. Locked.

"Well, *that's* an easy enough problem," she muttered, pulling a hairpin loose. When she got back to 1913, she would have to find her old hairdresser and tell her how dead useful these pins had been over the last year. She inserted it into the lock and, biting her teeth, twisted until she felt something catch. The door creaked open. Grinning, Dorothy stepped through the door and into a dimly lit hall, the words *East Wing* written in faded, peeling paint in front of her.

She turned, pushing the hair out of her eyes—

And saw the corner of a dark jacket whip around the corner.

"Professor?" She frowned, hurrying after him. Her heart was beating in her throat, and blood was rushing in her ears. It seemed to whisper to her, *At last, at last.*

She followed the dark jacket through the door and found herself in a stairwell. She could go up, or she could go down.

"Professor?" she shouted. Her voice echoed, and she thought she heard the sound of footsteps, someone running toward the roof. Heart pounding, she ran, holding her breath as she plowed up the stairs.

Each step she took shuddered through her, rattling her bones and making her knees ache. Eventually, she reached a heavy door. She pushed it open and stumbled outside.

Sunlight hit her full in the face. She shielded her eyes, squinting into the glow.

A man stood before her. He had dark brown skin and hair, and a black beard speckled with gray. He looked different from what Dorothy had been expecting, in his jacket and loose black T-shirt. Dorothy's throat closed up. He looked just like Zora.

He was humming to himself, fumbling with something that appeared to be a small gun. Dorothy eyed the gun, wondering whether she should be worried. He didn't seem dangerous, but . . . well, it occurred to her that he *might* be a little crazy. She'd read his journal. He might be more than a little crazy.

Then again, she'd come all this way. She cleared her throat.

The Professor looked up.

"Ah!" he said, brightening at the sight of her. Dorothy didn't know whether it was her modern clothes or her white hair, but he seemed to know, instantly, that she wasn't from this time period. "Have you come to fetch me, then?"

For some reason, his casual demeanor made Dorothy uneasy. It occurred to her that he didn't have a clue what was happening in his own time. She didn't particularly want to be the person to break it to him.

"Professor," she said, taking a step forward. "Do you know who I am?"

He narrowed his eyes, taking in her tattered clothes, her white hair, and scarred face. "Are you a friend of my daughter's?"

Dorothy's lip twitched. "Uh, something like that," she said, trying not to picture the look of horror that would surely cross Zora's face if she were to learn that Dorothy had referred to the two of them as friends. "I was coming to see whether I could convince you to come with me."

"Ah . . ." The Professor frowned, his nose twitching. "I see. It's just . . . I was rather hoping I'd have a *bit* more time."

"Professor, the future is a mess just now. The earthquakes are getting worse, and there's a man trying to take over New Seattle, and time travel—"

She was cut off by the sound of footsteps. She turned, her heart hammering. "Blast. I must've been followed."

"Actually, I think they're after me," the Professor said. He was looking down at his gun now, fumbling with something that Dorothy couldn't see. "I really shouldn't be here." He looked up, eyebrows lifting above the frames of his glasses. "Then again, I doubt you're supposed to be here, either."

"Definitely not," Dorothy admitted, glancing anxiously, over her shoulder. The footsteps were drawing closer. "How are we—"

"Ah, that." The Professor lifted his gun. "I've been working on something special."

"Time travel without a vessel," Dorothy said, staring at the gun.

"Without a vessel, without an anil, without anything." The Professor stroked the sides of his gun, his grin widening. "That's why I've come back here, as a matter of fact. To see if I could arrange for a way to travel through time without causing the earthquakes. I do believe I've done it. One shot of this, and we can vanish anywhere in history without remotely disturbing the structure of the tectonic plates."

Dorothy cast one last glance at the door behind her. She didn't exactly have time for second thoughts. She could either trust the Professor, or face whatever was about to come through that door.

Swallowing, she asked, "Does that need to be injected into my aorta as well?"

"Oh, no, dear, any arm will do." He looked at her now, holding out the gun. "May I?"

She nervously offered the old man her arm.

Here goes nothing, she thought, squeezing her eyes shut.

It was like getting pricked with a needle, just a quick jab, a flicker of pain, and then nothing. Dorothy opened her eyes in time to see white light swirl beneath her skin and then vanish.

"Oh my," she said, amazed.

The door burst open and soldiers spilled onto the roof, surrounding them.

"Ah. Well, then." The Professor pushed his glasses up on his nose with one finger. "I suppose we are a bit later than I intended. Best make this quick." He aimed the gun at his own arm and pulled the trigger again, cringing a little. "Time to go," he said to Dorothy.

Dorothy was confused. "Go?"

Instead of answering, the Professor wrapped an arm around her shoulders and pulled her over the side of the roof.

Bullets filled the air around them. People shouted. Dorothy saw the ground rushing toward her face, trees and sky blurring as they fell faster and faster—

And then, like a blink, they vanished.

28

ASH

JUNE 12, 1913

Ash was sure he was dreaming again.

The pain was there, and everything was all swimmy and blurry, like he was just waking up. He'd been lying on his side in bed, staring out the window at Seattle circa 1913, and trying to keep himself from falling asleep.

It hadn't been easy. They sky was full and gray and heavy with clouds. It seemed to hang very low, and Ash had the feeling that if he opened his window and reached outside, he'd be able to touch the clouds themselves. He remembered wondering if they'd be soft, like cotton, or if they'd be wet . . .

And that must've been when he'd drifted off. Because, the longer he watched, the darker those clouds became. At first the change was so gradual that he hadn't even registered it. It was like watching paint darken as it dried, the change so subtle that it's only noticeable after, when one compares the mental images.

Ash watched the darkening clouds and, when they were

near black, he realized, dimly, that a storm must be coming. But—it was the strangest thing—see, the storm only seemed to be brewing in this one, very specific part of the sky. If he turned his head either to the left, or to the right, the clouds were still light and fluffy.

Weird, he thought. He'd seen a lot of storms in his time, but he'd never known them to act like this.

His eyelids were growing heavy. Lightning flashed, and he thought he felt thunder rumble through the earth, the vibration moving up his bed. His pillow was so soft. . . .

And then, smoke appeared. He smelled it before he saw it, that acrid, engine smell leaking through the glass in his windows. His eyes fluttered back open at the exact same moment that the shapes of two people appeared in the clouds. Ash watched, drearily, certain he was dreaming as the people fell to the earth, their bodies thudding into flattened grass. For a moment, they were still. Ash wondered whether they were dead. They hadn't fallen a long way, but it had certainly looked painful.

He began to drift. He was stuck in that halfway point between sleep and waking. He wasn't entirely sure whether his eyes were open, and everything felt so heavy, so warm.

The two people who'd just dropped out of the sky began to move. They crawled to hands and knees, and then stood, dusting off pants and shaking out their jackets. The smoke around them began to fade, and the clouds overhead lightened and thinned. One of the people was a woman—

Dorothy, Ash realized dimly. What was she doing?

She knelt, offering a hand to the other person. Ash squinted. It was a man in a tweed jacket, his salt-and-pepper hair strangely familiar. . . .

Okay, Ash thought, grinning stupidly. This was definitely a dream. Because that wasn't just any man, it was the Professor, and he happened to know that the Professor was dead. He'd died at Fort Hunter complex in 1980. He and Zora had seen the footage, and they'd stood on the bloodstained rooftop, so he knew it was true. The Professor was long gone.

So he couldn't be standing outside just now.

Couldn't be.

Ash's eyes closed. He felt himself sink farther into his pillows, drowsiness washing over him in a wave. He hadn't fully recovered from his stab wound, and he needed rest to heal. Rest, and some morphine, preferably. Why couldn't Dorothy have taken him to a time period where they had better drugs?

Sleep, he thought groggily. Sleep sounded so good right now.

But something nagged at him.

All the other dreams he'd had while unconscious, they were of the past, of things that had actually happened. There was the time he met Dorothy in the clearing outside the church, and that first moment he saw Quinn Fox's hair on a security camera and realized that she was going to be the one to kill him. But the only time Ash had ever seen the Professor and Dorothy together was at the Fort Hunter complex.

And . . . well, now that he thought about it, that was a pretty strange coincidence, seeing them together. When had it even happened? Dorothy had never mentioned going back to Fort Hunter with Roman. And what had she wanted with the Professor, anyway? As far as he knew, the two had never met in real life. She'd have told him if they had, wouldn't she?

My daughter just left, Loretta had said. Ash had tried to get her to tell him more, but she'd refused. She'd stood, saying that he needed his rest, and then she'd left his room without another word. Ash hadn't given it much more thought— Loretta had been right, he *had* needed his rest—but now he frowned.

What the hell?

Curiosity was enough to get him to pry his eyes open again. The last of his drowsiness had faded, and the scene outside his window wasn't quite so swimmy and strange. He could clearly see the Professor and Dorothy walking across the grass. Talking to each other.

His heart began to beat a little faster.

"Professor?" he murmured. He pushed himself up to a sitting position, groaning deeply. Everything ached. He felt like he'd been hit by a truck. It took him several tries to get his legs out of the bed, and several more tries before he could put any weight on them at all. He grabbed for the wall to steady himself, thinking, *Easy now*. He moved one foot and then the other. It wasn't until he walked all the way to the end of his bed that he trusted himself to move his hand away from the wall. He swayed, a little, but managed to stay upright. So far, so good.

He hobbled across the room, toward the door. The door

was heavy, and it took all his remaining strength to pull it open, but the hall outside was empty. Ash felt his heartbeats falling like hammer blows. He wanted to run, but he didn't want to end up flat on the floor, so he forced himself to move slowly, carefully. It was excruciating, how long everything was taking.

Ash limped out of his room and down the hall. By the time he made it to the staircase, he'd managed to convince himself that he'd been hallucinating. He *had* to have been hallucinating. The Professor was dead. He couldn't have been outside. He *couldn't* have been.

Slowly, slowly. Each step down the staircase was agony, but he would have gone down a dozen staircases if that's what it would take to know the truth.

He made it to the first floor and stumbled up to the front door seconds before it burst open and Dorothy appeared, silhouetted against the light.

"Ash?" She reached for him, worry lines etched across her face. "What on earth are you doing out of bed? You're ill—"

"I—I saw you . . ." Ash murmured, looking past her. "I saw you with—"

The rest of his sentence died on his tongue as a man stepped inside the house. He wore a tweed jacket covered in bits of dust and debris. He had his head bent, absently brushing it off, but he looked up when Ash spoke.

The Professor had always looked alarmingly like his daughter. He had Zora's strong jaw and dark eyes, and his mouth had the same way of twisting into an ironic smile whenever someone said something that he thought was a little stupid. But there were lines on his face that Zora didn't have yet, deep frown lines around his mouth, creases that cut across his forehead and fanned away from his eyes.

"Jonathan," the Professor said brightly, smiling.

Hearing his name brought tears to Ash's eyes. It was the Professor, really and truly, after all this time. Ash opened his mouth, but he didn't trust himself to speak.

The Professor took a step forward, clamping a hand down on Ash's shoulder. "It's good to see you again, son."

29

DOROTHY

Dorothy thought it best to let the Professor and Ash have a moment alone. She backed away as the two men embraced, feeling like she was invading on something very personal, a reunion between a father and son rather than a teacher and student, for instance. When she saw that she would not be missed, she darted through a door and down the hall.

She wandered Avery's house for a while, at a loss as to where to go. This place had never felt like home to her, not even in the weeks leading up to her wedding when she and her mother had lived here. It had a museum-like quality to it, the ceilings soaring above her, the walls all ornately papered in the most expensive oriental fabrics, the floors and trim gleaming with fresh polish, even though Dorothy had never actually seen anyone dust or mop them. Even the furniture was over-the-top, lavish, intricate. Settees covered in velvet, elaborately stitched cushions, tables carved with tiny animals and flowers. It was too much, and Dorothy was surprised to feel a sharp ache of homesickness as she walked through the halls now.

She thought of decaying, brocade walls and waterlogged carpets, the top of a domed skylight peeking out from below the black waves. Her hotel. Her real home.

She found herself entering the sitting room, which had always been . . . well, it seemed disingenuous to call it her *favorite* room in Avery's house, but it was at least a room she didn't actively despise. It was small and narrow, with heavy, velvet drapes and thick carpets that made it feel a bit like a child's fort, almost like it had been built entirely of blankets and pillows. And there was the fact that Avery rarely came in here. Always a plus.

A teapot and several cups were laid out on a small table near the love seat, probably her mother's leftover service from that morning, Dorothy realized. It was likely cold by now, but Dorothy poured herself a cup, anyway. Caffeine was caffeine, and she hadn't gotten a proper night's sleep in she didn't know how long. She stirred in a few spoonfuls of sugar and sunk onto the sofa, thinking of the Fairmont. It had truly been the only place in her life that had actually felt like a home. Would she ever be able to go back again? she wondered.

She took a sip of cold, bitter tea.

"Well," said her mother's voice, from directly behind her. "That was quite a show you put on."

Dorothy cringed and nearly swallowed the tea wrong. She

forced herself to return her cup and saucer to the table beside her before turning to find her mother standing in the sitting room doorway.

Loretta swept into the room and took the seat beside Dorothy's. She poured herself a cup of tea as well and grimaced as she drank.

"That tastes dreadful," she murmured, placing her cup back on the table. "We should call for a fresh pot." She looked around, as though expecting a maid to step out of one of the walls.

"Leave the servants alone; the tea is fine. In fact, I think it's quite good." It was a silly lie, but Dorothy was feeling contrary. She took another careful sip of her own tea, sucking her lips in so she wouldn't inadvertently grimace. Her mother gave her a look of utter disdain, clearly not falling for it.

Swallowing, Dorothy said, "So, I take it you were watching?"

"Your little stunt out in the field?" Loretta lifted an eyebrow. "Yes, I was watching. You and that *man* seemed to have appeared out of thin air, clouds of smoke billowing around you. How *very* exciting."

There was a catch to her voice, as though all of this were an elaborate prank, but there was something complicated happening behind her eyes. Dorothy felt her mouth twitch. No matter what her mother said, she could tell that Loretta's curiosity was getting the better of her.

"You still don't believe me?" Dorothy asked, working hard to keep the smile from touching her lips.

Loretta only stared at her. Looking back at her mother, Dorothy remembered a story she often told, of attending a séance with the Fox sisters long before Dorothy was born. The Fox sisters were the most famous mediums of the nineteenth century, and they'd managed to con most of the country, claiming they could communicate with the dead through mysterious knocks and raps. But Loretta had noticed that the noises these "ghosts" were supposed to be responsible for only came when the sisters' feet were on the floor, or when their dresses were in contact with the table. She confronted the women after her séance was over and was given a stack of cash to keep her mouth shut.

Thinking of this story now, Dorothy found herself unable to suppress a grin. It must be killing her mother that she couldn't explain how Dorothy was doing the things she was doing.

After a moment, Loretta said, "What exactly do you plan to do now?"

With that, any semblance of a smile dropped from Dorothy's mouth. What now? How could she begin to answer that question?

She thought of the Fairmont, half-flooded, with its ruined carpets and lovely columns. She thought of Zora and Willis and Chandra, and the horrible future that awaited them. Blackened sky. No sun. A lump formed in her throat. She thought of Roman, dear Roman, who hadn't deserved to die the way he did. All alone in a bleak and terrible future.

And, on top of all that, Mac and that dreadful woman in

black were still holding New Seattle hostage. Dorothy lowered her face to her hands, gently pinching the bridge of her nose between two fingers. It made her head spin to think of it all.

"We have to go back," she said eventually. "Soon, I hope."

"Go back?" Loretta lifted an eyebrow. "To the"—she grimaced, as though it pained her to say it—"*future*?"

"Yes, Mother," Dorothy said.

"Will you ever return home?"

Will I? Dorothy blinked, surprised to find that she hadn't fully considered that question. She certainly hadn't planned on returning, but now that she thought of it, she realized that she wouldn't be able to, even if she'd wanted to. Once they got back to the future, they would need to find a way to destroy the remaining exotic matter. It wouldn't be possible for her to come back.

For some reason, knowing that she wouldn't be able to return made it all so much harder to face.

"I . . . I won't," she said, blinking hard. Were those tears in her eyes? How strange. "Which means this is goodbye, I guess."

Loretta studied her for a long moment, her expression unreadable. She'd always been hard on her. Cruel, even, Dorothy thought. But now that she knew what it was like to try to take care of herself in a world where she'd had nothing—no friends or family or money—Dorothy thought she understood where that cruelty came from. She'd become a monster, too, after all.

After a moment, Loretta sighed and reached out to touch her daughter's ruined face with her own badly damaged hand. She traced Dorothy's scar with her thumb, and, for a moment, Dorothy was sure that her mother was about to say something terrible about how reckless she'd been with her beauty. She steeled herself . . .

But Loretta was quiet. Something passed between them, and then Loretta took her hand away.

"What will you do in this future world?" she asked, sniffing. She glanced over her shoulder, toward the hall, where Ash and the Professor were still talking. "Will you be with him?"

"I—I'm not sure," Dorothy said, her cheeks coloring. She hurried to add, "There are other things we need to take care of, much more important things."

Loretta lifted an eyebrow, and Dorothy could read what she was thinking as clearly as if she'd spoken the words out loud.

More important than marriage? Does such a thing exist?

"There's this terrible man, Mac Murphy," Dorothy rushed to add. "He's sort of a crime lord in New Seattle. He wants time travel for himself, and the only way to stop him is to make time travel impossible." Dorothy stared down at her tea, feeling helpless. "So, that's what we're going to do."

Loretta was studying her now, frowning. She looked disappointed, which made something inside Dorothy ache. Even now, after all this time, there was still a part of her that desperately wanted to please her mother.

Eventually, Loretta picked up her abandoned teacup and stared down at the dregs inside, nose wrinkled. She swirled the tea, thinking.

Finally, she said, "Mac Murphy is this man's name?"

Dorothy frowned. Her mother had a way of asking questions so that they didn't actually sound like questions. It was as though she already knew everything and was only waiting for her to confirm it.

"Yes," Dorothy said, "that's his name."

"And he's something of a crime lord?" *Crime lord* said with a curl to her lip, as though the idea were a joke.

Dorothy took another sip of her awful tea. "He is," she said, swallowing. "He has the entire city in his back pocket."

"Happy man, is he?" Loretta cocked an eyebrow. "Lots of friends? Family?"

"Well . . . no." And now Dorothy frowned. She'd never given that much thought to Mac's personal life, she realized. He'd always just sort of . . . existed. "I don't suppose he has any friends or family, now that I think about it."

A small smile twitched at Loretta's mouth. Dorothy knew this smile well. It was her mother coming up with the beginnings of a con. Her heart quickened.

"What?" she demanded, setting her teacup back into its saucer. A bit of tea sloshed over the side, filling the saucer with weak, brown liquid. "What are you thinking?"

"It's just that I'm a bit disappointed with you," Loretta said. "Men like that, men who have power but no relationships, men who are lonely. How have I taught you to treat them all this time?"

"As a mark," Dorothy said, feeling numb.

"Exactly." Loretta slapped her ruined hand against her knee, making a point. "Men like that are weak, no matter how much power they seem to have accrued. They are blind. They think that their wealth and their influence will save them, but they've left themselves open and vulnerable. What do we do with men like that?"

Dorothy felt her lip twitch. "We ruin them."

"Exactly," Loretta said, with cool triumph. She took another dainty sip of her tea and said calmly, "We ruin them."

30

ASH

Ash and the Professor had retreated to a small sitting room. It was a fussy sort of room, Ash thought, all small and crowded, the furniture slightly dainty, like he might break it in half if he moved around too much. Ash felt much too big for it. He balanced at the edge of a floral-patterned love seat, one hand pressed to the bandage on his abdomen. His knife wound was starting to sting, and something perfumed hung in the air, making his nostrils twitch.

The Professor took the seat across from him, and, for a long moment, the two of them sat in silence.

Ash shifted his gaze down to his knees. He'd spent the last year going over and over what he would say to his mentor if he were ever sitting across from him again, but, just now, he found his mind completely blank.

No, that wasn't quite true. His mind wasn't blank—it was too full. It felt like that static he saw on old television sets when he couldn't quite find a station. That was his brain right now: white fuzz and, every few seconds, a word, the beginning of a question, gone before he had a chance to ask it out loud.

He was happy to see the Professor again. Of course he was happy.

But he was angry, too.

This man let him think he was dead. He let his own *daughter* think he was dead.

And not just for a few days—for over a *year*. He vanished in the middle of the night and left them behind to clean up the mess he'd made of their city.

Why? That was the question that finally appeared in the static of Ash's brain. Ash took a deep, steadying breath and looked up to see that the Professor was staring back at him, a sort of sad smile on his face.

"I suppose you're wondering why I left," he said apologetically.

"Among other things," Ash muttered.

The Professor shifted uncomfortably in his seat. "Well, I'm afraid that's quite a long story."

"We got a hundred years or so to kill."

"Ha, that's funny." The corner of the Professor's mouth curled. "You told a little joke."

Ash didn't laugh. He found himself wishing he had a drink in his hands, just to give them something to do. With nothing else to focus on, they'd clenched together, fingers practically white, the skin at his knuckles pulled tight.

He spread them out wide, clenched them again, trying

to get his muscles to relax. When the Professor didn't say anything, Ash lifted his eyes. "The earthquakes. Start there."

"I see you've done your homework." The Professor leaned forward, propping his arms on his knees. He took off his glasses and began cleaning the lenses with the hem of his T-shirt. "The earthquakes. This all started because I wanted to find some way to avoid them. After Natasha . . ."

His voice cracked. He closed his eyes for a moment, seeming to need to regain his composure. A beat later, he continued, "After Natasha, it seemed important to figure out why they were happening, maybe even find some way of predicting them in the future. Years ago, Roman had been looking into that sort of thing, studying tectonic-plate and fault-line activity. He'd even built some computer program that was supposed to predict how the earth's crust might move in the future, but he'd given all that up when I recruited him to our team. I went back in time and borrowed his research, to see whether he'd been onto anything."

"And he was," Ash guessed.

"Oh, yes." The Professor lifted his eyes. "I'm not sure Roman himself was fully aware of what he'd discovered. There were patterns, you see, numbers that proved there was some correlation between time travel and the earth's movement. It was all very fuzzy science, of course. Nothing conclusive. But it was a start.

"Once I saw the trends, I couldn't just look the other way. I had to know more. But the city was still recovering from the flood. I needed resources, a clean place to work, a lab, books . . . I tried to get in touch with the few allies I still had in the Center, but they weren't interested in helping. The earthquakes weren't affecting them. And WCAAT, well, all the research we'd spent years developing, everything, it was all gone."

"So, you went to Fort Hunter," Ash said.

The Professor nodded. "Once I realized I needed to travel back in time to gain access to the sort of resources I needed, the entirety of human history was open to me. It made the most sense to go back to a time when they were investing in the exact type of science I was looking into. In the 1980s, Fort Hunter spent an enormous amount of time and money delving into the world of environmental modification. The plan was to attempt to weaponize it, I believe, but the program was shut down later that decade after some political pressure. I thought it seemed worth a look, so I went back.

"I only spent a day there, but it was enough. More than enough. Within hours, I was able to verify my theory that the continued use of the Puget Sound anil would only lead to larger and more devastating earthquakes in the future."

Ash thought of the scrawled notes he'd found on the windshield of the *Dark Star*, each a date and a magnitude number, the promise of more devastating earthquakes to come.

"So why didn't you come back then?" he asked, his throat closing up. "You could have helped us. You could have warned us."

"I wanted to." The Professor frowned, deep lines appearing around his mouth. "Jonathan, you have to believe that all

I wanted to do was go back to New Seattle and save you from that future. But there was more work to be done. Now that I knew what caused the earthquakes, I couldn't use time travel any longer, not until I'd figured out how to mitigate the damage I was doing every time I went through the anil. I was able to pinpoint that the size of the earthquake correlated directly to the amount of disruption the anil experienced at the time of travel."

Ash frowned, the Professor's words spinning around in his head. "Sir? I don't think that I understand. . . ."

"To put it in layman's terms, a larger ship created a great deal of disruption, while a smaller ship created less." The Professor held open his hands. "And no ship . . ."

"Means . . . no disruption?" Ash guessed.

"*Exactly*." The Professor clapped his hands together, the sudden sound making Ash jump. "I got the idea from my research with Nikola Tesla. Tesla, you see, had long theorized that time travel without a vessel was possible. And not just without a vessel, but without direct access to the anil itself. It involves using the earth's energy to access the power of the anil wherever you stand in time and space."

The Professor pushed his glasses up his nose with a flick of his hand. "To be perfectly honest, I thought he was mad! I thought it was impossible. But if it worked, it would mean that there was a way to travel through time that wouldn't upset the earth's tectonic plates, a way to stop the earthquakes once and for all. But it's tricky science. I'd only just finished the prototype when your friend arrived." The Professor's eyes shifted to the door on the other side of the room, almost like he expected to see Dorothy standing there. "She told me I was needed here. So, I came."

Ash stared down at his palms. He didn't know what to say. It made sense, all of it, and it killed him to know that they could have found the Professor weeks ago, if only they'd looked harder, if only they'd trusted that he was still alive.

He closed his eyes and saw the Fort Hunter rooftop, Zora's devastated face as she realized that her father wasn't there. He felt like he might be sick.

"I—I thought you were dead," he admitted, his voice thick. "Zora, too. We all did."

The Professor slid his glasses back up his nose. His eyes, behind the lenses, looked deeply pained. Ash waited for him to ask about his daughter, but he didn't.

"I had no intention of causing either of you so much heartache," he said instead. A small, sad smile. "I was trying to prevent all of this, believe it or not."

Ash nodded, understanding. He *did* believe it. Time travel, he was starting to realize, had a way of muddling things, of messing things up.

The Professor removed a small, silver gun from his coat pocket. It was strange-looking, almost like it had been cobbled together using spare parts from his ship, but the Professor held it in his palm like it was something precious.

He said, "Humans travel through time more easily than a clunky ship. All we need to do is take a small amount of EM into our bodies, which this gun allows."

The Professor tilted the gun, and Ash could see that there was a very small amount of exotic matter stored inside, held in place by a clear glass capsule.

"That thing really works?" Ash asked, skeptical.

"It brought me here," the Professor said. "No bumps or bruises, no horns growing out of my head."

Ash rubbed the back of his head. He felt uneasy. It was something about that tiny bit of exotic matter stored inside the Professor's gun, the knowledge that there was so much power stored inside of something so small. Anyone could get their hands on it.

He wet his lips and said carefully, "If someone like Mac Murphy were to get ahold of this thing, there's no telling how—"

A creak on the other side of the room, the sound of a door opening. Ash stopped talking and looked up.

Dorothy and her mother stood framed in the doorway. Looking at them, Ash realized he couldn't say exactly how long they'd been there. It was entirely possible that they'd been listening this entire time.

"If you two aren't too busy," said Dorothy. "I believe we might have a plan."

PART FOUR

There's no place like home.

—The Wizard of Oz

31

DOROTHY

Dorothy and Ash stood on the docks overlooking the Puget Sound. The night was still, and the only things that disturbed the flat surface of the water were the distant boats circling the anil. Dorothy counted the ripples as they drifted toward her, sending water lapping against the docks.

"They think we'll be coming through the anil," Ash said, pushing the damp hair from his forehead. It wasn't raining, but the air was still thick and wet. Dorothy felt her own cloak sticking to the back of her neck, her hair plastered to her forehead and cheeks. She shivered.

"It appears that way, yes," she said. In actuality, they hadn't needed to use the anil at all. The Professor's new technology meant they were able to appear a comfortable distance from the Fairmont itself, on a bit of old docks that Dorothy happened to know were rarely used. From here, they could see what was happening at both the anil and at the hotel, without getting close enough to be spotted.

That, of course, wouldn't last. It wasn't part of the plan.

Ash touched the spot below his ribs, gingerly, grimacing, and Dorothy felt a moment of doubt. He shouldn't be here. He was still injured; they should've given him more time to recover. They'd had plenty of it back in 1913, after all. Time.

But Ash had insisted on moving sooner rather than later. He didn't like the idea of hiding out in the past.

"Anything can happen while we're here," he'd told Dorothy. And then, nodding at the Professor, he'd added, "Look at him."

She supposed he'd had a point. The Professor had spent a single day in 1980 but, by the time he found his way back, an entire city had fallen apart. And so, she'd agreed to return sooner rather than later.

Doesn't mean I have to like it, she thought, taking in Ash's pale skin, the sweat on his brow. Surely, things would have been fine if he'd given himself even a week longer to recover?

"Let's get this over with," she said, and her eyes flicked back to the waiting Freaks. She felt her heart begin to hammer inside her chest. "Come on."

Ash nodded and lifted his arms above his head, and, together, the two of them stepped out of the shadows.

The night was heavy with fog, making it difficult to see how many Freaks had converged on the docks in front of the old hotel. Dorothy could make out the ghostly lights of the hotel windows, and the hazy shapes of people moving, but nothing else.

She held her breath as they drew closer. This was the most dangerous part of their plan. They were going to simply give themselves up, and if the Freaks decided to shoot one or both of them, well then that was that. This would all be over before it had even started.

They made their way across the docks, first one Freak turning and spotting them through the fog, and then three, six, many. A cackle went through the crowd, and Dorothy stiffened, waiting for the crack of a gunshot to split the silence. None came. It bothered her that this was such a relief.

"So far so good," she muttered, under her breath, as the circle of Freaks parted. Ash nodded, but his gaze was trained straight ahead.

Mac had just appeared at the top of the Fairmont steps, gun stuffed lazily into his waistband, face twisted into a snarl. The woman in black stood just behind him, her head bowed, silent as ever.

"You here to surrender, Quinn?" Mac asked.

Dorothy wet her lips, nerves tightening her muscles. They'd considered many versions of this plan before landing on this one, discarding them all one after another. Disappearing into the past meant leaving this world to rot, and taking on Mac directly meant that they would almost certainly be outnumbered and killed.

And so, they'd decided on *this*. Showing up unarmed, alone. It had seemed like their only option, at the time. Now that they were here, though, it was clear that this was lunacy.

Please work, she thought as she raised her hands a little higher, to show that she had no plans to reach for her daggers.

Eliza had separated from the fog and was by Dorothy's side in a second, ripping her arms behind her back with more force than strictly necessary.

"Good choice," she snarled into Dorothy's ear. She began to pat Dorothy down; clearly, she had no intention of trusting that she was unarmed.

Dorothy tried not to grimace as the rest of the Freaks surrounded them, guns drawn.

"I'm here to make a trade," Dorothy said, working hard to keep her voice calm. She saw, from the corner of her eye, that Bennett was patting down Ash.

Mac lifted his eyebrows. "A trade?"

"That's right." Dorothy offered a slow smile, her eyebrow twitching. "Ash and I are prepared to hand over what's left of the exotic matter and lead you to the location of the *Black Crow*. Now, if you'd like."

Mac chewed on his fat lips for a moment, thinking this over. "And you're doing this out of the goodness of your own heart are you?"

"Of course not." Dorothy felt the corners of her lips tighten. Holding the smile was becoming difficult. "In exchange, you'll call off the bounty on our heads. No more Freaks following us wherever we might go, no more threats. You get your time machine, and we get our freedom. Everyone's happy."

For a long moment, no one said a word. The only sound was the wind over the water, the shuffle of boots against damp wood, the dock's disapproving groan.

"There's no trade without a pilot," Mac said, eyes narrowing.

Dorothy kept her eyes trained straight ahead. She'd done many questionable things in the year she'd spent as Quinn Fox, but she'd always been able to justify them as necessary. She'd been building a better world, a better future. If there were people she needed to step on along the way, so be it.

But she'd never thought of herself as a selfish person before. Not until now.

If she looked at Ash, she knew she wouldn't be able to do what she'd come here to do. And so she kept her eyes straight ahead, a muscle in her jaw tightening.

"I've brought you a pilot," she said evenly.

Out of the corner of her eye, she saw Ash's head swivel around, his eyes boring into the sides of her face.

"Quinn—" he said.

Dorothy felt a muscle in her jaw tighten. The sound of his voice twisted something inside of her. He sounded so betrayed, so hurt.

"Now you and I are straight," she said, and she took a few intentional steps across the dock, so that she was standing beside Mac, the two of them facing Ash, together.

One of the Cirkus Freaks laughed, the sound cruelly cutting through the fog. They began to draw closer, circling him.

"No." Ash's face was terrible, confused and hurt.

Dorothy forced herself to meet his eyes, even though it pained her to do so.

He looked from Mac to Dorothy and said, as though trying to appeal to some humanity inside of her, "What are you doing? We were going to take Mac on together. That was the plan!"

"Ash, be reasonable. If we did it that way, I'd have Mac and his men following me for the rest of my life." Dorothy felt a rush as the truth of this statement filled her words. Her mother had been the one to point this out. She'd known men like Mac her whole life, and she was certain that Mac wouldn't give up until he'd found a pilot. The only way to be rid of him for good was to give him one.

"I'm sorry," Dorothy said, ashamed to hear her voice breaking. "There simply isn't another way."

To Mac, she added, "You have everything you need now. Tell me, do we have a deal?"

Mac was considering her, lips twitching with glee. He seemed to be enjoying this immensely. He rocked from the heels of his feet to the balls, hands stuffed in his trouser pockets. Dorothy held her breath, waiting. She could practically hear the words on his lips.

We have a deal.

But, after a long moment, he shook his head, almost sadly. He pulled his gun from his waistband and used it to scratch his temple.

"The thing is, princess," he said, with a short laugh. "I just don't trust you."

And he pointed the gun at Dorothy's face, drawing the gun's hammer back with his thumb.

32

ASH

Ash felt his spine stiffen as Cirkus Freaks surrounded him on all sides, his head spinning. He hadn't liked this plan one bit, not from the moment Dorothy and her mother had shown up to pitch it to him. It sounded dangerous and complicated and . . . well, stupid.

But it'd been the only plan they had. And, so, he'd agreed. *Stupid, stupid, stupid.*

Now he swallowed his fear and looked around, trying to calmly assess the situation. There were four Freaks to his left, another five to his right. Too many to fight his way through and, with Dorothy standing next to Mac, he was a little short on allies. The Fairmont wall was directly behind him, cutting off any means of exit, and the sound was just ahead, flat, black, and cold. He wouldn't be making a swim for it, not tonight.

He was pretty well screwed, no matter which way he looked at it.

"No." He forced the word out of his mouth, the taste of it bitter on his tongue. Turning back to Dorothy, he said, "What are you doing? We were going to take Mac on together. That was the plan."

Meanwhile, he lowered a hand to his gun, his fingers curling gently around the hilt. The metal felt damp in the foggy night air and cold to the touch. It brought him some comfort that he had it with him. Screwed or not, he wasn't going down without a fight.

Get ready, he told himself. His muscles pulled tight, waiting.

Across from him, Mac yanked his own gun from his waistband and used it to scratch his temple.

"The thing is, princess," he said, "I just don't trust you."

He pointed the gun at Dorothy's face, drawing the hammer back with his thumb.

Ash felt an old urge roar up inside of him. He wanted to leap at Mac, push him away from Dorothy. Was he really going to stand here and watch her be shot in the head like an animal? He didn't think he was capable of that, no matter what she'd done or said.

And yet he held himself still, barely breathing.

Dorothy's eyes flicked to him, and away. If she was frightened, she didn't show it. Her face was emotionless, giving away nothing.

"Don't call me princess," she said, offering Mac a thin smile.

Mac seemed to think this was funny. His bitter laugh cut

through the night. "I suppose those last words are as good as any other." He licked his fat lips and squinted down the gun's sight, aiming. "It was nice knowing you, little—"

"No!" Ash had his gun in his hand in a second, his heart beating at his chest like an animal but, before he could pull the trigger, the ground in front of him exploded, showering him with wood and water.

Dorothy danced backward, swearing, as Ash blinked into the cloud of dust, trying to find something to shoot. The Freaks were closing in, firing. He heard another crack of a bullet—this one whizzing past his face—and then the air cleared enough for Ash to make out Mac standing at the top of the Fairmont staircase, debris falling like snow around him.

Ash moved his eyes away from Mac for a fraction of a second, squinting to find Dorothy in the darkness.

"Wait, please!" She was crouching a few steps below him, a thin line of blood cutting across her face. She fumbled with something in her cloak, and Ash heard a sound like scraping metal. "I have the exotic matter right here. I'm telling you the *truth*—"

A gunshot cracked through the air, and a bullet caught Ash on the arm, spinning him around. Grimacing, Ash tightened his grip on his gun, firing back. He felt dazed, overwhelmed with disgust and fury.

He pressed a hand to his injured arm, breathing hard through his teeth. He could already feel the blood soaking his shirt.

Bullets whizzed past Ash's legs and hit the wall behind him. *Ping. Ping.* Ash managed to crack off a single shot before the third got him in his thumb—bright white burst of pain—and then he was jerking his hand back, and his gun was thwacking into the ground.

He ducked back behind the Fairmont wall, chest rising and falling, heavily. *Shit.*

"Mac, please," Dorothy was saying, "Listen to reason!"

Ash thought he heard another gunshot, a *thud.* Despite everything, horror flooded through him. He peeked around the edge of the wall.

The exotic matter was lying on the ground three feet away. He didn't see Dorothy anywhere.

He moved his eyes back to the exotic matter. It was too far for him to reach. If he wanted it, he'd have to lunge for it.

It was only three feet away. Not far at all. He could make it. Probably.

The muscles in his leg tensed. His heart beat hard and fast in his chest.

He dived—

The second his hands closed around the EM, he heard a click. He looked up and saw Mac standing on the Fairmont stairs a few feet above him, one hand curled around Dorothy's shoulders, his gun aimed at her head.

Smiling, Mac said, "Hand that over, son, or your girl dies."

33

DOROTHY

Dorothy held her body perfectly still, trying to breathe despite the cold press of the gun at her temple. The Freaks had stopped shooting. They stood in a loose circle around the three of them, glancing at one another anxiously, eager to see what was going to happen next. Dorothy found Donovan and Bennett in the crowd and was pleased to see that they looked worried. Eliza stood a few feet ahead of them, looking excited by the potential for bloodshed. Dorothy couldn't stand to look at them, and so she shifted her gaze to the woman in black, who stood still as a shadow, saying nothing.

Everything is a con, she thought. Her fingers twitched.

"What'll it be, kid?" Mac said gleefully. "You going to hand me that canister nicely? Or do I put a bullet in her pretty little head?"

Dorothy swallowed, finally letting her gaze drift over to Ash's face. She was standing above him on the Fairmont steps while he knelt on the docks several feet below, his head lifted, a worried crease between his brows. He stood very slowly, the canister of exotic matter clenched in one hand.

"Why would I care what happens to her?" he asked. He was dusting the dirt from his trousers, and so Dorothy couldn't see his face, but his voice was thick with emotion. "She just tried to sell me to you."

"He has a point, sweetheart," Mac said.

Dorothy felt his breath on her ear and had to work hard not to cringe.

"Ash." She had to force his name through her lips. He looked at her, his eyes narrowing and for a long moment, Dorothy just stared back at him, studying those golden eyes and thinking of the first time they'd met. What had he said to her?

Excuse me for saying so, miss, but it seems like you meant to get lost.

She smiled now, remembering. Her mind felt strangely blank.

Ash frowned, waiting for her to speak. To beg for her life, perhaps, or else beg him to trust her again. She had no intention of doing either. Everything she could think to say seemed so small and stupid. What's done was done and, now, all they could do was wait to see how the rest of this would play out.

She said simply, "I wouldn't trust him, if I were you."

The edge of Ash's mouth flicked, the beginning of a smile.

Mac swore, his grip around her shoulders tightening. Dorothy heard a click.

Down on the dock, Ash shouted, "*No—*"

Dorothy was vaguely aware of movement, Ash struggling to make his way up the stairs, the Freaks closing in around him. All of that seemed very far away just now. Dorothy clenched her eyes shut, every muscle in her body pulling tight—

Mac pulled the trigger, and a sound like fireworks filled her ears, the blast crashing around the inside of her skull. She tried to take a breath, but it was as though someone was holding her lungs in their hand, squeezing. Black lights burst before her eyes and pain tore through her. And then . . .

Well, and then there was nothing for a little while.

34

ASH

The shot echoed through Ash's head, seeming to ring in his ears long after it should've gone silent.

Time hitched. He almost thought it was a time-travel thing, how the world around him seemed to slow down so that he saw every moment of what happened next in vivid, excruciating slow motion.

Dorothy went limp in Mac's arms, her head lolling to the side as blood spread over her temple. Ash stared at her, his eyes not quite focusing. He couldn't make himself believe what had just happened.

Mac stepped away from her, allowing her body to hit the ground just as the smoke from his gun cleared.

"I'm done playing nice," he said, smacking his lips. "Seems to me that both of you had your chance to make deals a long time ago. We're at my hotel, surrounded by my people, and I'm currently the only one holding a gun, so I'm going to go ahead and make the rules."

Mac hadn't holstered his gun, Ash noticed. He glanced to where he'd dropped his own gun. Still a few feet away. Too far.

Ash lunged for it, but he was still a good foot away when Mac shot. He ducked the bullet, slamming into the ground, his fingers twitching, his mouth filling with dust and dirt. Wood scraped into his cheeks, and remnants of shattered glass bit into his skin.

He coughed, hard, and tried to push himself back up, but Mac was too quick. There was a click that could've been a thumb sliding over the hammer of a gun—that was *probably* a thumb sliding over the hammer of a gun—and then cold metal pressed up against the back of Ash's neck.

"The two of you have been pains in my ass for too long," Mac said. "Why don't you just hand over that canister and we can both—"

Ash threw his head back, his skull connecting with something hard. A grunt, and a spray of blood told him it'd been Mac's face.

"You son of a bitch!" Mac snarled. He still had an arm angled across Ash's back, holding him down, but his weight had shifted, and Ash knew he was probably struggling to retain his grip on him, his gun, and his badly bleeding face. Taking advantage of the chaos, Ash hauled himself up to his forearm and threw his elbow behind him.

A sharp *clang* told him that Mac had dropped his gun, too. They were both unarmed.

Mac curled an arm around Ash's neck and tried to drag

him backward, but Ash was larger than Mac, and he hurled himself to the side, sending Mac off his back and rolling through the ashes. He was seeing stars, and his arms and legs felt like jelly, but he made himself push up to hands and knees, blinking.

Where was his gun?

There—a flash of metal in the ashes. Ash grunted, crawling for it, and that was when he noticed Mac a few feet away, eyes locked on something in front of him.

Mac reached his gun first, and he pushed himself up to his knees, swiveling around. His gun was before him, finger at the trigger—

A half second later, a gunshot cracked through the air.

Ash clenched his eyes shut a moment before the bullet hit him.

35

DOROTHY

Dorothy lay on the Fairmont steps, her eyes clenched tightly shut. Pain beat in her temples, but it was a shallow pain, almost like the beginnings of a headache. She felt a throbbing ache in her shoulder from where she'd smashed into the stairs, and she was pretty sure the fake blood was getting in her hair.

She opened her eyes a crack and saw that everything around her had gone dim and cloudy. People were blurry, unfocused. The edges of her eyesight seemed to pulse.

Blast. It was possible that she had a concussion.

She eased her eyes open just a bit wider, and now she could make out a glimmer of light in Ash's hand. He was still holding the exotic matter. Good.

The sound of the gun shot came from far away, like she was hearing something that had happened in another room of a very large house.

The bullet hit Ash on the right side of his chest, jerking him backward. He swayed forward, landing on the ground cheek-first, plumes of dust and ashes billowing up around him. The canister of exotic matter skidded away from his body, rolled into the side of the Fairmont—and shattered.

There was a popping sound, and a small explosion, like a firework. Dorothy saw sparks of blue lightning, and then soft, crackling flames, and then the exotic matter disappeared in a cloud of thick, gray smoke.

The ashes obscuring Ash's face cleared, and then he was staring at her, his eyes not quite focusing. He swallowed, with difficulty. Dorothy watched the slow rise and fall of his Adam's apple beneath the skin at his throat.

And then—he winked.

All was going according to plan.

36

ASH

Playing dead was the hardest part.

Ash had to work to keep his breathing shallow so that no one would see the rise and fall of his chest. The air was thick with dust. His nose twitched. This was embarrassing but . . . he badly needed to sneeze.

He'd closed his eyes before the canister of exotic matter had hit the ground, and so he never saw the moment it smashed. He heard the sound of shattering glass, though, and that's how he'd known that very last store of exotic matter on the planet was gone.

Something inside his chest clenched, painfully. It had been a bittersweet realization. He knew it had to be like this, but the exotic matter had changed his life. It'd changed a lot of people's lives. He didn't like thinking that there was no longer any of it left. That time travel was now a thing of the past.

Well, mostly.

Footsteps pounded against the dock, and, a moment later, Ash felt the toe of a boot nudge into his arm. He had to remind himself to keep still.

"He dead?" a woman's voice asked. *Eliza*, Ash thought grimly, remembering her name. A couple of days ago, she'd helped torture him to within an inch of his life. He wasn't her biggest fan.

"We didn't need him," Mac answered. His voice was gruff, but Ash could hear an undertone to his words.

"He knew how to fly the time machine," Eliza pointed out.

"You read those pages, same as me. We don't need a time machine anymore." But Mac didn't sound as certain as he had a moment ago. His voice was wavering, weak.

He was getting nervous, all right. The thought made Ash want to laugh out loud.

Good.

Eliza seemed to pick up on this as well. The dock beneath Ash's cheek trembled as she stood and crossed over to the Fairmont stairs. "We needed that canister, though, didn't we?" she said, and, in contrast to Mac, her voice filled with barely concealed anger. "That exotic matter or whatever it was . . . you can't travel through time without it, can you?"

"We don't know that for certain . . ."

"We *do*."

Ash bit down on the inside of his cheek. Now that Mac

had gone and screwed everything up, the Black Cirkus was turning on him, just as Dorothy and her mother had said they would.

Their plan was coming together beautifully.

He was dangerously close to smiling again.

Play dead, he reminded himself. *You're supposed to be dead.*

The con started more than 150 years ago. Loretta had been the one who'd come up with it.

"According to my daughter, this . . . Mac Murphy has been causing some trouble in your city," she'd said.

They were back at Avery's house, in the stuffy sitting room, and Loretta had been handing out lukewarm tea sweetened with far too much sugar.

"He has," Ash had admitted, taking the teacup Loretta had offered him. It felt too small in his hand, like a toy.

"Thank you," Ash murmured, and took a sip, trying not to let his lips pucker.

Loretta placed the tea tray on a table and perched on the edge of a chair next to Ash, eyebrows lifting.

"A lonely man with too much money and power and not nearly enough allies." Loretta had sniffed, unimpressed. "What we need is a good con."

"I'm not sure that man can be conned," Ash had said.

"Anyone can be conned," Dorothy said. "The key is to make them believe they're in control. Mac has too large a head to think he could be played."

"We can use that, of course," Loretta added. "Men with

that much power have blind spots. They've spent far too much time grasping for money and respect. It makes them weak. Now, all we need is something he wants. Tell me, what does he want?"

"Time travel," said Dorothy, frowning. "Exotic matter, the Professor's notes . . ."

Loretta had waved all of that away. "No, no, none of that will work. He's already planning on going after you and Ash, isn't he? What else?"

Dorothy had frowned, thinking. "I'd say he needed new muscle after losing me and Roman, but . . ."

Her voice had trailed off, her eyes lighting up. "Oh," she'd said. "I . . . I think I have an idea. A good one."

Ash frowned, not following. "Do you care to share with the rest of the group?"

"It's something my mother said that made me think of it. . . . Men like Mac, they tend to not have a lot of personal relationships," Dorothy added carefully. "It's how my mother and I managed to make so much money so easily. Powerful men are so used to everyone around them cowering in fear that they have no idea when they're being played. It makes them easy marks."

"So you're going to . . . .what exactly?" Ash asked Dorothy. He took a sip of his tea, thinking, and when the idea occurred to him he nearly choked it back up. "Seduce him?"

Loretta and Dorothy exchanged a look, grinning.

"Not me," said Dorothy.

37

DOROTHY

Dorothy's eyes were open, but only just.

She watched a pair of black boots make their way through the screaming crowd. The boots stopped a few feet before her and paused. A voice cut above the shouts.

"Eliza! Bennett! A little help with the bodies."

It was Regan Rose. Dorothy was careful not to breathe too deeply, lest she give herself away, as someone slipped their hands beneath her armpits and hauled her up off the ground.

"She looked a lot smaller before she was dead," Bennett grumbled.

"You think *she* looked smaller?" Eliza grunted. From the labored sound of her voice, Dorothy guessed she was busy hauling Ash.

"Enough," Regan said, and there was a sudden, sharp sound of a clap. "Take them into the back where we won't have to look at them."

Dorothy held her breath to keep her chest from ballooning.

She didn't dare open her eyes any more than they already were, and so she couldn't see Ash being dragged around behind her, but she could hear the sound of his boots thudding over the ground, and so she knew he was right behind her.

Good, good, she thought.

The sounds of shouting and arguing faded as they were dragged into a back room, far from the other Cirkus Freaks. Eliza dropped Dorothy onto the ground, which hurt, and she heard another thump, which had to mean that Ash had been dropped beside her.

"Let's go, I want to see what's going on back there," said Bennett.

"Yeah," said Eliza, and there was a shuffling sound of footsteps and the two of them were gone.

Ash and Dorothy were alone with Regan.

"You can open your eyes now," Regan said. "They've gone."

Dorothy eased her eyes open just as her mother slid back her mask.

"You did well," Loretta said. Then, glancing at Ash, she added, "Both of you. If I hadn't known any better, I would have believed you were dead myself."

38

ASH

They'd taken Loretta back first, to September 2077. There, they'd given her a costume, some money, and instructions on who to make contact with.

Loretta had curled her lip at it all. "This world may be new," she'd said, "but the game is older than I am."

"Even so, I'm not leaving you here to starve," Dorothy had told her mother, shoving the money into her hand. "Take it."

Loretta looked unconvinced, but her hand curled around the crumpled bills, and she'd shoved them deep into her pocket.

"Eliza introduces you to Mac in a little over two months," Dorothy told her. "By then, you have a reputation around the city for being cruel. That's what gets Mac's interest. You need to make sure that reputation holds. Can you do that?"

Loretta blinked slowly at her daughter. "I admit, I'm new

to all this," she said carefully. "But I believe that, if you saw it happen, I must be successful. Correct?"

Dorothy had to admit, her mother had grasped some of the more complicated aspects of time travel rather easily. "All you have to do is gain his trust," she continued. "And then, on November 13, when Ash, the Professor, and I return, you'll need to replace the bullets in his gun with blanks." Here, her throat seemed to close, just a bit. "If you fail . . . all of us will die."

Loretta met her daughter's eyes and said, her voice firm, "Then I will not fail."

Now, Ash, Dorothy, and Loretta quickly gathered their things and crept silently through the Fairmont, through dark and moldy hallways, down narrow staircases until, finally, they reached the entrance that dumped out onto the back docks.

No one had seen them. They'd been like ghosts.

Dorothy got the door and swung it wide, eyes peeled for movement as she ushered her mother and Ash through. She pulled the door closed behind her, shivering as she stepped onto the docks.

A boat was already waiting. Zora sat in the front, one hand propped on the motor.

"Let's go," she said, starting the engine.

Their little boat flew past aisle after aisle of old dinghies, motorboats, and the odd yacht that'd seen better days. They kept low, in case there were other Cirkus Freaks about, and the boats rocked on the waves they left in their wake. Otherwise, the night was still. Dorothy squinted into the darkness, her nerves on edge as they approached the library. She knew they were safer here than almost anywhere else in New Seattle. Mac and what was left of the Freaks were still back at the Fairmont, and it was unlikely that anyone had noticed them missing yet. But, still, she worried.

Dorothy was soaked to her knees and shivering by the time they docked in front of the library's doors.

"Hurry," she said when Zora cut the engine. "It's already getting late."

Ash had a hand cupped over his chin, fingers nervously tapping the side of his face, but he smiled at her and said, "Aye, aye, boss."

"Get a room," Zora muttered, rolling her eyes at them both.

They climbed out of the boat and hurried inside, weaving through the stacks, to where the others waited.

The Professor stood near the window, anxiously flicking a curtain aside every few minutes, his left eye twitching. Chandra appeared to be trying to decide on something to wear. She seemed to spend a long time straightening T-shirts and picking invisible pieces of lint off the hems of the jeans.

"You're back," Willis said, standing. He had to crouch to keep his head from knocking against the ceiling. The shadows in the library painted his face in harsh grays and blacks, making him look like a man hewn from stone.

At the sound of his voice, the other two looked up.

"Well?" said Chandra, her eyes moving anxiously between the three of them. "How'd it go?"

"Do we look dead to you?" Ash asked.

Chandra frowned. "Well, no . . ."

"So, it went okay."

Chandra opened her mouth but, before she could respond, Zora had elbowed him. Ash grimaced and rubbed at a spot on his arm.

"We need to move." Zora's expression remained the same, but her shoulders tensed beneath her stiff shirt. To her father, she said haltingly, as though choosing each word very carefully, "How did things go back here?"

Everyone went quiet, watching Zora and her father while trying to seem like they weren't watching. It was awkward, and there was a part of Ash that wanted to tell them all to snap out of it. But the other part, the bigger part, wanted to listen in himself.

He'd been present for the first reunion between Zora and her father and it had gone . . . not well was somewhat of an understatement. Zora had spent the last year wondering where in time her father had vanished, and the last four weeks certain that he was dead. Then, just a few hours ago, he'd walked back into her life, not dead, not even close.

Ash could still remember the emotion he'd seen play out on his closest friend's face when she saw him. Zora's expression had hemorrhaged between hope and despair, joy and confusion. And, because it was Zora, it had quickly morphed into anger, like so many of her emotions often did. The Professor had tried to hug his daughter, but she'd only crossed her arms in front of her chest and said, her voice deadpan, "You're late."

Now, the Professor grinned at his daughter, eyes glistening, like he was looking at the sun. She stared back, and Ash could see that she was trying very hard to maintain her stony disposition. It wasn't working. The tip of her mouth was curling into a grin, no matter how she tried to stop it. It was a strange expression to see on Zora's face. Ash liked it.

Zora saw him staring. "Shut up," she murmured, and tried to bite the smile back. When it still didn't work, she groaned and turned to face the window.

"Everything went swimmingly," the Professor said. "The exotic matter has been administered." He nodded at the counter, where the gun that once contained the remaining EM now sat, empty. Dorothy glanced at it but said nothing. Everything was in place.

"We should probably hurry," Ash said. "Mac thinks we're both dead, but he's bound to figure out the truth when he goes to the back of his workshop and sees that we're all missing."

"Would that really be so bad?" Chandra asked. "The Cirkus turned on him, right? He doesn't have any power any longer."

"Their betrayal depends on them thinking that he's failed, that he's killed us and lost them their very last chance of getting to use time travel for themselves," Dorothy explained. "We've bought ourselves just enough time to get out of here before Mac sends the rest of the Cirkus after us."

"Not to worry. We'll be gone by then," said the Professor. "Only one question remains. Where would you all like to go?"

PART
FIVE

The end is in the beginning and lies far ahead.

—Ralph Ellison

39

Light pressed into Roman's eyelids, the sensation so strong it was almost like physical touch. It coaxed him from the darkness of sleep, pulling him back up, up to . . .

Where? His eyes were still closed, but he could tell that he was lying on something. There was a stiff, cool pressure beneath him, and the faint weight of something draped over his body, a sheet or a light blanket. Behind him, the sound of distant voices, footsteps. He inhaled, and his nose filled with the smell of beer and fried food.

A bar, then. He was in a bar.

Open your eyes, he told himself, but the command had no effect on his physical body. His eyelids felt glued shut, two strips of flesh held tight by something sticky. He tried again and, this time, a slight groan escaped his lips. Light burst across his retinas. The brightness was overwhelming. Pain shot straight through his skull, shocking him so much that he closed his eyes again, on instinct, grimacing.

He took deep, even breaths through his nose, waiting for his heartbeat to steady before he tried again.

The room was long and narrow, with a single window on the far side, a thin curtain hanging over it. He was lying on a bed, and he appeared to be wearing his own clothes, but they were bloodstained, dirty.

He tried to lift his head, but pain prickled up his neck, and he let it drop back down onto the pillow, eyelids fluttering.

Something very bad had happened. He knew that for sure. He closed his eyes and tried to remember what it was.

He'd expected to find nothing, empty space and darkness, but the memory was still there, right where he'd left it. He reached for it, and it was like a current dragging him downriver, gasping. Once he started the memory playing, there was nothing he could do to stop it again.

He saw the time machine and Quinn. Mac. The future. The gunshot.

A hum rose in his skull, the sound blocking out all other noise. His fingers curled toward his palms, fingernails digging into skin. The room felt very small and very dark, and a terror like Roman had never felt before took hold of him.

He'd been shot.

His hand leaped to his chest, nervously, searching for a bullet hole. He found a bandage, still damp with blood. His breathing started to steady.

"Well, look who decided to wake up," said a voice.

Roman eased his eyes open and saw a girl standing just inside the door of his room. She was wearing light-wash jeans and a white sweatshirt, hair falling over her forehead in soft tangles.

She smiled at him as she came inside. "We were thinking of taking bets on whether you'd ever wake up at all. My money was on yes, but Pop says I'm an optimist."

Roman tried to speak. "Where . . . where . . ." His voice wasn't working like it was supposed to. The inside of his mouth tasted strange. Stale. Like he hadn't brushed his teeth for a very long time. And, damn he was thirsty. His tongue felt like straw.

He swallowed, trying to force saliva down his scratchy throat.

"You are in the lovely town of New Seattle, at a charming little bar called the Dead Rabbit," the girl was telling him. "We found you here two days ago, bleeding from a bullet wound, of all things. Pop was the one who brought you back here and got you stitched up. Although, I have to be honest, he does have a bunch of questions for you. Gunshots aren't super common around these parts, not in the last few years, at least."

She crossed the room and yanked the curtains open, letting in a shock of bright, white light. "Why don't you relax while I go find him. He's the one whose been taking care of you, and I know he'll be able to explain everything."

Roman blinked, trying to make sense out of all the things she'd just said. He was in New Seattle? At the Dead Rabbit? And what did she mean, gunshots aren't common?

The girl was almost to the door. Roman cleared his throat, trying again to use his voice. "What . . . what *year* is it?"

The mention of the year brought the girl's chin up. She stared at Roman for a long moment, and then she said, very carefully, "It's 2082. Why?"

Roman exhaled. He could feel his heart beating at his temples, see the blood pulsing through his lids.

The year 2082, he thought. Well, that wasn't so bad. He was in the future, but not so far in the future that he couldn't live something like a normal version of his life. And . . . well, things certainly seemed different from when he'd come here with Dorothy. No ashes and blocked-out sky. No city in ruins, at least as far as he could see from this bed.

They must've done something, he realized. Dorothy and Ash and the others. They must've changed things.

The thought brought a thin smile to his lips.

Good for them.

When Roman opened his eyes again, he saw that the girl was still at the door, staring at him.

"What is it?" he asked, frowning.

"It's just . . . I was wondering if you were a"—she lowered her voice—"a time traveler?"

Roman felt himself go still. His heart was pounding in his ears, a slow, steady drumbeat. "Why would you ask that?"

Now the girl looked nervous. "It's nothing," she said in a rush. "It's just that there are a bunch of people outside and . . . I thought they were crazy, but they said that they're time travelers, too. They seem to think they're friends of yours."